CW00351402

CYBER CIRCUS

and

BLACK SUNDAY

Kim Lakin-Smith

One of a Special Edition, Signed by the Author
Limited to just 100 numbered copies
This is number:

91

CYBER CIRCUS

and

BLACK SUNDAY

Kim Lakin-Smith

NewCon Press
England

First published in the UK by NewCon Press
41 Wheatsheaf Road, Alconbury Weston, Cambs, PE28 4LF

NCP 040 (signed hardback)
NCP 041 (softback)

10 9 8 7 6 5 4 3 2 1

ISBN:

978-1-907069-29-1 (hardback)
978-1-907069-30-7 (softback)

Cover illustration by Vincent Chong
Cover layout and design by Kim Lakin-Smith

Editorial meddling by Ian Whates and Ian Watson
Book layout by Storm Constantine

Printed in the UK by MPG Biddles of Kings Lynn

For my father,
Nev Lakin

CYBER CIRCUS

ONE

1937. Sore Earth, population – 3120 souls.

Darkness. Deep treacly dung-scented darkness. Made incandescent by the appearance of thousands of tiny weak stars in the heavens. The air is a cloak of intermingled breath. Bodies shift. Slowly the stars brighten.

The ringmaster smiles. He is a squat dumpling of a man. Red suited in tail coat and knickerbockers, with a head that shines under the spots up in the rafters. In his hand, the hat for which he is famed; a crest of soft green velvet, sprouting feathers like spines. Hat of the king pin, owner of Cyber Circus. Herb wields it before the crowd. To the roll of a solitary kettle drum, he slowly, teasingly, places it on his head.

Applause. A storm of it, whipping up from the front stalls and rolling back. The calliope begins to pipe, contours shining. Fibrous sponge beats behind the ornate metalwork. Air drains through fine copper veins. Tucked in under the ribs of the giant instrument, the boiler is a stomach of greenish glass. Water steams and bubbles inside.

Herb leaps into the centre of the ring. A dancing maggot.

"Welcome, one and all, to the sensational, lavational, electrisical, metaphysical Cyber Circus!" A flourish of a hand. Oohs from the crowd. "On this most exhilarating night, you will witness wonders from the outer reaches of our land of Humock where only the devil and lost souls dare venture. I bring you strange people, weird people, and some who aren't people at all!"

He runs the circuit of the ring, coattails flapping. "Cower in the presence of Wolf Girl. Feast your eyes on the electrifying Desirous Nim. Behold the half-child half-crab Scuttlers. Marvel at the aerial daring of the tantalising Lulu. Come face to face with a HawkEye…" A nod to acknowledge the audience's gasp. "Indeed, ladies and gentlemen. A bona fide HawkEye who, wearied of the lone battle, has joined our family of freaks and appears for you tonight, fully armed and watchful." Herb points two fingers at his eyes then directs the gesture out. "And if that wasn't enough, on this very stage, inside this very canvas, we will unleash not one but two hoppers!"

Eerie, the collective stop of breath. Then a shock wave of applause. And Herb is dancing again, hat's plumage shivering at the impact of each step, the brown egg of his belly poking out from below his braided jacket.

"Strike up the band!" he calls to the calliope, and seemingly it hears him. The tent fills with watery mechanical music.

Herb gestures to a painted curtain. He lights his smile.

"I give you Wolf Girl!"

"How is she?" Lulu's mouse-like eyes shone with tears.

"Scared, I suspect." Hellequin kept his arms folded. His shadow loomed against the silk drops that separated the living quarters from backstage.

"Oh, my poor baby doll. A downpour of hawk shit on that mark! He's a suckerloop, a villain!" The ladyboy wrung his hands. Kohl ran beneath his lashes.

The HawkEye frowned, emphasising the twin bone ridges at his forehead that protected his circuitry. "He's not a mark. He's a pimp. A lowlife grubbing in others' suffering. Herb shouldn't have set down here. Not if he wants a good clean show."

"But what are you gonna do? It's not like you and Nim are sweethearts." Lulu dropped his voice. "She gets wind you're on guard out here and, oh my, you seen the sparks flying offa her recently?"

Hellequin's steel eye telescoped. "Just blips in her circuitry. Comes of shoddy workmanship when the mods were installed."

Lulu fanned his fingers against his smooth cheeks. "I hope you're right. I'd hate to scorch this pretty face." When Hellequin failed to respond, the ladyboy clucked his tongue and popped out a hip. "Not that a hard heart like you would notice. Even with all that fancy hardware." He waved a hand in front of Hellequin's face, aggravating the HawkEye lens into fresh adjustment.

"Bitter much?" Pig Heart muscled his way through the silk curtains, dragging a rope attached to a pallet piled with bone and meat.

"Drink swill from the donniker!" Lulu flicked his white dreads back off his shoulders.

The pitchman showed a mouthful of tusks. "Love you too, Lulu." He dragged a hand across his large glistening nostrils, leaving a smear of blood there. "Come on. Let's pucker up."

"You are a revolting swine!" Lulu danced back.

Pig Heart arched his back and let out a belly laugh. "By name and nature." The pitchman tapped his breast. "Whatever dead hog gave me this ticker made sure of that. But I see you checking out my porky ass, Lady Lulu. You wanna piece of this, doncha?" He gave his generous rear a slap. Snorting, he picked up the rope again and started for the entrance to the ring.

"Nim. Is she going on tonight?" said Hellequin sharply.

The pitchman stopped. He craned his bristled jaw over a shoulder. "Maybe you ain't been here long enough, Hellequin, but ain't none of us carnies the keeper of the other. Nim's got a problem visiting Sore Earth, it's her choice to tell Herb, or put up and shut up."

Lulu clucked. "Like any of us have a say where Herb chooses to pitch down."

"Ever known Herb change his mind once he's on course?" Hellequin focused on the pitchman.

The rope fell from Pig Heart's hands. The pitchman strode back, arms swaying at his sides like joints on hooks. Hellequin stayed rigid, his back to the flow of silk. Lulu skipped on the spot.

Pig Heart's pale damp eyes fastened on Hellequin's revolving lens. "Ten years back, we hit a dust storm. Came outta nowhere so fast it seemed the devil had parted his ass cheeks and farted. We dipped inside the caverns west of Zan City. Seemed there was no way we'd make the gig at an old tunnel town called Drieur. Our only option was to let the marks keep their dollar – which Herb was having none of – or travel under the storm and navigate the caverns." Pig Heart dragged up a shirt sleeve. His forearm was scarred with three deep lacerations.

"Hoppers." Lulu clutched his throat.

"Some crew weren't so lucky, which was how Herb ended up changing course. Once." Pig Heart inclined his head towards Hellequin.

A tremendous clacking noise prompted all three to stare at the stage curtain.

"Herb's getting his iron rattler in a twist. I'd best feed Rust before she sinks her jaws into them marks out there. You kids play nice now." Pig Heart showed his fat teeth. He took up the slack on the rope and hauled the pallet after him, meat slopping like jelly.

Lulu took a lace handkerchief from one cup of his bustier and dabbed his temples. "I need to climb aboard the spring pad. The mood Herb's been in recently, I'll be one dead cannonball if I miss my entrance." He shook the handkerchief towards the silk drop behind Hellequin. "Let's get in and out of here as quickly as possible. For *her* sake."

Hellequin turned around to see a lamp fire up behind the flimsy walls. The change in light replaced his shadow with an hour glass silhouette. His chest tightened.

"I got my eye on Nim," he muttered.

Lulu waved a talon at the gadgetry stitched into the soldier's face. "Indeed you have."

Earl macerated a wad of leaf. "I'd like to play buckaroo with that wild dog!"

D'Angelus sucked the stub of a Cherokee smoke stick, cheeks working like bellows. "She'd give the John a bang for his buck, that's for sure."

"What they feeding that bitch anyway?" Earl's voice thickened with revulsion.

"I don't know." D'Angelus flicked his smoke stick, exaggerating the red glow at its tip. The scent lay upon him and around him like the perfumed skin of a woman. "Even if it's the butchered slop of the Saints themselves, it'd be a price worth paying. Look at her." He stabbed the smoke stick at the ring where a she-wolf was pawing a cracked femur and slathering marrow into her mouth. The red mane that tickled her coccyx was threaded with gore. Blood streaked her cheeks like war paint.

Watching from the back of the tent, D'Angelus felt a strange longing. Owner of the Elegance Saloon, he had peddled skin for a lifetime, enjoying many varieties of black, gold and lilied flesh. But all that carnality had done nothing to sate his deepest need. No matter how he mixed tears into their smiles with the lash, or how many of their mouths suckered him, he could not achieve a true, beautified sense of his own fleshness. He wanted to be properly devoured. To be feasted upon.

"Reckon the circus owner'll sell her on?" Earl gobbed his mouthful of weed onto the soil floor.

"Why risk asking? I'm thinking once the wolf girl's done supping and is stowed back in her cage, the boys just step behind the curtain and attain her." D'Angelus bobbed his trekker head towards the fifteen strong crew in his employment.

Earl's eyes tightened. "They got a HawkEye."

D'Angelus revealed a mouthful of recycled teeth, taken from dead men and screwed into the gum. "I betcha the HawkEye is just some bum in a mask. Ink him with a regiment's colours and the townsfolk who roll in once a year ain't gonna question it."

He watched Earl retrieve a battered tin from his pants' pocket, pinch a wad of leaf and squash it inside a cheek. The man was all kinds of ugly, thought D'Angelus. He liked that about him.

"Alright," said Earl. "'Cause I ain't never heard of a surviving HawkEye, only what you get by way of tall tales out at Grenyan's Bar. Like how they'd take to their lung baskets and be able to spy a jewel wasp infesting a cockroach with her lava from the sky. All those wires and bits of metal inside a face? How'd a man do that to himself, D'Angelus? By the Saints, I gotta tell ya, it's a dark use to put the body to." He shuddered and chewed his cud.

A Saint Sister edged around on a nearby bench, grey wimple angling stiffly from her head to her toes like a shroud. The face which poked out had gone off with age.

"By every Saint in the blue, will you pair of suckerloops shut your traps?"

"Beg your pardon, Ma'am." D'Angelus nipped the brim of his hat.

The Sister scowled, further corrupting her dried features. She turned back to the action just as the wolf girl sunk her jaws into a side of wet meat and shook it like a dog. Blood sprayed the crowd. The Saint Sister rocked back, hands to her face, muttering in disgust. She kept her seat though.

In the realm of the circus, blind fascination won out over revulsion, D'Angelus mused. And he liked the wolf girl even more then because her savage nature was on open display and not disguised behind religion and a wimple.

"Forget the HawkEye," he told Earl. "Let another couple of acts play out. Allow the wolf to get comfortable in her cage. Then you and the boys head backstage and acquire her." He broke out his ghoul smile. "Reckon we should introduce her to a new breed of predator. Our clientele."

Pig Heart manhandled the stripped pallet out of the ring and to one side of the stage curtain. He let go of the rope and eased back his shoulders. Bloody pulp ingrained his hands. Pig Heart resisted the urge to suck his fingers. Instead, he slipped back into the shadows and rooted in a pocket for a smoke stick. He struck a match and applied the flame to the tip. Releasing a piquant mouthful, he let his eyes settle on the wolf girl.

Rust was performing a weird ballet along the low wall surrounding the circus ring. Her legs were short and scrub-covered, her breasts drained of fat and pendulous, more like teats than the usual soft mounds. She threw back her head and howled to intimidate both enemy and prey. Or was it a call to her kind, wondered Pig Heart? Smoke bled from his wet nostrils.

Limbs skittering, Rust chased her shadow round the ring. Pig Heart ate her up – the patch of fur between her legs, the scarred flesh of her rear.

"Quite a performance," said a nasal voice.

Pig Heart whipped his head aside. It was D'Angelus's man, Earl, the one with eyes so small it was impossible to see a chink of decency. Earl tucked in alongside him in the shadows and churned his jaw – sign of a leaf chewer.

"Not too gory for you?" Pig Heart snorted as Rust found the steak he had disguised beneath a mound of sawdust and, without pausing to brush it off, started to gnaw the meat.

Earl shot aside a slug of leaf. "Rabid beast ain't my flavour. Nim, on the other hand..? Well, I sure would like a second taste of that delicacy. When's her spot?"

Pig Heart grubbed in the bristles of his chin. He felt rage at the mention of Nim – rage at her for presenting him with this opportunity by returning to Sore Earth, rage at himself for taking advantage of the fact.

"After Rust's finished, it's the aerial act. Nim's up next after that."

"Mr D'Angelus is keen to see what his protégé has been doing with her time these past few months. Travellers off the dust trail claim she's quite the attraction."

The pitchman took a fresh drag. He narrowed his eyelids against the bloom of smoke. "Nim gets menfolk squirming in their long johns, that's a fact. But not even her kootch show distracts from the true blowoff. Ain't many folk shared tent space with hoppers, which is how they ain't never gonna know the beasts are mostly harmless. 'Cept when they swarm." A dark impression played across Pig Heart's mind… the scrape of chitinous limbs, fibrous neck folds, burred tentacles. He took the last lungful off the smoke stick and ground the nub under a boot heel. "Make a good show though," he appended gruffly.

"Shame to miss it, but I got a feeling Mr D'Angelus will be collecting on our exchange before this evening's grand finale." Earl smiled, teeth gangrenous with leaf pulp.

Their conversation was interrupted by a grinding noise. A camshaft, fat as a salt pillar, corkscrewed up from the opposite end of the ring, just as the stage curtain drew back so that Rust could make her snap-jawed exit. On top of the camshaft stood Lulu, white-gold dreads cascading over a shoulder, one shapely leg kinked against the other. In a jewelled bodice and tutu, his appearance tricked many assembled below. The air filled with trills of appreciation. The audience's lust was interrupted by the crack of gun powder and the chime of the propeller's spring release.

Lulu flew the length of the tent at a steep trajectory. Catching hold of a trapeze disguised in the black canopy overhead, he swung out over the heads of the crowd, looped back in and dropped down, one leg hooked over the apparatus, arms extended in an upside-down V.

The crowd broke into applause.

Pig Heart leaned sideways. "So, I let you know where Nim was. Time to pay up and I don't want no carnie roll of one dollar bills with a higher note wrapped around. I want the notes separated."

Earl squinted sideways, a touch of mockery to his lips. "We

gotta see the merchandise before we hand over the reward for her whereabouts. A creature of integrity like yourself has gotta see that, ain't you now, Mr Swine Heart?"

"Pig Heart," muttered the pitchman. He whipped another smoke stick between his lips and watched the acrobatic antics of the ladyboy. Soon Nim would take to the stage and he could pocket the reward, and none in the troop would be the wiser.

TWO

The ladyboy touches down on the apex of a colossal iron scaffold. He curtseys and steps out of view. The lights grow dim. Applause fades out.

All eyes lift to the ribs of the tent where pearlescent light feeds down to the fibrous mass of the calliope. It breathes. The instrument actually breathes. Folk turn to poke their neighbour and point and nod – they are sure of it. The intricate pipework steams. It speaks to them, the calliope, in a voice that is dry and fluting, its purpose being to distract the crowd from the figures who rush from the wings and unroll thin canvas over the floor of the ring. Hammers chime as Pig Heart's pitch crew secure the waterproof skin inside the rim of the low wall. They disappear and return moments later, shouldering prisms which they arrange around the outer rim. The calliope sings its strange song. The pitch crew melt back into the shadows.

The stage is bathed in a soporific glow. Water tumbles from a perforated sluice in the central rib overhead. Secret mechanisms grind into life and the prisms begin to weep like waterfalls. Spotlights burn greenly from below the shallow pool.

A woman steps from one of the larger prisms as if passing through glass. She is tall as a reed and curvaceous. Her face is full with a pinch of bone at each cheek. Red hair loops down onto pale shoulders. She wears silk pantaloons and a corset of ribbons. In her ears are silver hoops. In her hand is an umbrella.

The air dusts with spray as she mounts the low wall and

steps daintily around it. At each prism, she angles her umbrella under the flow, sending water spurting over the heads of the crowd who hoot in delight and sway to the pipe of the calliope.

Coming full circle, she swings the umbrella upside-down, places it on the water and steps inside. Few among the marks hear the soft click of a pressure pad or understand the revolving magnet patched onto a slim track. Instead, it is an apparently cognisant umbrella that conveys its beautiful cargo about the ring.

She casts off her soaked pantaloons. Men whoop and whistle. Her undergarment is of the same wet ribbon as her drenched corset.

The umbrella glides to the centre of the ring. As the lights dim further, she appears as an hour glass silhouette. But the transformation goes further. She is suddenly alight. Her mouth shines, as do the outlines of her breasts, each nipple visible between the slats of her ribbon top, and too the curve from hip to inner thigh and the plump of each buttock.

The song of the calliope is replaced with a discordant clang that gathers pace. Faster and faster the umbrella twirls to the guttural music. And she is a light cell, a blur of shine-shot neon. Colours grease the air in her wake.

“Ask me, the wolf bitch can’t hold a candle to our Desirous Nim” whispered Earl in the glowing dark. “Helluva show.”

Pig Heart stared at the impression of Nim’s form left behind by the light trails. She was seductive in the way a pin-up in a peepshow pamphlet gave him something to jack off to. But she didn’t speak to his essence like Rust. While Nim was all about erotic suggestion, Rust was a force of sexual nature, incapable of manipulation or artifice. Her desires came from instinct, which was how on several occasions now, she’d crawled into his bed and pinioned him, her louse-riddled hair spilling onto his naked chest. Their rutting had a bleak urgency, which was not to say it was without sentiment. He’d found himself longing to join her in her nest, to taste her bloody mouth, while there’d been a suggestion of need in the tug of her hands at his jowls, in her drinking him in.

"Nim's a crowd pleaser," he muttered. "Me? I don't get the appeal of a whore all lit up with directions for awkward Johns."

"No?" Nim's neon pinwheel reflected in Earl's pupils. "Each to their own, hey, Mr Swine Heart. I'm just eager to get our girl back in the stable she bolted from. Mr D'Angelus, though, he's taken a fancy to the wolf girl. Seems we'll be depriving Herb of two attractions this evening. And since you were the man to direct our eye here, you get a few extra dollars." Earl took the band from around a fat bank roll and fanned the notes.

Pig Heart didn't move, not even when Earl pressed the notes into his hand. Regret burnt inside his chest like a brand. Not only did D'Angelus intend to re-secure Nim but he had his sights set on a new pet, Rust. The pitchman rubbed a sore spot at his brow. What in the devil's name had he unleashed upon her?

Nim concluded her act and Earl slipped away, leaving Pig Heart alone with his frantic thoughts. There was no way he could take on D'Angelus's men – grunts with rock rifles slung over their shoulders. At best, he'd maul a couple before they took him out with their impromptu ammo.

He raked a hand through the spines at his head. He could warn Rust, but how'd he explain without admitting his part in Nim's betrayal? The money they'd paid wasn't enough for him and Rust to run away on. Hell, it'd buy them temporary shelter with a desert caravan at best. But maybe that would do for the time being.

Lights blazed. The Scuttler children rolled into the ring like balled woodlice. Pig Heart's gaze darted off to the outskirts of the tent where D'Angelus and his gang appeared distracted by the Scuttlers' clown antics.

Sweat oozed down the rough matting at Pig Heart's back. He despised the wolf girl for putting herself in the way. At the same time, he was infested with need for her.

He slipped behind the stage curtain. Backstage was littered with debris: boom trampolines – skins stretched to varying degrees of tautness so each produced a different note when bounced on – alongside sooty fire rings, stage flats painted to resemble cacti, sandships and tunnellers, coils of hemp rope, lighting rigs, and the huge gilt wagon that housed the hoppers. Down the left side ran a wall of flimsy curtaining designed to separate off the dressing rooms from the frantic energy of backstage. Right of him were the crew's living quarters, rows of tin-rib cells packed in tight against one another and, hard ahead, the steaming lift rig leading to the three platforms above.

Striding past the milling pitch crew, Pig Heart leapt up onto the rig as it began a fresh ascent.

"Howdie, Pig Heart."

"Got a light, boss?"

Two of his pitch crew rode the rig alongside him. Kid with a beltful of dried rat carcasses – exterminator by trade, Pig Heart suspected, forced into carnival labour by the recent sandstorms which had taken out the year's glut of land vermin. Also, a red skinned Jeridian with a ladder piercing of two-centimetre-long steel strips down her throat.

It was the woman who touted the smoke stick. Pig Heart tossed over his match book, snatching it from the air seconds later when the Jeridian tossed it back. The lift rattled to a halt at the first of three platforms that were bolted onto the side of the tent above the living quarters and that were supported by a great exposed ribcage of iron scaffold.

"Catch ya later, boss."

"Thanks for the light."

The exterminator and Jeridian strode off into the partial dark of the first platform – the mess hall.

An iron lever as tall as man's hip drove the rig. Pig Heart yanked it towards him. In a burst of steam, the lift continued its assent, past the second platform that housed the ornate carcass of Herb's personal quarters with its green silk shutters and lingering stench of incense. Up to the third level, the zoo. He stared out across the great hull of the Cyber Circus tent as the rig climbed. Backstage took up one third of the interior. Beyond lay the vast circus ring and, at the far end, the sprawling calliope – a great pulsating mass of sponge, copper filigree and air pipes – with its narrow balcony, spiralling steps and boiler tucked in beneath.

From that distance, the tumbling scab balls of the Scuttler children looked as small as roo rats. Yup, when it comes to Cyber Circus, we're just amoebas crawling over the skin of the thing, Pig Heart thought to himself.

The rig reached the third platform, known affectionately as 'the zoo'. Pig Heart stepped off and made his way down the central walkway. Either side were stalls, sectioned off from one another by a patchwork of corrugated iron sheeting. That high up in the tent the air was fresher and tinged with the earth scent of purple sage lining the beasts' beds.

To his left, the stalls were dedicated to livestock. Roo rats bickered in their city of interconnected pipes, ramps, scratch posts and dust baths. Their nutty flesh served the soup pot well. Next door were giant tortoises, the meat of which was fried in spiced oil or dried into thin gnawing strips, the shell made into bracelets or trinket boxes for sale during pre-show parades. Next were the wrinklenecks, shoulders hooked and feathers ruffled like Jeridian medicine men, and, after, red horned goats that tore at dry grass in wall-mounted mangers.

To his right, every stall was occupied by clothhods. The creatures stayed in the shadows, necks looped back to allow their long muzzles to rest in the folds between their broad shoulders. One moved to drink from a high trough. Keratin hoofs swished through the strewn sage.

The larger beasts were housed to the rear. Where the hoppers' wagon was usually located, the floor was littered with calcium deposits; the giant nymphs wept milky bile from their ever churning mandibles. Rust's wagon was parked alongside.

I hear the wind making music in their wings, she had told him.

Gore at her lips. Lice in her hair.

One side of Rust's wagon faced out from the wall and was masterfully carved with jewel coloured mouths and eyes that served as the face of the circus during pre-show parades. It also provided Rust with privacy should she desire it. Of course, she wasn't really quarantined to the zoo, but free to come and go as she pleased about the tent. But she preferred to keep to her own. As Pig Heart understood it from the brief moments she was more woman than wolf, she'd crawled from the ruins of her parents' desert dome when it and her entire family were lost to one of the great dust storms. The lone survivor, she had found shelter with a pack of cave wolves until she reached puberty. Only when hunters shot dead the alpha-female of the pack did she skulk back to her own kind, furred, spit-jawed and fit only for the circus.

I bring you freaks, strange people, weird people, and some that aren't people at all! Herb's patter. Pig Heart grabbed the banister and swung up onto the step at one end of the wagon. He prepared for her backlash; Rust hated to be disturbed, which was how some young grunt off the pitch crew usually got stuck with the task come show time. The rush of claws coming at him through the bars made him flinch in spite of himself.

"Rust! It's me. I gotta talk to you. I gotta let you know somethin' and we ain't got long, baby."

Eyes pulled up to the bars. Wet, black, spider-lashed.

"Pig Heart." She touched her tongue to a corner of her mouth. "Is it here to rut with me?"

Pig Heart shook his head. He was used to her distanced treatment of him. For Rust, the only creatures she truly associated herself with were those in the adjacent stalls and cages. He, on the other hand, was still an unknown. An 'it.'

The spider eyes ate him up. "What's it want with me then?"

"Rust. I gotta tell you. There's men among them marks down there. Bad men. Want to cage you for real. Want to let other men rut with you without your will or say so. I ain't the sort of mucker to want that to happen. I'm putting it to you now…"

He shut off midsentence, hearing the rattle of the lift rig alongside the muffled noise from the main tent area. The lift didn't ascend to their level, presumably having conveyed a fresh batch of pitch crew to the mess hall. Pig Heart returned his attention to Rust.

"I got money. Not much but it's enough to get us part passage on a desert caravan. Maybe we'd get as far as Zan City before they dump our asses."

"Zan City is a nest of blood worms. The bare-man, Herb, says it often."

Pig Heart scrubbed at his bristled head. He was sweating profusely. How long until D'Angelus and his men invaded backstage with their rock rifles? How long until they strong armed some poor grunt into showing them the lift rig that led to the zoo?

"Yeah, Zan City's a hole. One you and me can get lost in."

She put a hand through the bars and batted his cheek. "And why'd I come with it? Why'd I leave my stink bed?"

"The men, Rust. Saints almighty, Rust, the men!" The pitchman was slopping spit now. His borrowed heart swelled and flabbed.

Rust swung open the door to her cage. Her face was a breath's distance from his in an instant.

"Wolves don't run to Zan City when the lion tracks us over the dunes or when the storm comes and we have to take to the caverns if hoppers swarm there or not. The bare men cannot tear me from my stink bed. I will claw out their eyes, bite the skeletons from their flesh."

"But they have guns, Rust. Rock Rifles. They will take you down just enough to keep your mauled body fit for rutting. We got no choice, baby. They're coming for Nim and they're coming for you."

The wolf girl cocked her head. "Nim. What do the bare men want with Nim?"

"They want her back, Rust!" he spat in her face. Had her time with the wolves sent the girl stupid? She seemed unresisting to her fate, like an exhausted jackrabbit in a trap. And still she eyed him with that liquid gaze.

"Nim smells happy now. She smelt sad when she came, but she likes it here. You will tell her about the bare men too."

"I can't, Rust. No time. Besides, she's got Hellequin for a shadow, whether she wants him or not."

Rust thumped at an ear with the back of a hand, chasing an itch. "The HawkEye." She seemed to roll the words around in her mouth, tasting their texture. Her gaze flicked past Pig Heart's shoulder. "It says there's bare men coming for Nim and me."

Pig Heart sensed a presence behind him. His breath stuck in his throat and he slowly turned around.

The HawkEye stepped from the shade. He held two squirming roo rats by their tails in one hand, a blood stained mallet in the other. Striding down the walkway, he unfolded an extra couple of vertebra. His grip slacked on the roo rats. The creatures fell to the floor and scampered back to the seeming safety of their roo rat city.

"D'Angelus has located Nim then. I wonder who helped him do that." In the centre of Hellequin's steel eyepiece, a bud of amber light strengthened.

THREE

D'Angelus tossed aside the glowing nub of his smoke stick. He adjusted the angle of his trekker hat. "Come on. I've seen enough."

Earl wore his disappointment like a child deprived of sweet root. "Nim ain't going nowhere, boss." His gaze wandered back to the ring where the Scuttlers propelled themselves from one tent pole to another in a great clanking of giant pincers. "Nimble little vermin," he snorted and, tucking his thumbs into his waistcoat pockets, rocked back on his boot heels and chuckled. He glanced at D'Angelus. His face drained of pleasure.

"I'll send in our guys." Earl deposited fresh leaf in one cheek. "You want it to go softly or us to mess things up back there?"

D'Angelus eyed the crowd. "No need to cause a ruckus. We don't want to ruin the show for these good folk." He showed the tics of his teeth. "Softly does it. We want to keep the merchandise pretty."

Earl strode away, signalling his men to move off to the stage curtain.

D'Angelus stayed behind. Knowing the wolf girl would spit, claw and buck in his bed that evening sent a crush of blood to his groin. As for Nim, she'd be enjoyed in a dark room where her erotic circuitry would guide many hands.

He stared at the clowning freak children with their claws and hoary shells and shrunken heads. Would that he had been born such, without the weight of his desires!

Rage congealed behind Hellequin's ribs and the internal clockwork of his steel eye. He sensed it not so much as direct emotion as a neural thickening. Nothing was as it had once been. The sucker bolts, bores, griplines and proton flasks that acted as spark plugs were hardwired into his brain, a process which meant he couldn't recall the depths to which he had once felt fear or anger or obsession. But he knew how emotion amassed and at that instant, it was locking his fingers into fists and stiffening his jaw.

Pig Heart's nostrils twitched. Hellequin saw the tiny movement as a widening of cartilage around breath.

"By the Saints, Hellequin, we gotta get these broads outta here."

There wasn't time to debate it. Nim's scream cut through the tent. From his high chair at the far side of the ring, Herb heard it and felt a patch of dread open inside. D'Angelus threw back his head and drank in the sound. Rust flinched at the door to her wagon. Hellequin broke into a charge towards the lift rig.

"They've got rock rifles," he heard Pig Heart call after him. No matter if they had the burning spears of the Saints themselves, he would fill the air with their death cries.

He pulled up short of the rig. Steam continued to rise at the far reaches of the tent, which told him that Herb was keeping the calliope in action and choosing to go on with the show. The marks' 'oohs' and 'ahhs' assured him that the hoppers had been set grazing in the centre of the ring. Soon the handlers would whip the beasts into flight and the crowd into terrified, maniacal applause.

Oiled to keep its motion down to a low purr during show time, the lift rig would still produce enough noise to alert those below to his assent. Hellequin opted to feed his hands around the fat steel cords of the steam winch and use his boot heels for grip. He slid down, taking in a panoramic view of backstage.

A Jeridian woman by the name of Asenath was secured, a blade pressed to her throat. Two more of the crew were on their knees, rock rifles pressurising their spines. Meanwhile, D'Angelus's men behaved like raw recruits on sentry duty at some dead outpost, talking softly and shifting from one boot to the other as if bored by their responsibilities.

Hellequin reasoned that unless they had cutting tools strong enough to slit the hide of the circus tent, the grunts would have to bring Nim through backstage and smuggle her out past the marks. Perhaps they'd brought a flask of Dream Juice for the purpose? Or perhaps they'd simply gag her and apply a rock rifle to her back. Either way, Hellequin saw no need to intercept the men below. He needed to get into the dressing rooms behind the silk curtain.

Keeping to the shadows, he eased over and under the crisscrossing scaffold where it fed behind the tented dressing rooms. Lamplight shone up through the silk; three men moved below. Hellequin guessed they'd been tasked with delivering their charge direct to the bossman. But even a hard hand like D'Angelus could not compete with the bewitchment Nim put men under. They had her at a grotesque angle between them, her nakedness betrayed by the flow of neon beneath her flesh.

Hellequin's head jerked, neurons misfiring. Memories flashed over his steel retina - staring down from the safety of his lung basket, a bird's eye view of a flaming farmstead below. His HawkEye homing in on the maul of weathered hands on young flesh. Out in the open. Where screams brought no one running.

The memory snapped off. He refocused on the tented silk below. Nim was silent, the acts the men enforced on her all too familiar.

His lens flicked right. He had noticed the figure approach of course.

"Whadda we do, HawkEye?" It was Pig Heart. The pitchman had slunk along the scaffold, his bulk belying the dexterity which allowed him to tread the upper gangplanks without ever disturbing the crowd below.

Hellequin wanted to crush the pitchman's windpipe and haul him over the scaffold. But the soldier in him saw the value in a simultaneous attack on backstage and Nim's dressing room. Better to deal with all of D'Angelus's men at once than give them chance to spread and take cover.

A great chittering arose from the main tent. The hoppers were in flight, the crowd gasping. It was time to act.

"You take out the men backstage. I'll deal with Nim."

"Like hell I will. By the shitting Saints, Hellequin, they've got rock rifles and our arsenal is back down in the living quarters! Let's take them out together then come back for Nim."

Hellequin gripped Pig Heart's stumbled chin and directed his face down to the tent where Nim was being used.

"Do you see?" he demanded in a dry rasp. "You give Nim over to *that* for a fistful of dollars." He slung Pig Heart back from the edge and wiped his hands down the worn blue frockcoat he wore at show times.

"Yeah, well, it's not like the whore ain't used to it," muttered the pitchman. But he kept his gaze away from the goings on below. "Okay, I'll cause a ruckus with the boys backstage," he spat at last, adding, "I gotta do right by Rust anyways."

"Right by your groin more like." Hellequin was losing time, losing patience. "Rock rifles have to kick back against a shooter's padded shoulder. Stay that same side of the barrel and, often as not, the ammo'll miss."

The pitchman nodded and moved away. Hellequin crouched down, one leg extended, fingers resting lightly on the scaffold. He homed in on the tented silk below, his mercurial eye in constant adjustment. Closer in, he zoomed. Closer, until he magnified the weave enough to see its shoals of silverfish. He found a worn patch.

Alongside the noise of the crowd and the clatter of hoppers' wings, he heard Nim give a sharp cry. Without further thought, he tucked in his elbows and leapt. He dropped like a lead weight. His boots made contact with the silk; it rent under him like spider's web and he fell through the ceiling of the dressing room.

Time narrowed as his HawkEye made a series of minute observations that prompted his body to react. The pole supporting the tent was in arms' reach; he felt its flaking rust under his palms and swung in tight while sliding down. His steel eye's shutter motion allowed him to simultaneously catch the first few seconds of reaction below. A three-backed beast broke apart to reveal Nim spread-eagled. Her attackers were saloon heavies judging by the cut of their cloth.

Two struggled into their pants as Hellequin slid to the ground. A third was in the process of raising a hand to his shoulder where he'd slung his rock rifle.

The heavy never completed the manoeuvre. Hellequin drew his bowie knife from its sheath at his hip. The hilt was clothhod leather, the blade, mottled blue steel. It glinted wetly in the gaslight. Mashing the blade into the heavy's neck, Hellequin severed the carotid artery. He kicked the man aside.

Shouts from the far side of the silk wall told him that Pig Heart was also making his presence known. A rock rifle fired, but it was a smaller silhouette than the pitchman's which slammed against the silk, clutched it and slipped down. A ribbon of red seeped through; Hellequin registered the fact while driving his arm through the air and plunging the knife into a second man's shoulder.

Blood exploded from the wound. Hellequin's steel eye focused in on a single bead, plump as a Jewel Fruit seed, tumbling sideways. His HawkEye refocused inside a microsecond.

Nim had a blank expression. Only the eyes gave her away, brilliant with tears and reflecting the third man with a rock rifle pressed to his shoulder.

A slug embedded itself in an upright landing mat close to Pig

Heart's head. The pitchman tore back his lips, baring yellow tusks. The sniper was tucked behind one of the flats at the far end of the backstage area; Pig Heart suspected an illustrated sand hill, where the faint plume of discharged spark powder lingered in the air. He dragged a hand across his nostrils. Before he could concentrate on the sniper, there were three more chumps to sock it to.

"Saints alive, you're a sight, ain't ya!" shouted a two-tone in a rag waistcoat and pants a size too big. He rocked from one foot to another, a knife to his young hostage's neck. Pig Heart recognised the belt of dry rat remains at the kid's waist. The hostage was the one-time exterminator who had ridden the lift rig with him earlier.

"Only one thing to do with a pig. Slit his throat and make him squeal," said a second, a Sirinese with brow locks that flowed either side each eye and a butting plate stitched into his forehead. His rock rifle was trained on a number of the pitch crew who were spread-eagled on the ground, faces in the dirt.

The sniper took a second shot. Pig Heart felt the slug nip his ear. The sting of it, alongside the blood which oozed down his neck, made him let back his head and loose a tremendous snort. Crumpled at the bottom of the silk drop was the man he had killed first. Pig Heart yanked a rock rifle from the man's dead fist. Swinging the butt in tight to a shoulder, muscular tissue bulging, he ran at the Sirinese.

"Take the pig out, Gribson!" called the Sirinese, presumably to the sniper. He kept his own rifle trained on Pig Heart's men and showed his black teeth.

Pig Heart had the measure of the sniper's angle. He kept the two-tone and the kid hostage between him and the gun. When the sniper failed to take him out, the Sirinese aimed his rifle at the nearest pitchman and fired a slug. The man's skull cracked open like an egg.

Pig Heart kept on coming. He and the Sirinese clashed with the force of two rhinehorn bulls. Pig Heart brought his club of a rock rifle slamming down. The Sirinese blocked the blow with his own rifle, braced between two hands. A slug of rock ammo pierced Pig Heart's thigh. He drove forward with new grit.

"Get up, you gimps! Drive these shitters out," he roared at his pitch crew.

"Easy, freak. Else I'll dust your boy here," shouted the two-tone while the exterminator kid yelped, "He got me, boss! He got me!"

Pig Heart wouldn't be held to ransom. He shunted the Sirinese in-between him and the sniper, with the vague idea of rescuing the kid once he'd disentangled himself. It was an idea which melted the instant he heard the zip of knife passed through flesh. The kid gurgled and fell.

It was distraction enough; Pig Heart felt a crush of pain and the world flooded black. He stumbled, blood draining from his split nose, the same cherry red smearing the butting plate at the Sirinese's forehead. The man's victory was cut short. Pig Heart crushed the butt of his rifle into the Sirinese's windpipe, heard him wheeze like a pair of bellows. The whip of a pocketknife near his jowl told him the two-tone was on him. A slug from the sniper punctured the ground where he'd stood a second earlier.

Convinced his crew had deserted him, Pig Heart cursed them as yellow-bellies. But then the two-tone started to shake violently as if suffering from a malady. It took a second glance for Pig Heart to see the splay of blood at the man's chest and the protruding curve of a scimitar. He didn't stop to thank his backup but charged at the painted sand hill.

Shoot me up, chump! Just you shoot me up, he dared the sniper. There was a whistling noise and a rock took a second chunk out of his already bleeding ear. Pig Heart tossed his head from side to side while snorting, and powered his muscular limbs.

A red figure streaked by – the Jeridian he'd encountered earlier on the lift rig – and she was phenomenally fast. Inside seconds, she made an arrow of her body and leapt over the flat, twisting into a revolving bullet as she travelled and so avoiding the two rock slugs the sniper peeled off.

D'Angelus's man knocked down the sand hill flat and started to run. The Jeridian landed in a roll of muscle, ripped the scimitar from the sheath at her back and flicked it clean through the sniper's neck. Pig Heart watched the head fall.

Earl didn't like being close to hoppers. He pressed back against the thick canvas wall as one of the two nymphs landed on a nearby tent pole, claws scraping the dark metal, wings folding with a rough clack-clack. The nymph was the size of a small burrowing machine – in fact, as Earl noted, its taupe and black exoskeleton had a lot in common with the panel work of those machines abandoned by the government at the country's inactive mines. That the creature was alive did little to detract from its stiff easing out of segmented femur and tibia, or the clockwork bob of its head. Resembling large black pustules either side the skull, the eyes appeared all seeing while the bright green cornsilk poking from between the forewings betrayed the creature's botanical DNA. The same plant feed which had turned Humock's farmland to dust was responsible for the crossbreeding of the original hand-sized greenkicks with a strain of air plant. To a man like Earl, the idea was as ludicrous as it was terrifying.

"Nothing natural about you," he whispered, pawing the canvas at his back as if to scale its height. The hopper twitched its head in his direction. Earl could've sworn it absorbed him with those huge swimming eyes.

With a brittle rub of motion, the hopper took to the air and joined its twin in circling the tent.

Forcing himself to move, Earl mauled the leaf lump in his mouth and eased around the edge of the circus tent to the backstage curtain. Having forced Nim to drain his juice, he'd thought it good for morale to let his boys poke the whore; they'd never afford D'Angelus's rates otherwise. "Swift as virgins getting their first tug-off," he'd warned, and slipped back out front to keep an eye on the boss.

But the minutes were dragging and the men were taking their sweet time. D'Angelus and the heavies he'd kept back were eating up the hoppers' act, but Herb reckoned the ringmaster would be rounding things up soon.

Finding the edge of the curtain, he pulled it gently aside. He needn't have bothered with subtleties. Jaxx, the Sirinese, came tearing through the curtain, followed closely by the swine man, sweaty and mad-eyed. Earl slunk back into the shadows as the pitchman leapt onto Jaxx's back, the two men careering into the ring.

There was a moment of hush as the crowd seemed to presume it all part of the act. Then a statuesque Jeridian woman strode out from backstage and raised her arm, the hair of a severed head intertwined with her fingers.

"Ahoj na vás, vražedné Bolest' Earth svině!" she cried in her native tongue, and the still of the crowd transformed into violent alarm.

Earl's eyes were tight bobbing beads; they scooted to the far side of the tent, settling on D'Angelus and his reserve of men. D'Angelus showed none of the courtesy he'd shown earlier, slamming the Saint Sister aside as she tottered out of her seat and tried to force an exit. His men crushed around him, marking out a path through the crowd with their fists.

Earl dribbled his wad of leaf onto the back of a hand and slopped it aside. *Devil in Hell!* Where were the men he'd sent in? And what now? What as the Jeridian threw the severed head into the dirt and took on the first of D'Angelus's men to reach her? What as the swine who'd pocketed D'Angelus's dollars a short time earlier took the full thrust of Jaxx's butting plate against his forehead and reeled, only to power back inside the second?

All around the ring, the townsfolk stampeded in a bid for freedom. The noise of panic was bloodcurdling. Having escaped to the calliope balcony, the ringmaster, that squat plug of fat, was hopping and gesticulating. Because the hoppers were still loose. Which meant the exit was stitched shut, Earl realised, his insides curdling.

He stared at the spot-lit heavens where the hoppers dashed against the side of the tent, motes of chitinous material dusting down. It was his job to fight alongside D'Angelus, Earl thought vaguely. But he remembered the hopper clinging to the tent pole earlier, and he felt the weight of its oiled black eyes, how it had seemed to stretch its sight inside him and leave some shred of itself tethered there.

There was an urgency to move; he felt it as acutely as a rush of leaf bitters to his bloodstream. One of the hoppers was skydiving. Twisting and tumbling, it swept around the circumference of the tent, slinking in and out the tent poles like a beast of legend. Earl watched, entranced and horrified by the whir of wings, and how, with each revolution, the creature dropped in height but increased its velocity. Nailed to the spot, he was vaguely aware of a blur of battle cries, the shift of bodies, and the tide of air against his face as the hopper swept closer.

"Saints alive, buddy!"

Herb's round face puckered. He shook a hand out as if freeing his fingers of the gore which splashed one half of the stage curtain. The hopper swooped up to a perch in the rafters and was swiftly lassoed by its handler, the man having installed himself at the edge of the zoo platform for the purpose. Herb felt a sense of relief, an emotion which strengthened when one of the pitch crew called up, "S'okay Herb. Hopper just took out one of the brawlers."

Whatta way to go though! From the safety of the calliope balcony, Herb cursed his vantage point. Seeing the pimp's man sliced from hip to rib was another stain on his memory. But wasn't that the price of the ringmaster's life? Cyber Circus was a difficult beast to control and it took every last bit of effort to keep its savagery in check. Occasionally it spilt over.

Herb gripped the gilded railing, leaning into it. There was only one option – leave. But before they rolled on out, it made sense to know what, or who, had caused the ruckus in the first place.

He turned his attention to the crowd. The marks were tightly herded at the edges of the tent, the canvas straining with the pressure of so many bodies fighting to get out.

Herb tapped the rail under his fingers and said softly, "Hang in there, old gal. Just a minute more." It was better to keep the marks circulating. Less chance of the troublemakers actually achieving anything.

In the ring, the Jeridian circled her scimitar above her head, other arm crooked out for balance. She faced three opponents – dust handlers from the looks of them. They had that 'stooped against the wind' stance. Pig Heart had it worse. His snout had been smashed. Blood soaked the pitchman's chin, neck and shirt bib. He was up against a Sirian – ex-cage fighter judging by the brow bolt plate and the slug of the man's fists. Pig Heart took it though and kept on standing.

Herb's eye was distracted by the pimp's black leather trekker's hat. Ahead of him, heavies cut a path through the marks. They appeared to be heading in the direction of backstage.

Whatta they wanna do that for? Herb hummed a slow sad song, the sort Jeridians sang at their torchlight funerals. The calliope played one sour note to harmonise. Staring across the length of the tent to the twisting iron mass of the scaffold, Herb finally understood. On the lift rig stood the HawkEye soldier with the courtesan, Nim, in his arms.

"Okay, old gal. Let's ring the changes."

Herb gave the rail an affectionate pat. On cue, the calliope expanded its gilt ribs and began to pipe a lilting melody that meant nothing to the marks and everything to the carnie folk. Herb saw the Jeridian slice a second head, spin about on a heel and leave the two remaining dust handlers in a footbath of blood. She ran a circuit of the outer rim, leapt at one colossal tent post and hung off the pitch crew's handholds. Watching her climb towards the rafters, Herb saw the second hopper reined in by its handler.

Nim, the hoppers... his main attractions were intact. Herb took off his hat, its soft plumage waving like a sea anemone.

"Adey up, old gal. Adey up,"

He settled his ass on a small stool, lent back against the vibrating pipes and added his hum to the calliope's swan song.

Concussed, Pig Heart found his world had become a blood-red dust cloud, the roar of thousands of papery insect wings in his ears. Out the corner of his eye, he saw the Sirinese's fist speed in again and he pitched sideways. The fist missed his lips by a finger's breadth, just as the pitchman heard the farewell pipe of the calliope. A hot gush of terror ran beneath his chest. He had to get out of the ring and back on board.

"Lost your balls, swine?" The Sirinese showed his black teeth. Blood greased the bolt plate at his forehead. Pig Heart's.

The insinuation fuelled a fresh attack. Pig Heart juiced his legs and charged. The Sirinese might have the advantage of a plated skull, but he had the advantage of pig-headedness. He butted the Sirinese in the left set of ribs.

Pig Heart didn't stick around to give his opponent time to recover. As the reedy music filled the tent, he ran to the side of the ring and attempted to pressgang his way to the backstage area. Rock rifles fired off in the heart of the crowd and he stepped up onto the rim of the ring to get a glimpse over the marks' heads.

At the calliope's cue, his pitch crew had rolled the steel shield across the gap between backstage and the ring. Just like he'd taught them. Dull prangs sounded from outside the tent, droplines being released. A sudden pitch in the tent walls told him that Cyber Circus was on its way out.

He didn't join in the screaming. A glance back confirmed that the Sirinese had sniffed him out and was on his way over, thrusting marks aside. At the same time, Pig Heart sensed the air heating all around him.

The circus was abandoning him, just as he had abandoned it. Just desserts, Pig Heart reminded himself with regret. The dollars in his pocket weren't worth shit now. And that one good thing he'd done in trying to keep the wolf girl out of the hands of the pimp D'Angelus, well, that might aid his legacy but it wouldn't keep the Sirinese from caving in his skull.

The calliope was puffing faster now, its fluting transformed into a low purr. Pig Heart recognised the sound as a heartbeat as alien as his own. His eyes squinted every which way. No time to climb the girders that supported the tent and which were retracting in towards each another, like a dying insect drawing its limbs in to its abdomen. No time to fight the swell of marks and appeal for entry at the backstage door. He stared up at the heavens. Only time to thank the swine's heart in his chest for a life stretched beyond its limits.

"Give me your arm!"

A figure interrupted the glare of the spotlight overhead. The face that lowered towards him was a timepiece. The roar of the crowd seemed to drop away. Pig Heart could've sworn he heard the whir of sprung-wound inner workings. Blood ran from his snout. Multiple blows to his skull had left him in a state of partial consciousness.

One of the Saints themselves, sent to escort me to the afterlife, thought Pig Heart, and he stretched up an arm, expectant of a soft flow of warmth and their joint accession. Instead, a firm grip fixed around his forearm and there was a tremendous wrench to his arm socket. The shock wide-eyed him.

In place of a divine being, he saw Hellequin – HawkEye telescoped down. Skin strained over the twin bone ridges at the soldier's forehead.

"Come on, you swine!"

The tent swayed dramatically, swinging them hard against one of the diagonal iron girders. Pig Heart felt a fresh slash of pain in one knee. He stared across the weave of girders and saw the Sirinese perched between the 'V' of two enormous struts. The man trained a rock rifle in his direction.

Pig Heart counted off his last breaths.

The marks reacted to their first glimpse of the HawkEye soldier, and the Sirinese was knocked off balance by the crush of eager bodies. It was reprieve enough for the pitchman to attempt one last fight for life. He locked his grip around Hellequin's forearm and together they were rising.

Pig Heart's tiny watery eyes took in the speed of their lift, the sides of the tent slipping by in a flash as they shot towards the roof. His stomach flipped as they started a rapid descent. But then the motion swept them sideways, Pig Heart's jowls dragging back off his tusks, the rush of air cooling his bloody snout. A gridded floor appeared under him and they dropped, landing on the deck in a painful mess of limbs.

Pig Heart breathed in gulps. He tasted the tannin stench of the zoo. The mesh beneath him reverberated and there was the oh-so-familiar buffering of heated air. He squinted past the rails that enclosed the platform. Lulu's black trapeze swung towards him, receded far away, then swept back in again. He glanced down and saw Sore Earth drop away.

FOUR

Hellequin watched the pitch crew heave the last headless corpse over the rail, the Jeridian having sequestered the heads for her private collection. He imagined the cadaver flick-flacking out the open skirts of the tent below, a smear on the evening sky.

"Strike me again and I'll chew your hand off," Pig Heart muttered behind him. The threat won the pitchman another heavy slap.

Hellequin turned around, arms folded, and put his lower back against the rail.

"I don't recall you adding that enthusiastic muscle to our fight, Lulu," he said quietly. His HawkEye revolved as he fixated on the ladyboy.

Lulu lost his steel and looked tearful. "Hellequin, you chastise *me*? After what the bad man did?" He waved his handkerchief towards the pitchman, now suspended off a great iron hook alongside the ornate egg sack of Herb's private quarters. A short girder was strapped across Pig Heart's shoulders – forming a makeshift patibulum such as convicts might be forced to carry – his arms bound to it by hemp rope, his lower body left to dangle.

"I cannot begin to comprehend why you would save the brute. He stitched us up. He stitched Nim up." Lulu gave Pig Heart a backhand, the pitchman roaring more in rage than anguish as he attempted to lurch forward. He only succeeded in aggravating the rope burns to his flesh. Wincing, he fell back.

"Enough, Lulu." Perched on the steps to his personal quarters, Herb rotated his hat's rim between his hands. Gone the theatrics and light he reserved for performances. His lips were tight, his eyes hard.

"You're all sissies," pouted Lulu. "Only reason any of us even got wind of D'Angelus's band was because Hellequin overheard Pig Heart and his bitch conspiring to run out on us." The ladyboy thrust a finger at the suspended pitchman, just short of a poke in the eye. "We should offload this shitter along with the rest of the dead bodies. See if pigs can fly."

"Maybe we will. First we gotta get the facts of what happened back there. Sore Earth isn't any old pitch – its ripe at the seams. Literally, which is how the mining boys got them great steaming worms eating up the land like they do. There's traders there, and forges, hardware, printin' press, apothecary, whore houses. Which attracts marks aplenty, all in need of a night out at the circus and the spending of new-mined dollars in their pockets."

Herb's face pinched. "So I gotta wonder what we gained and what we lost back there. Taking off before the end of our show is gonna stitch us up good. Then there's the question of the marks we sliced and diced. And for what?" He pointed at the zoo platform overhead. "To save our women, hmm, Pig Heart? Was that the way of it? Thought you'd sell one piece of ass then take exception when D'Angelus wanted a second into the bargain. Ain't that touching?" Moving up to the top stair – a needless boost to his height since Herb relied on iron will and not size to intimidate – he gestured to the pitch crew as if welcoming their agreement. "Pig and wolf rutting it up."

The sourness of the image reflected in the pitch crew's murmured distaste.

Herb cut them off with a raised hand. "Only, this ain't a summer dance and I ain't no matchmaker." He fed his hat under an arm and strode down the steps. With the might to hire and fire at will, he caused a small shuffle of polite feet among the pitch crew. A few flopped off their caps.

Cyber Circus's king pin eased under the dangling pitchman and brought his head in near to Pig Heart's.

"No one asked you to beat on D'Angelus's men," he hissed.

"D'Angelus was gonna peddle Rust as a whore. She's one of us. Don't that mean something to ya, Herb?" Pig Heart's muscles bulged. The hemp rope rubbed against his flesh with a papery whisper.

"Us? So there's an us now, hey, Pig Heart? And there was me thinking there was only a you." Herb gave the pitchman a push, prompting the patibulum girder to rock slightly on its iron hook. Turning away, he stared at Hellequin and slung a thumb over a shoulder. "So what motivated you to keep ahold of this grunt?"

Hellequin parted his frockcoat and put his hands on his hips. "No carny's the keeper of the other. That's what he told me earlier this evening. I decided to prove him wrong."

"Ain't you the fool!" Herb's mouth got mean. "I don't know what they taught you about comradeship in the military, but here that don't mean shit. When it comes to who gets a handshake and who gets spit on, I'm in charge! Only thing you need to worry about is the money in your hand and how to keep them marks happy."

Hellequin watched Herb cross back to the steps, the readjustments of the HawkEye transposed into small jerks of his head.

"And Nim? Isn't she an asset worth defending?" His tone was measured.

Herb rested a pulpy arm on the stair banister. He let out a sigh. "Hellequin, Hellequin. Day I start treating Desirious Nim like an asset is the day she'll pack up her unmentionables and jump ship. You got a hunk of hardware stitched into your eye and you still can't see the truth about those around you. Nim asks for protection anytime, I'll see about getting her some muscle offa the crew. But so long as she don't ask, I'm gonna presume she's had her fill of guards at the door. I'm gonna presume the real freedom she earns here is worth the imagined dangers."

"Nothing imagined about those gimps raping her this evening." Hellequin drew up to his full height, a hand hovering at the hilt of his sheathed bowie knife. "The pimp was never going to pass up the chance to get Nim back. Why'd you bring us here, Herb?"

A beetle's wing of gilt green opened up in Herb's coach. Nim stepped out of the door and down onto the top step. She wore an angular black robe with a wide red sash.

"Because, as Herb says, Sore Earth is a rich seam and Cyber Circus is a business," she said choppily, adding, "Thanks for letting me rest up a while, Herb."

The ringmaster nodded.

Nim's spectacular red eyes settled on Hellequin. "D'Angelus's men. You halted their assault." She drew the sign of the Saints' arc across her brow with a fingertip and inclined her head. "I am indebted to you."

"You don't need Saints' oaths with a HawkEye. The desire to protect is written into my Daxware." Hellequin's steel eye was still at last, focused fully on Nim. His hand left the hilt of his bowie knife.

"So now we get to it!" Herb tapped Nim's hand as if she was his confidant, but the volume of his voice spoke to all. "The HawkEye didn't save the pitchman because he thinks us carnies look out for our own, even if they are despicable sell-their-own-motha shysters. Oh no, he saved the pig because his hardwiring gives him no say so in the matter."

Hellequin crossed his arms, exposing the frayed fabric badge of the HawkEye platoon on one shoulder – a circle within a circle, stitched in off-white thread. The pocketed grey pants he wore were ripped at the knees. His boots were black clothhod leather, steel plated at the heel.

"I still think for myself," he muttered.

"Oh no you don't. Not if you work at Cyber Circus." Herb went to push past Nim. He paused to allow her to step down then put a foot inside his front door. As an afterthought, he turned his head towards the assembled company and shook his hat at them. "Whatta we do with Pig Heart then? I gotta have a chief pitchman and he's it. Has been for the longest time and I'm loathe to let a good man go. But he's got a pocketful of dollars from betraying us. So do we sling him overboard or let him chop it in the breeze a while? Pitch crew come and go so I'm gonna stick with asking the main acts. Lulu? I got an inkling I know what you're gonna say."

The ladyboy ran delicate hands over the tutu lace at his hips. "Toss the bastard."

"And Hellequin? I'm guessing you're for keeping the swine alive?"

Fixated on Nim, Hellequin said, "Let him chop it in the breeze if it will satisfy a need for retribution."

Herb's finger of command passed to Nim.

"Whaddaya say, Nim?"

"If the pig'll sell us out once, he'll sell us out again."

"I'll take that as a vote to dump his ass. What about you kids?" Herb squinted at the far end of the platform where the fat burp pipes of the heating system wove in amongst the polyps of float bladders. "Come outta the dark a second will ya and let's get this over with."

Armadillidium balls, the colour of inner eyelids and the height of Hellequin's knee, rolled out into the gaslight. Each pinkish exoskeleton unrolled to reveal a soft inner belly shaped like a child. Two girls, one boy, unfolding gangly red-crusted legs and two great claws.

"Tip him over," said one girl. Her face had a puckered quality, like skin soaked in water.

The other girl gave her sibling a knock on the carapace with a club-hand. "I like the pig man. He rolls me in the dust to buff my shell."

"Keep him. His head makes a good scratching post," said the boy, speaking with the same fat vowelled lisp that affected all three.

"Two for, one against. So far we're drawing even." Herb looked agitated. "Guess it's left to me to be the one to call it."

"What about my say, you sack of shitters?" called Pig Heart, rattling on his cross. Slaver dripped from his mouth to the ground.

"Forfeited your say the second you pocketed D'Angelus's blood money," shot Herb. "Ah, to hell with it. Send the pig overboard. I ain't got time nor inclination to watch my back for fear he'll stick the knife in." He slapped a hand through the air, dismissive of further appeal from Pig Heart, and went to shut the door.

"Bare men mustn't kill the pig. Its mine," interrupted a sibilant voice. Long fury limbs appeared over the lip of the platform overhead and fed slowly down onto the railing enclosing Herb's personal platform. Rust squatted on the rail, ratty hair amassed at her shoulders, black eyes shining out from a filthy face.

"Just because you and the swine can't resist your bestial impulses does not give him room for reprieve," cut in Lulu. He flinched as the wolf girl leapt down and raced towards him on all fours. She drew up just short of the ladyboy, fingers bracing the metal floor, her muscular thighs skimming sideways.

"And it with titties and a shlong." Rust gnashed, a glint to her eye. "Cyber Circus is full of beasts and freaks. The pig is mine. Give it back. I will tear out its heart if it does bad stuff again."

"You're vouching for the pitchman, Rust? It'll be up to you to keep him in line else I'll have you tossed back out onto the salt plains where I found you."

Rust nodded. Herb slumped at the shoulders, tired with it all.

"I ain't no hunk of flesh to be whored out or mithered

over." Pig Heart buckled against the strut at his back. "Hell, Herb, fifteen years you and me have been working Cyber Circus. We've been through the lot of it, and you're gonna rat me out on one mishap?"

Herb squinted over. "You sold me out, swine. Me! Not the whore. Not the wolf. You sold out my acts and put the real lady here in danger." He held up his hands and gestured to the reverberating cavern around them. Tenderness came into his eyes, replaced with a razor edge as his gaze returned to the pitchman. "History don't mean nothin' if you're gonna switch sides and play a different game."

He thrust a finger at Hellequin. "Bitch gets her wish. Pig Heart stays. But he pays and you're gonna make sure of it." His finger shifted to the Jeridian woman. "Name?"

"Asenath." The Jeridian titled her chin, exposing her throat piercings. She wore her hair in a giant Mohawk. Her red skin glistened.

"You will assume Pig Heart's duties." He pointed to the hessian sack the Jeridian carried, the bottom of which was wetly stained. His lip curled. "Whaddaya gonna do with those heads anyway?"

"Remove the skull, scrape out the brains, pack the eyelids with seed, pin the mouth, boil the head in herbs, and rub it with ash to keep the spirits out. Then I string it from the top mast to warn the motherfuckers to leave us be."

Herb tugged on his shirt collar. "Sorry I asked."

His attention returned to Pig Heart. "One thing the Jeridian's right about – Cyber Circus has gotta have blood." He eyed the pitch crew. "Chop him to the breeze, fellas!"

The ringmaster stepped inside his cabin and slammed the door shut.

FIVE

The country of Humock was 3,268,601 square kilometres. Wherever there was a mine in need of burrower drivers and dust handlers, a well shaft to be maintained, or a ranch to be staffed, there were men. And wherever there were men, there was a whorehouse, and a bar stocked with smoke sticks and Jackogin, and a hamam with sweat rooms and soft hands to lather up and rinse the day away. The workers had other needs too – cobblers, general stores, haberdasheries, clothhod stables, armouries, banks, print presses, and apothecaries, alongside markets selling water, bio-toughened sage, soap flakes, and other bare necessities. And while the sun beat down like a curse, and it was difficult to know where the once fertile land began and the deserts ended, Humock was still a promised land in comparison to its neighbours.

To the east, the bedrock creased to form huge black mountains. Beyond lay the much smaller country of Jeridia, and Sirin, which was tinier still. When the civil war broke out in Humock, both countries had rallied to its aid, but both had endured the fallout in isolation. All that remained of the once fertile Jeridia was a scab of bedrock. Since few of its citizens were able to eek out a living, most became refugees in the dry expanse of Humock. It was a similar story for Sirin. The fists and plated skulls of the Sirinese were useless against the erasing gas wielded by Humock's militia. Like the Jeridians, the Sirinese were forced to abandon their homes, schools, workshops, spirit huts and graveyards, and cross the border into the selfsame country which had bombed it.

Ten years on, Humock had become a melting pot for the disenchanted, a place where men were employed to shovel dust out of the mines in the certainty it would drift back in, where a respected flesh handler like D'Angelus would rather waste the breath of every employee he had if it meant victory over Cyber Circus, and where a Sirinese warrior like Jaxx would work for blood money in an alien land, all the while despising his employer.

"What's the state of play, Jaxx?" D'Angelus straddled two squat limestone columns, hands on his hips, trekker's hat shadowing his face.

"Das says we can board now. He's got a handful of men to spare, harnesses for ten in the cargo hold. Machine was used as a dust carrier fairly recently, but we can stick the men in filter masks, tell them to rest their eyes until we come up for air. Supplies are loaded. Das is asking if you want to head north via the swallow hole or stick to the bore tunnels 'til we reach Haven Springs?"

D'Angelus took a nip off his smoke stick. "Haven Springs. Swallow hole takes us through the old cave system and I'm not a man to trust in Mother Nature." He exchanged the smoke in his nostrils for an invigorating breath. "Herb isn't the sort to skip the dollar. He'll want to haul up at one of the pitch sites close to Haven, else he'll have no choice but to hit Zan City to refuel."

"Shuck." Jaxx produced the sound from the back of his throat. "I'm all about avoiding that shithole. And she's worth it, this Desirious Nim? The whore weaves a pretty dance, but is she worth us spitting time and energy her way?"

"Oh, this isn't about Nim anymore," said D'Angelus, tugging the last dregs off the smoke stick. "Although I intend to reacquire that whore and put her to use. No, this is beyond that. Those circus freaks sliced my boys." He smiled. His cannibalised teeth shone under the moonlight. "Bet you'd like a rematch with that two-faced pig too."

"I'm in no hurry," said the Sirinese without inflection. "My people have a saying. Walk simply. Find the light."

D'Angelus grunted. He dropped the stub of the smoke stick between the limestone columns. "What the hell does that mean?"

"Means I'll get my rematch with this Pig Heart maybe tomorrow, maybe half a lifetime from now. But I will get it."

"I say screw the maybe. I say a man makes his own luck."

"So we go after them now. But what about the HawkEye? He's unnatural." Jaxx scratched the scar matter edging the butt plate at his brow.

"None of us got a real look at that suckerloop. Sure, he comes in last thing to snatch the pig out. But why'd he act coy unless he's a grifter with fake ink and a tin eyepiece?" D'Angelus shrugged. "Only thing that matters is the goon took out three of my men. Not a problem if our raid had been successful. A few dust handlers in exchange for a whore worth her weight in gold? It's business. But we got our blood spilt and for nothing. What's more, I missed out on the wolf bitch too and that is one lost opportunity too far."

He stepped down off his limestone pedestal. Slinging his head left and right, he took in the men who milled at the entrance to the mine, a vast maw in the face of the blasted cliff. Dust handlers for the most part, he concluded, men whose spines had hooked from labouring under sacks filled with the stuff. There were also a few wheaters who'd exchanged that useless livelihood for thuggery. They carried their rock rifles under an arm like the farmers they once were.

The only figure who intrigued him was a solitary Zen monk, wearing a black robe secured with a belt full of relics – shrivelled dead things and blooded scraps of fabric alongside strings of bottle-tops, the clinking of which was designed to ward off the devil. A traditional sackcloth hood covered the man's head, belted at the neck with twine. The mouth was partially buttoned to allow for breath. The eyeholes were gorged out.

D'Angelus squinted across at Jaxx. "I lost Earl this evening so I'm promoting you. There's leaf wad, crates of Jackogin and whores aplenty for your trouble." His mouth hardened. "Help me track the bitches and bring them in. And while you're there, tear each of those circus freaks a new asshole."

Jaxx nodded. "We navigate the bore tunnels and intercept them. But you should know I can't use my tracker skills this side of Zan City. That blood nest leaves its crust in the air." His nostrils flared.

"This side of the Zan we're no worse off then. Should the hunt stretch out beyond that hole, we've got an extra trick up our sleeve."

D'Angelus started for the mine entrance. Jaxx accompanied him.

"Want me to pick ten men?" Jaxx kicked up dust as he walked.

"Fill up the cargo space. There's space for four up front: you, me, the driver, and one more."

D'Angelus stopped.

"You religious, Jaxx? Your savage ways been tamed to those of the Saints?"

Jaxx shook his head, moonlight glancing off his bolt plate. "I'm a spirit man, boss. The Saints are too…" He considered his phrasing. "Stiff."

"I should hope so. Saints wouldn't be much use to us alive!" D'Angelus patted Jaxx's shoulder. "If it's all the same to you, I'll keep religion on my side." He showed his tic teeth.

"Father!" he shouted at the hooded figure. "The miners can live a day without your silent ministering. You and I, we're going underground and, by the Saints, you'd better bring me luck."

"I'd have preferred to grease up Old Billy there." Das nodded across the cavern at a huge bore machine. The thing boasted five drill heads, each a quarter long again as the main cab. "But there's still a hairline fracture in one of those pretty drills. Given the time scale, I went for the next best. Wanda-Sue."

Jaxx eyed the smaller burrower. The cab was covered in titanium scales. A great sweep of the metal rose up off windshield, like a hopper's bone crest. Out front, a giant corkscrew captured the glow of gaslight inside the cave, its surface moving liquidly.

There was a femininity to the machine, Jaxx gave Das that much. Something about the decorative scales – although the design was purely practical, geared to have the shale and water pockets sluice right off the burrower. He didn't believe in a monk's ability to bring them luck. But he did believe in spirit signs, and the look of those scales reminded him of the silver slab bolted to his scalp.

D'Angelus was clearly less concerned with the look of the machine and more with its speed. "I'm thinking they've got fifty knots on us by now. Headwind means they'd be fools not to head southeasterly. You're the map man, Das. Where'd we need to come out to track the freaks down?"

Das sucked in his cheeks. Fishing the miniature tin scroll of a Mapbox from an overall pocket, he typed in co-ordinates with a grimy finger. "We got a straightish run, boss, through some of the widest bore tunnels. We're pushed on time but, Saints willing, we'll come out at Hide or Bromlin in time to catch the circus landing."

"Hide has the permanent site," said Jaxx. Bigger towns had year round pitches for the travelling circuses and other vagrant performers, consisting of fixed wooden seating and a concreted dust ring. Some even had gas lamps dotted around the showground, just begging for a struck match.

D'Angelus clapped his hands. "No point standing here gassing about which way Herb'll swing that floating puffball of his."

A ripple of heavy chains echoed about the cavern and the

monk flinched instinctively. But they were not in the freshly cracked chambers below where sound had a far deadlier impact and the men paid him no heed. Instead, the hatch at the rear of the burrower lowered to form a gangway. Securing filter masks over their faces, the ten men Jaxx had selected transformed into insect hybrids – the hard black leather air chamber protruding off their faces like mandibles, the reflective visor resembling one large compound eye. Striding up the ramp and disappearing inside the cargo hold, they fell into a herd-like symmetry. The rub of chains resounded about the cavern again and the hold buttoned up.

Das stabbed a finger at the Mapbox. "Yep, that's the way of it."

He pocketed the device and slumped off to the front of the burrower. Cracking his shoulders to loosen them, he took hold of a winch handle and revolved it with effort. Jaxx considered knocking Das aside and performing the task himself. It surprised him to find that Das, a sack of skin and bone, had some muscle to him. The titanium head crest levered up, providing access to the cab.

D'Angelus gestured to a metal ladder.

"After you, Father."

SIX

"You see him?" Rind had her wrinkled face to the gap.

"I'm looking." Tib was impatient. Sights like this were rare, even in the harsh world of Cyber Circus. It would be a crying shame to miss it.

"I spy with my little eye..." Rind's siblings tried to crowd her spy hole.

"...a great fat pig flapping in the wind." Ol finished her sentence, over enunciating her words with relish.

They were tucked in behind the calliope. The great spread of the instrument lay on the other side of a mezzanine of pipework. Only the Scuttlers had the strangeness of limb and agility to fit between the calliope's flesh and folds. Crouched down on pinched knees and hard forearms, hoary shells perched above like ovipositors, the children squinted through gaps in the fibroid floor. Suspended under the front rib of the circus, and visible now and again when the clouds dissipated, was the patibulum girder. It was attached at the bough by steel guide ropes, but otherwise free to revolve in the tremendous airflow. Every so often, they would hit turbulence and the stretcher would buffet up against the toughened sponge at the breast of the ship. The Scuttlers watched the crucified Pig Heart get dragged across the barnacled sponge.

Rind fed the tip of one clawed limb between her lips and sucked it. "He's a gonna," she said, seemingly sad of the fact.

Nim watched the tassel fly's lazy looping flight near the ceiling silk. Its wings were a glorious sunset bisected by veins of blue neon. The thorax and head were coated in that velvet blackness peculiar to insects, softness that provoked a desire to touch alongside bristly abjectness. Nim shivered and stretched her long pale limbs across the bedcover. The satin felt good beneath her skin and she needed that. Something gentle after the violence of the men hours earlier.

The tassel fly circled above in a whisper of wings. Nim remembered the attack in waves; the first slap that knocked her sideways, a man pinioning her, another gnawing her breasts, a third bruising his way inside of her, slop-jawed and territorial.

She moved her bare legs up and down the silk sheet. Think of the good. That's what she'd always done when put to work at the Elegance Saloon. So she concentrated on the purring undercurrent of the circus in flight. The powder pink ribboned corsetry which she had so carefully stitched... Prying hands and lustful faces washed across her mind again. Nim tensed her neck muscles and forced the memory aside. Her heart was a tight punch behind her ribs. The good stuff. The smell of spiced incense from the pierced metal resin burner. The tremble of a thread of tiny bells suspended near the doorway. The swiftness of the ship through the night.

A voice spoke from beyond the screened doorway.

"Can I come in, Nim?"

She recognised the timbre. Hellequin. The HawkEye. It hurt her that he was so quick to cash in on her Saints' oath. Not because she expected him to be above desire, only that her own flesh felt like a weight. But the tears would heal, the bruises fade.

Forcing herself up onto an elbow, Nim wondered if he would prefer the gas lamp dimmed. The current spat like hot fat below the surface of her skin; if he was intent on her colours, he might not notice the stains the other men had left. She kept her robe closed for the time being though and answered, "Yes, I am ready."

A hand parted the soft flow of fabric at the doorway.

Hellequin entered the dressing room. He'd discarded his frockcoat, the striped waistcoat showing more of his skin. Nim's gaze lingered on the blue and red hawk tattooed on the outside of both his upper arms. Signature of the HawkEye regiment.

She stared at his face. After several weeks encountering the soldier on board, she still couldn't make sense of the clockwork left eye. It made her gut sore to think that this apparently cognisant man had chosen to butcher himself in such a way. She was aware of the arguments of self-sacrifice, the promise of excellence in the field of war craft. But in simple terms, Hellequin had agreed to his own deconstruction and rewiring, and Nim could not begin to comprehend why. What she did understand were the consequences of biomorphing. Hellequin might have chosen where she had enjoyed no such choice, but in the end they were both made freaks by the process. Both at home in Cyber Circus.

She tried to remind herself of their similarity while easing her legs off the bed and slowly walking towards her guest.

"These are my terms and they are not up for discussion. This is a one time thing. Outside of this hour, you will not call on me. You will not presume to act familiar with me before the crew, and you will not loiter outside my dressing room anymore. I may not have the strength to always fight off my attackers, but while I'm living in this circus, I will live as a free woman. I will not be guarded!" She stalked over to the thin gilt stalk that grew up from the floor and served as a bedside table, grasped a large hour glass and turned it over.

"I'm not here for that." His hand closed around hers as she started to undo her robe.

Rage enveloped her. "This is the only thing I have to offer you, Hellequin. I have no Jackogin, no smoke sticks, no leaf wad, and I'm all out of patience. So let's screw or else take your unwelcome ass back out the way you came." Her blood eyes flashed. Not a man alive could break her.

The soldier dipped his chin. "I came to see how you were."

"Just dandy. Thanks for asking." Nim pointed at the doorway. "See you around, Hellequin."

The manufactured eye telescoped in on her, amber lens burning. "How are you, Nim?"

"You've asked me that already and I've answered."

"Are you hurt? I can have Herb call in a doc next time we land." Hellequin tipped back his head. The steel eye whirled and adjusted. "Still got that rip in the ceiling where I came though earlier. I'll see Herb about that too. It's letting bugs in." He stretched up a hand and swatted the tassel fly.

Nim imagined she heard the tiny knock as the insect hit the floor. She clutched the rails at the end of the bed and peered over. The fly was beautiful brokenness.

"Want to know how I feel, Hellequin? Rip the skin off my bones and crawl under if you could? Thing is, I don't fit neatly into your view of the violated. I have been gangbanged before and, every time, I lock up the fact and throw away the key." She got off the bed and stood up, her spine immaculately straight. "Your prying concern means shit. There'll be no display of sobbing hysteria. Those men robbed me of nothing… except a peaceful evening." She gestured curtly towards the doorway.

The HawkEye toughed up. "I'm not asking you for details. There's been damage inflicted and it strikes me as right that someone should check on you. Pig Heart's being keelhauled as we speak for his part in it. He's no innocent, but he's been with the circus long before either of us came along, and today Herb had to dole out that hellish punishment on his chief pitchman because you want to live as a free woman." Hellequin shook his head. He exhaled heavily. "Saints almighty, Nim, you peddle a dangerous trade. Even if D'Angelus doesn't force you back to his stable, there's always gonna be some goon fixated on a beauty with the mods you've got. So you don't appreciate me watching your back? I say tough."

Nim swallowed painfully. "You're trying to pin Pig Heart's punishment on me? The man betrayed us!"

Hellequin gave a sharp laugh. "And that's the only thing you take away from everything I've just said. Desirous Nim, you are one self-occupied doll. I'm talking about you putting the whole troop in danger and unnecessarily so."

"You are not my keeper, Hellequin. Said yourself, the need to protect is hardwired into you thanks to Daxware."

"Just explain this to me, Nim. If everyone in this troop is so convinced they are their own agents – owe no mind to anyone, just keep their eyes on the money – then how come Pig Heart's guilty of a crime? And if there's no idea of belonging to something, why'd men die for you today?"

"Because they were in D'Angelus's way, plain and simple. And don't forget I wasn't the only prize he was eying. Rust was on the list too."

"Rust's used to having blood on her hands. She can protect herself."

Hellequin's hands went to his hips. Nim saw the shift in muscle beneath his tattooed upper arms. She was more attuned to the ebb and flow of the body than most – it was her job to be. Despite the violence she had experienced so recently, she was instinctually drawn to the HawkEye. His arms looked like hard-packed leather with tattoos stitched in.

Lust was alien. She felt immensely tired suddenly. "What exactly do you want from me, Hellequin?" she said softly.

"I want your permission to do as I am coded."

"You want to stand guard over me?"

"Yes." Hellequin lost his soldier reserve. He worked a hand around his jaw. "More practical to stand guard outside the door, I suspect."

Nim wore a faint smile. "I suspect it would be."

The soldier squatted down at the end of the bed. Nim heard the concentric rings of his steel eye revolve as he examined the carcass of the tassel fly.

"Fragile little bug," he said softly.

Time was a tumble of hurt bones and muttered half words for Pig Heart as he hung crucified beneath the front rib of the ship. Wind stung each ear flap. Muscles strained. Flesh bled where it had been sliced open at each impact. The scream of air slipstreaming around him was added to suddenly by the drag of chains.

Pig Heart sensed a square open above him. Seconds later, he was drawn upwards at a measured pace. The instant he was winched inside the ship, the hatch bolted back down and the noise cut off. Peace settled around him.

The iron patibulum was dragged aside from the hatch and he was lowered to the floor, a hand guiding the crucifix down so that he lay face up. His head sang with vertigo. And his body – oh, his body! – it seemed to tear into itself over and over. He blinked repeatedly. His vision stayed blurred, the fibrous ceiling overhead reduced to an incongruous mass. He tried to move. The agonies intensified and he yowled.

"Hush, Pig Heart," said a sibilant voice – salve to his hurt body and mind. "A bad bad thing it did talking with those bare men. But it's suffered enough."

The hemp rope slackened then fell away; Pig Heart felt its imprint remain in the blistered flesh at his wrists, upper arms and waist.

"It must crawl now to Rust's den."

Pig Heart felt something wet and rough at his throat. Rust raised her head. Tangled hair hallowed her face and spilt down. She kept her tongue poked out, stained with his blood.

"Legs won't carry me," he mumbled.

"Pig's too fat to drag. Crawl."

Only for Rust. Only for that grime-spattered bitch. Rolling off the patibulum, he felt the stiff matter of his clothing against his raw flesh like hornet stings. It took every last trace of energy to persuade his hands and knees to support his weight.

He started to crawl. Waves of agony broke over him. He hurt down to his soul.

SEVEN

D'Angelus nipped at his smoke stick, temporarily misting the view pane. The drug did little to soothe him. He was all about the flesh trade. This subterranean world was bloodless. No amalgam of fibre, fur, sweat, colour and death. Miles below Humock as they were, there were only the bore tunnels – great caverns blasted out the limestone, which reminded D'Angelus of a flameless hell.

The Sirinese, Jaxx, was strapped into the bench seat to his left. He brushed his elbow against the sleeve of the monk strapped in to the right of him.

"A home fit for the devil himself, hey, Father?"

The monk belonged to a silent order and wouldn't answer of course. But it didn't stop D'Angelus wondering if the monk knew something he didn't about the integrity of the rock surrounding them? The superstitions of the miners certainly suggested as much, which was why a Zen monk always accompanied blast parties to the rock face. But the bore tunnels were well established; any unstable rock had long been mechanically sheared off, or netted and bolted to a seam above.

D'Angelus let back his head and howled. Seeing the monk flinch instinctually, D'Angelus strained against his harness, laughing from the pit of him.

"Forgive me, Father. Don't think me without faith. But these black pits, well, they give me the willies. Gotta have a sense of humour."

"Oh yessy," Das mumbled from the driver's bucket seat up front. The navigator fixated on the windshield as the burrower's headlamps glanced off tessellated rock. "Gotta have a joke if you wanna survive the mines. Dust handlers got filthy mouths on them."

D'Angelus grunted. "Don't I know it! Come pay day, the fuckers end up in my joint. Wanna trade a dollar for snatch. Not that it's in my interests to complain. A dollar's a dollar, hey, Father?" He gave the monk's arm another knock and showed his ghoul teeth.

But just thinking about the Elegance Saloon brought to mind the rich blaze of chandeliers, his stable of warm, languid girls jacked up on Dazzle Dust, the scold of Jackogin, and his smile drained. He didn't like it below ground. Didn't like it one bit.

Seated alongside D'Angelus, Jaxx seemed to sense his boss's apprehension. "Not long until we surface now. That right, Das?"

"Yep'um. Just entering the old farm tunnels."

Jaxx glanced across. His eyes were slits of jet. "It'll be dawn once we surface. Nowhere to hide in that dust bowl. For Cyber Circus or us."

The farmhouse had long since run to ruin. A windmill that once pumped water for livestock stood motionless. The porch was crumpled in. The roof had sloughed most of its tiles; those that remained were the colour of rust.

Across the yard were a water tower and tumbledown barn. The water tower reservoir advertised 'Soul Food' in faded red lettering. The door to the barn stood ajar. Inside were a great many hessian sacks stored for the transport of the plant feed, now buried under dust.

The farm appeared hastily abandoned, with many remnants left in place to rot. Delivery trucks were still parked out back of the barn, tyres fallen in, the sun and wheat sheaf logo bleached across their bonnets. Out in the nearest field of dust, the traction reaper had seized mid-furrow, jaw craned wide, its scythe-like teeth blooded with rust. Chaff plates ran the length of the reaper's spine. Two squat chimneys sprouted up back like testes. Other machines were scattered as far as the horizon: corrugated burrowers, steel Jack O'Lanterns with their eyes gone out, a stack of reserve trespass mines from the end of the farm's operational life when it became necessary to guard against the protestors and those whose land had been destroyed.

Dawn brought with it a new intruder – a large dirigible drifting overhead. The unusual craft boasted a brightly striped hide, open skirts that frilled and ebbed like living fungus, and strings of coloured lights streaming from its twin masts. Smoke spilt off the backend, leaving a grey snail's trail across the sky. As the sun rose over Soul Food Farm, the dirigible advanced with bursts of steamy engine sound and soft putt-putts of expelled air.

In the barren field below, dust started to bounce a centimetre above the ground. Moments later, the surface broke with an audible crack that echoed off the quiet landscape. A metal corkscrew wormed up, expelling dry dirt like sputum. It grew in circumference, revealing a huge titanium crest, faces behind glass and a scaled abdomen that tapered to a steam-sealed trapdoor.

Sledging up and out of its hole, the burrower propelled itself through the dust, belly flicking side-to-side to drive momentum.

"You can't be serious about putting down." Hellequin stared at the ringmaster.

"Someone explain why we've gotta land," Herb threw out as he strode between the pitch crew, busy oiling the fleshy rigging either side of the gangplank.

"Need to refuel," answered Asenath, the Jeridian with a penchant for severed heads and who now headed up the pitch crew.

"Precisely." Herb stopped walking and rested his elbows on

the brass safety rail. He peered down into the air-filled hull. "My girl here is running on dregs. She needs to suck on a water pipe." He gave the rail an affectionate if begrudging pat.

Hellequin dragged a hand through his hair. "The pimp's gonna have acquired a new chain gang of heavies."

"It'll take D'Angelus two days to navigate the dust trail to Haven Springs. Plenty of time to get a bellyful of water." Herb kept his gaze on the grey landscape below. "Plenty of time to set up pitch and relieve the marks of their dollars too."

"You want to put on a performance at Haven Springs?" The soldier's steel eye tucked back into its socket, revolted at the fact.

Herb tutted. "Hellequin. I've been straight with you all the way since you and I first bumped gums. You need a way of life that'll distract from the madness you know is coming. I need acts. Simple as. So when I tell ya Nim's a nice girl, but in my eyes, just another asset, I'm guessing you gotta believe me. You keep guard outside your girlfriend's dressing room if you want. But for the rest of us carnies, the show must go on!"

The ringmaster walked away, patting his belly and nodding knowledgeably as he inspected the handiwork of each crew member he passed.

Hellequin leant forward and draped his long arms over the railing, aware of the warmth of the metal through the sleeves of his frockcoat. Below, the open hull gave out onto the dust plains – or as he remembered them, fertile prairie until Soul Food sucked the life from it. He caught sight of something then, a silver dash in the desert. The HawkEye implant telescoped in, its twin rings performing alternating revolutions. He saw the tip of a vast metal nose cone, the splatter of dust mid-motion…

"And what if the pimp's caught up with us already," he called out.

Rubberised silk blasted up into the sky, propelled from spinnerets to the rear of the burrower, Wanda-Sue. Most fell short of Cyber

Circus. Two threads struck home, one attaching to the stump end of a brass vein, the other to a kite line. Each gob of silk burst apart into hundreds of micro-fine threads that wound round and round their anchor points, securing purchase. The noise of the ship deepened as it buckled against the restraints. Far below, the burrower wormed its backend into the dust.

"They're bedding down. Everyone grab a hold!" cried Asenath, abandoning her maintenance task to grip the rail alongside Herb and Hellequin.

"What in the name of the Saints does that mean?" Herb's eyes widened with the sort of surprise that didn't strike the ringmaster often.

"Means D'Angelus has got himself an ex-military burrower. Machine fitted with cannons capable of shooting rubber silk at the enemy."

The Jeridian was right, Hellequin realised. Focusing on the feed jet at the base of one spinneret, he saw the flight of the silk bundles in fractured snapshots. He switched his attention to Asenath, steel eye retracting and refocusing.

"Who'd you serve with?"

The Jeridian batted a hand off her brow. "Ninth platoon. Home of buffoons, loons and idiots."

"Ninth platoon?" Hellequin took in the ladder piercing at the woman's throat, the rock ammo scars at her high forehead and a shoulder, the scar of a stab wound running from an inner elbow around to her collarbone, a dark blue symbol at one ear lobe. Tattoo of a sickle blade. Sign of one of Zan City's gangs.

Hellequin kept the knowledge to himself. The woman was well versed in military technology, and, just then, that was all that mattered. She was also Cyber Circus's newly appointed chief pitchman and all about giving orders.

"Herb. You'll take the bridge, ya? Be ready to drive your lady hard once we've broken free of the tethers."

"Hold it there." Herb jiggled his generous belly with his hands, freshly agitated. "This is my ship and I don't take kindly to being ordered about by a Jerdian bitch who's newly elevated but who can just as speedily be removed from the post."

"Yes, this is your ship. You speak to its heart and lungs. You've known this vessel the longest and have the most experience as its sailing master."

There was a sudden jolt. Asenath's dark green eyes acquired the same intensity as Hellequin's metalmorphised gaze.

"They're reeling us in. I am asking you to take the wheel for this hour only. After that, you can don your hat and order us around again." A flash of silver and Asenath's scimitar arrived just short of Herb's throat. She grinned. "I'll even let you keep your head."

Herb considered his new chief pitchman with an appraising eye. "Uh huh." The trace of a smile at his lips suggested the ringmaster was secretly pleased to be tasked with saving his ship. He strutted off in the direction of the bridge, knocking into the rail either side now and again as the circus struggled against its tethers.

Returning the scimitar to a black leather scabbard at her back, the Jeridian clapped her hands briskly. The pitchmen responded, apparently having already fallen in with her abrupt style of leadership.

"We need volunteers to climb out on top of the tent, locate the parasite ropes and cut us free. The devils have landed three shots last count," she told them.

"You want some sucker to climb out on the rigging while Cyber Circus is in flight?" spat one pitchman, chowing down on a smoke stick as if it was his last taste of life and he intended to drain every bit of flavour. "We ain't got a hope. The Saints alone know where the gobs landed," said a second, and a third, "We ain't paid enough for that kind of shit!"

"D'Angelus will set snipers on anyone who goes up top and tries to free the craft," said Hellequin. He pursed his lips. They hadn't much of an alternative. The closer they got to the ground, the greater the likelihood that D'Angelus's men could pin down the ship.

"You need an athlete to navigate the exterior while avoiding sniper fire." Hellequin stepped inside of himself a moment, to the night he had been tasked with removing the civilian contingent from the goods' store at the township of Graymo. Tucked in behind a shot-out truck tyre, he'd sketched out his manoeuvres in the dust. He would send in men from the rooftop. He would cover them – that was the purpose of the HawkEye soldier. To see what was coming before others did. To be one step ahead. To volunteer the lives of those more disposable than his own.

His mind snapped back to the present. "Lulu should do it."

The surprise on the faces of the pitch crew gave way to a dawning inevitability and murmurs of "The ladyboy should do it," "Only one with the skills," and "Whaddaya say, Jeridian?"

"My name is Asenath," the woman emphasised coldly. She scrutinised Hellequin with her dark green eyes. "And how do we persuade Lulu to do it?"

"Let me handle Lulu," said Hellequin.

"Drag them in! Drag them in!" hollered D'Angelus.

Jaxx drove the giant winch by its handle, stretching onto tiptoe each time the wheel moved around to its highest axis. The sleeves of his kurta shirt strained across his tensed muscles. The brimless white kufi hat he wore grew dark with sweat.

Das was at his elbow. Crossing his wiry brown arms, the navigator squinted up and gave a low whistle. "Now that is one strange critter you've harpooned there, Jaxx. Oh, yessy yes. Oh, yessy yes," he repeated softly.

All around the burrower, D'Angelus's men were drinking in the fresh air after the hours in the hold, stretching their legs, sharing jokes and occasionally shadowing their eyes with the flat of a hand and staring up at their catch.

You think it's all over, thought Jaxx of each, including the saloon owner. His Spirit belief system led him to consider another path though. One that allowed for a small seed-like shape flickflacking down the side of Cyber Circus's tarpaulin.

Lulu took to his ass and slid down one panel of the tent's roof at speed. The bowed fabric at the bottom formed a makeshift trampoline. The instant his feet made contact with it, Lulu softened his knees, absorbed the tremor, and kicked off. He knew all about tumbling through space inside the tent, where the spotlights burnt down from above like balled fire. But this was a different degree of vastness. Arms pinioned to his sides, feet pointed out of habit, he imagined himself catapulted up to the heights of the tent's twin peaks. Except, there was an endless stretch of blue sky above him this time. Nothing to cling onto. No net below.

He tucked his fear beneath his breastbone. He was Lulu – tantalising, mesmerising, the marchioness of flight! There was nothing new about this performance. It was simply an alternative venue. And a tougher crowd, he realised as a couple of rock ammo shots fell short of him.

The attack brought his latent testosterone to the fore. Soaring over the first peak of the tent, propulsion hollowing his cheeks, he found a new motivation to succeed. Yes, he'd extracted a promise from the HawkEye in exchange for his help, but it was reward enough to spit in the eye of the bad men below. Men who'd take a prize like Nim and scratch their initials into her. Men who'd abuse gentler souls and leave them fit only for the circus, he reminded himself, pushing darker memories of his own misuse aside.

His toes made contact with the far side of the tent. He somersaulted sideways and down, nimbly avoiding the snipers' pot shots. Beneath him, the tent billowed and sighed with each wound.

A clot of the parasitic silk clung to the brass rod that ran around the edge of the tent roof. Lulu tucked his feet under the warm metal and leant back against the canvas to make himself invisible to the snipers. Reaching over a shoulder, he extended a corrugated hose from the small fuel case strapped to his back, aimed it between his feet and squeezed the trigger. Flames splurged from the mouth. The knot of silk melted back in layers, but still the fibres tried to re-knit. Lulu kept up the outpour of flames, narrowly avoiding scorching the more delicate tarpaulin as he fell sideways suddenly when that particular grip on the ship released. He let go of the trigger. The fire rescinded instantly.

"Oh, my sweet heart!" He patted the spot above one set of ribs.

The craft lurched, the bridge tipping skyward. Just as suddenly it rocked back. The ship was being towed towards the ground again.

"What the devil is Lulu doing up there?" Herb wrestled the ship's wheel at full lock, his squat hands moulding with its frills. Cyber Circus bucked, objecting to her restraints. The ringmaster was momentarily thrown against the chart coil to the left of the wheel, a navigation system worked via a foot pump and which drew a calico cartography strip through twin brass winders. He steadied himself, stepped up onto a foothold in the stalk of the wheel and tried to manipulate the pulley system overhead.

"Got to get us some leverage here."

Nestled in the viewing pit, Nim pressed her face to the grimy window. The bridge was a pustule of ribs and glass, located at the front of the ship and accessed via a gangplank above the head crest of the calliope. To the rear of the room was the ship's wheel and associated apparatus. To the fore, a cushioned viewing pit.

Nim peered up and saw a fresh glob of silk arrive alongside the shredded remains of the first.

"They've got a replacement gripline attached," she called back.

"Shit me backwards. That nimby, Lulu, better hurry his ass up and cut us loose already," spat Herb, voice strained with the effort to keep the wheel from spinning.

"We need someone else up there."

Hellequin stood at the entrance to the bridge, holding back the muscle sheet of a curtain. The whir of his internal clockwork made him just another part of the craft.

"Go!" Herb cried enthusiastically. "Any of you, go!"

Nim pressed her hands to the glass and stared down. She saw D'Angelus, the motherfucker, in his signature trekker's hat. His men swarmed below. Like fire ants, they deserved to have boiling water poured over them.

She turned around sharply. "I'll do it."

Hellequin parted his lips to speak. The red hot magma of her eyes was enough to torch his objections.

D'Angelus tucked behind one of the burrower's giant spinnerets; sooner or later the circus crew would get in range to start using their rock rifles. He squinted up to see a second figure emerge at one of the peaks of the circus tent. While the first had proven a slippery little sucker, flickflacking to avoid his snipers' best shots, the newcomer had a fluid elegance.

"Like a dancer," murmured the salon owner. He nipped at his smoke stick and savoured its aroma. "You!" He addressed the nearest of his dust handler grunts. "Give me your binoculars."

The man removed a pair of field binoculars from around his neck and handed them over. D'Angelus shook back the strap and brought the device to his eyes. One lens was pitted, the result of exposure to Humock's torrential dust storms, no doubt.

"How'd you see through these damn things," he muttered, adjusting the zoom to admire his prey in detail as she opened her black umbrella, brought it under her and leapt inside. Nim set the umbrella spinning in her descent. The snipers were forced to weave their barrels every which way in an effort to sight her.

"Fighting back, Nim? Well, I never." He flicked up the rim of his trekker's hat to get a better view.

Nim slid down to the fat brass vein running around the circumference of the roof. She stepped out of the moving umbrella and twirled it up over one shoulder.

"Lulu!"

"Miss Nim?" called the ladyboy from below. He appeared over the edge, face blackened by the backdraft off the flame hose. "The devils sent you out here to do a pitchman's job? The yellow-bellied stink swines!" Lulu pulled his lace handkerchief from the cup of his bustier, went to dab his temples then remembered his manners and offered it to Nim first.

She shook her head vehemently. "I volunteered, Lulu. Those men down there, they stole time from me, and other stuff. I'm here because I want to be. Understand?"

The ladyboy nodded and sucked a corner of his handkerchief.

Nim took the lead. "I want you to destroy all but one bit of the rubber silk. Secure that last length over the side here. I've a use for it."

When the ladyboy looked dumbfounded, Nim took one of his delicate hands in hers. "Get me that strand before the bastards yank us any lower."

Lulu swallowed, his Adam's Apple betrayed. His mouse-like eyes drank Nim in. "A valet doesn't desert his mistress. Even when she opts to flee. You and me, Nim. We're never gonna be free of our bondage to D'Angelus until the day we break that fucker's skull open."

The ladyboy disappeared over the side. Nim heard the roar of the flame hose. Her heart punched in her chest. She heard the whistle of rock ammo, listened for Lulu's scream as the bullets struck. But the roar of the flame stayed constant.

She said a silent payer, to whom she'd no idea. The Saints? Crusted divinities from a time period when things still grew in the ground and when Soul Food referred to a lovingly prepared meal and not the diseased plant feed which had spoiled the land.

Likewise, she'd no capacity for the spirit beliefs of the Sirinese, harbouring enough ghosts of her own. Or the blood voodoo of the Jeridians. Although she had a taste for their murderous instincts.

Rock ammo speckled the sky. The sound of the flame hose ceased. Nim felt the twist of dread in her gut. What if the ladyboy hung below from a tangle of silk, belly popped by a rock slug? Was it worth risking her neck to a bullet to peer over the side?

Nim's riding skirt pooled about her knees as she crouched. She brought her chin to the very edge of the roof, where the brass vein wove around the circumference like a rose stem. The ladyboy's face appeared directly opposite hers; she felt a surge of panic followed by blind relief.

Lulu clambered over. His shoulder was bleeding where rock shot had smashed the flesh off the bone. He dragged a thick rope of rubber silk onto the roof.

"I've torched the root. The rope'll still stretch and bind for you though. So what now, my darling?"

"Now we fight free of the devil."

A minute later, and despite Lulu's protest, Nim had the rubber silk tied around her waist. Where she'd split the weave in two, she knotted it up over both shoulders and behind her neck.

"Thank you, Lulu." She tossed him her umbrella. "We'll be out of here before you can count the rings on your fingers and bells on your toes."

She leapt en pointe and began to circumnavigate the fat brass vein. Faster and faster she ran, looping the fantastical rubber silk around the metal rim. She tried to forget the rock rifles. What was the point in D'Angelus pursuing her if only to have her gunned down? But he could instruct his snipers to inflict a superficial wound, or shoot out her footing and have her dangle off the edge, tangled in the silk and helpless.

Nim stepped off the edge, feet pointed in that beautifully contorted way of the dancer. She was plummeting then, and the sensation was as sweet as it was terrifying. Nothing could contain her. Not even air. But then the rubber silk whipped tight and she was spinning around the side of the circus in a wide arc. Grabbing hold of the silk rope with both hands, she tensed her arms to gain control over the swing.

Strength had been built into her. Years of drawing water from the well as a child, and playing punchbag for a father who came home vomit-soaked and drunk on Jackogin. She circled the underbelly of the ship, and she saw them – two gobs of rubber silk. Enough to keep Cyber Circus tethered while fresh gobs were released from the tremendous clanking burrower below.

Rocking out beneath the ship, back out and then in, she built momentum like a pendulum. She reached over her shoulder, extended the hose of her flame thrower backpack, aimed at the parasitic bundles and fired.

Hellequin stalked back and forth before the glass wall, his steel eye telescoping in on events below.

"For the love of the Saints!" spat Herb, doing battle with the ship's wheel, his face shiny-red as a jewel fruit pip. "Hellequin, do what you soldiers do best. Stick your nose in where it ain't wanted."

It was as good as an order to Hellequin. He exited the bridge and strode down the narrow gangplank where pitch crew leant over the side, firing off rock rifles as well as their own makeshift missiles; dried dung-cakes from catapults and splinters torn off the frames of old scenery flats and fired from short bows. He even saw the oilskin liner from the zoo dung dump set alight and tossed overboard.

"We got a boatswain on board?" he demanded.

"Yep'um," grunted a man with the dust handler's stoop. A worn-in type. Hard working.

"Can you disconnect any methane pipes around here?"

The boatswain batted his hands off one another and gestured towards the fat bottomed end of the ship, located off down a walkway behind the backstage lift rig. "Majority feed out via the engine room. But there's a couple up here we can unhook." The man squinted. "Thinking of giving our friends down there something to complain about?"

Hellequin nodded. He walked off down the gangplank. Inside the minute, the clank of the boatswain's pliers and the rip of brass panel work echoed through the hull.

He paused on the gangway and stared over one set of railings. The expanse of the main tent gave out onto empty air and the burrower below with its skirts made up of D'Angelus's men. Hellequin's amber lens took in fingers at the flintlock of a rock rifle, the pump of kinetic muscle as a huge Sirinese worked the winch to wind the circus in. He was distracted by the appearance of a rope of rubber silk that dropped away from the ship, threads thrashing at its severed end. The rope landed in the dust below with a tremendous whip-crack. Seconds later, he saw a second rope swing in under the ship. His steel eye focused in to see Nim hanging in a makeshift rubber silk harness, flame hose retained on a short blue lick of light.

"No!" Hellequin threw himself against the rail. The boatswain had done as asked – the unscrewed methane pipes hoisted off their brackets and directed at the gaping hole below, their streaming gases set alight. Except Nim wasn't meant to swing in at that instant, her safety rope of rubber silk scorched by flames from above. Now she hung suspended under the ship, a drop of flesh on a fraying line.

The pitch crew panicked and yanked up one pipe by its lagging, a stream of flames burning up the side of the hull. Cyber Circus bucked. Struggling to rein in the makeshift weapon, one man was crushed hard against the rail then flung over as the pipe flailed. The man dropped away through the open hull, clawing for a handhold.

Hellequin didn't stay to watch the fire fighting.

Nim heard the voices of D'Angelus's men below. There was laughter, and comments made in a filthy tone she recognised. She was suspended in the remains of her harness at a savage angle, head lolling, spine bowed. It was impossible to even attempt to reorganise her limbs and climb up. She hung under the ship by a sliver.

Lulu appeared at the edge of the roof, one arm extended down in a desperate bid to reach her. Counting off the seconds before the last thread snapped, Nim prayed the fall would kill her. *Don't let me be preserved in any way, a new attraction for D'Angelus's sicker clientèle*. Her aching body rotated.

The angel, when he came, had faded blue wings. He leapt between the circus guide ropes, spectacularly fast, phenomenally accurate, propelling off each to catch the next with strong momentum. Swinging down, around and underneath, he scooped her up into a solid grip. At the same instant, Cyber Circus broke free of its weakened bonds. They rose in an incandescent whirl, light streaming off Nim's skin in neon blues and pink and orange.

She looked into the face of the angel. He was flesh and metal.

The ship melted away at the horizon.

"I can't take Wanda-Sue under Zan City. That devil's playground is built on a solar strip." Das ran his hands down his sunken cheeks, adding to the smears of oil there. "Ain't a burrower in existence can take on salt laid that thick or the sea of brine beneath."

"Indeed there isn't. So it looks like I'll be following the Spirit Man philosophy today." D'Angelus glanced across at Jaxx. The Sirinese was slick with sweat from winding the huge winch.

D'Angelus stared back out at the drifting speck. "Cyber Circus is welcome to entertain the masses of Zan City. Meantime, we'll cross the solar strip and make our way beyond. Herb'll never double-back. Lose all that tasty revenue by turning up at pitches he's just worked? A showman like Herb would never do that." Rotating his hat's brim between his fingers, D'Angelus settled his mind to the fact. "Yeah, I go with your philosophy,

Jaxx, and trust we will encounter that merry troop again before too long."

EIGHT

The sky was a brilliant blue. Below, the solar strip endured in powdery, still white silence. Dots of movement betrayed the whereabouts of desert tinkers – nomads peddling the contents of patched water bladders, and who travelled the solar strip on sleds pulled by clothhods. The only other sign of life was a large shadow moving determinedly towards the scab of an island. Cyber Circus, her engines set to a low purr as if loathed to disturb the hush of the landscape. Heading for the brown hem of Zan City, where the cacti grew tall and fat.

"Mother of all Saints, I hate Zan City." Relieved from his post at the ship's wheel by a member of the pitch crew, Herb was nonetheless keen to oversee their docking and sat pinched into a chair at the front of the bridge. "Give her a wide berth," he called back to the navigator, who turned the wheel accordingly.

The ship curved around the vast salt column, a lookout tower left over from the civil war. Herb nipped his nose between two fingers and peered down. "They cram the mothers in," he said softly as they passed over hundreds of lump dwellings. The island looked diseased.

"We're a day ahead of schedule. What if there's another troop occupying the showground?" Lulu sucked his bottom lip. While Herb had felt need for a chair, the acrobat had settled amongst the faded floor cushions in the viewing bay. The shock of earlier events lingered in the slight shake of his hands. Every so often, he took a sip from a beaker of Jackogin.

"There won't be. Only Cyber Circus got acts queer enough to appease the Zan City temperament," said Herb with bragging emphasis. "Plus, this close to Hamatan, with the dust storms hotting up? My guess is we'll have a clear run at it." The ringmaster fed his chubby hands under his armpits. He nodded, as if reassuring himself of the fact.

No one replied, not Lulu, the navigator at the wheel or the Jeridian stood in the doorway... although she wanted to speak. Asenath's kohl-rimmed eyes flicked between the lookout towers and lump houses, the sprawl of the souk and the colossal salt walls of the prison. She'd no desire to return to Zan City. Things always got ugly.

Asenath kept her thoughts private. Instead, she pointed to a small hill and said, "The pitch site, boss." She raised an eyebrow at Lulu. "No other tent in residence. Seems we're in luck."

Salt. The ritual purifier. Funeral offering. Manna from the Saints. In Zan City, it was the absorber, desiccating all inside its sour ribcage. A small city which seemed to know its days were numbered, Zan oozed salt from every pore – the rag curtained windows of lump dwellings, the patchwork of stone that made up the sidewalks, the prison walls that rose up into the sky.

There was no relief. Hellequin knew that much from a day spent amongst its cacti when he'd headed up his platoon. Having secured the services of a desert tinker to repair a tear to his lung balloon's envelope, he'd let his men wander the souk. By the time it came to leave, one soldier had already got himself maimed in a bar brawl. Another never returned. "The sirens of Zan City drained his blood," was the whisper, inviting the dirty reply, "His cock more likely." In those days, Hellequin had made no allowance for missing men. He was the HawkEye – a role which made him lieutenant as well as lookout. The rest of the platoon? Just muscle with guns. Forgetting the lost soldier at once, he'd taken to the sky in his mended lung basket and steered the platoon away from the city, back out across the solar strip.

Five years on, Hellequin was grateful for Zan City's bleak nature and overpopulation. D'Angelus was unlikely to follow them here when he could wait it out on the outskirts and not have to bother with Zan's inhabitants. Plus, if they turned the show around quickly, they could earn the water they needed to fuel the boiler and be back in the air before the sun rose on a new day.

The flap of the circus tent had been hooked aside, letting in the blazing daylight. Hellequin watched Herb strut out of the tent, the thumb of one hand tucked in a waistcoat pocket, trailing his hat with its extravagant plumage in the other. A gang of bare-chested Sirinese approached, clubs in their fists and bodies which had been carved, stitched and re-carved. Prison wardens.

Lesser men might have faltered, but Herb crowed his ballyhoo and looked to all appearances like a djinee granting wishes. Meanwhile, the pitch crew ran outside to peg down guides ropes which whipped either side of Herb in a motion that was almost protective.

There was a strange connection between ringmaster and the wondrous beast of Cyber Circus, Hellequin mused – something that often distorted Herb's eye to the reality of their predicament. As now. The ringmaster squeezed off a handshake from each warden and strode back inside, announcing with a flourish, "We're on! We can slake this old gal's thirst with water from a pumping station out back in exchange for a show. But first, they want a full blown ragamuffin parade, and we're the fellas to give it to them!"

"I take it the plan to get in and out of Zan City as quickly as possible is abandoned?" Nim stood at the entrance to the ring. Overhead, pitchmen worked to lash the huge iron girders of the tent poles in place. The magnetic paths essential to Nim's act were exposed in the floor of the ring below; she stepped up onto the rim and walked around the edge, arms folded over her robe.

Hellequin knew the adjustments of his HawkEye gave away his every glance. He concentrated on the ground.

Herb got an empty look. "Business sympathises with no man. Woman of your intelligence understands the way of it. And if the marks are dusting off their dimes at the thought of a parade, well, the least we can do is give it to them."

"If you hadn't noticed, Herb, we're on the run," said Hellequin. He felt Nim's exquisite eyes burn into him but refused to meet them.

Herb snorted. "I notice everything, HawkEye, but nothing's gonna stop Cyber Circus when she's rolling. Not the pimp D'Angelus, not a whore peddling herself as something finer, not an old soldier with a headful of wires, not the Devil's own dust storm!"

He slung a squat arm towards Nim. "You – get dressed! Parade, rehearsal, and lights up at seven. And you…" The arm swung in the direction of Hellequin's breast. The soldier looked up, steel eye truncated. "I gave you a slot because all marks like a freak with medals. But your kind go bad over time, and by bad, I mean your skull's insides turn to mush. Don't give me an excuse to dump your ass already." Herb rolled his eyes towards the upper reaches of the tent. "Meantime, since you're such pals with Pig Heart, you'd best check on his progress. And tell Rust to get ready to take a ride. It's time to show Zan City the goods!"

Hellequin had witnessed all manner of unholiness in his life. But the rutting of Rust and Pig Heart intruded on the part of him that had known fresh bed sheets once and kid brothers sleeping on his chest and sea air in his lungs. The hoppers watched from behind bars. There was a chaffing of wing cases as they adjusted to his presence. Their churning jaws gave off small ki-ki noises.

"Herb wants Rust in the parade in fifteen minutes!" Hellequin called. He backed off to the clothhods' stall and stared through the bars for distraction. The bovines stretched their long necks to eat from high mangers. Their fine limbs swished through the sage.

"Fifteen's all we're need!" Pig Heart choked against a great lungful of air as Rust pressured down.

Images of Nim danced through Hellequin's mind. Her ribboned corset, dark with water like the glimpsed areola. Light pulsing beneath her skin. The crest and fall of her hipbones. He forced the thoughts aside.

"Herb says I gotta check on you too." Hellequin kept his tone neutral.

"Bastard Herb." There was the sound of a tussle and Pig Heart snapping, "Un-cock yourself, Rust! I've gotta crawl outta here."

Hellequin's amber lens caught a shadow of movement. He turned around to see Rust slink off to the opposite corner of her wagon.

"Rust not finished, but still it bucks her," she spat, hunkering down on her four limbs. "And after I rescued it from the ship's belly. After I licked the filth off it. After I pissed on its hurt spots."

"Aw, come on, girl. It ain't like that." Pig Heart levered up onto an elbow, revealing a spine transformed into beaten, raw flesh. The movement seemed to aggravate the wounds anew. With a cry, he fell back and curled in on himself.

Hellequin's steel eye played a series of images across his retina like a flick book: the bruising over the greater part of Pig Heart's body, the disjointed snout, the rip and fold of flesh, the metal splinters at a shoulder.

"I can ease him," he told Rust. Striding up to the cage, he saw a protective glint in her eye.

"Stay out!" she warned with a low hiss. "Rust's wagon is not for bare men."

"I'm offering to help your mate." Hellequin stared her down.

"Let the fucker in," moaned Pig Heart. Deprived of the anaesthetic qualities of sex, the pitchman was clearly drowning in pain again.

The wolf girl crawled up to the bars. She cocked her head,

spider eyes dancing over Hellequin – and for an instant, he understood what drove Pig Heart to take his pleasure from the filth-encrusted creature. He saw intelligence, and sexuality stripped back to its glistening, blooded nub.

"He helps the pig. Nothing more. Else I break every bone the bare man got."

Hellequin dipped his head. "I hear you."

Two minutes later, he squatted alongside Pig Heart in the cage, his amber lens magnifying the flesh at the pitchman's bare shoulder. Using swift, light motions, he tweezed out the metal slivers with his fingernails.

"There, at least, will heal now." He went to stand but Pig Heart's bristled hand gripped his arm.

"I've been slugged, crucified, and keelhauled for my crime. Every time you step in. I ain't a flavour you're looking to sample, so what's gives?"

Hellequin shook off the hand and unfolded to his full height.

"I've seen enough suffering."

Pig Heart snorted. He shuffled to gingerly rest his spine against the closed side of the wagon. "Haven't we all, pal?"

Hellequin squatted down, long limbs folding like a hopper's back limbs. His intensity had Rust shift forward on splayed claws, heckles raised. A hiss escaped her lips.

The soldier spoke in a harsh whisper. "Travelling in my lung basket, I've seen flies feast at a dead man's lips, bruises bloom under a child's flesh. I've seen suffering from a distance and at magnification, and it never. shuts. off."

Rust crept back onto her haunches. She twitched her head at him.

"Know your problem?" Pig Heart winced at some internal agony. He took a rattling breath. "You signed up to the sight of the Saints themselves. The eye of the holy. Always on watch. Never to rest again." He showed his tusks. It was a sympathetic grimace. "Now, what the hell did you do that for?"

NINE

The parade trawls through Zan City. Salt workers line the streets. Lured from their dry ghetto, the citizens welcome their queer visitors with quiet gusto. *Happiness is this*, they whisper to babes in arms and children at their feet. *Here is the circus. Here are the travellers who carry pocketfuls of scandal and political gossip for sale, and who live such lives!* Oh, the people are happy to see the circus, even if they blink their eyes against such vivid colours.

But it does not last, this well-received stroll through the old town. Soon the cacti tail off and the squeeze of salt block dwellings is replaced with an even starker utilitarianism. The cold heart of Zan City – the mausoleum of a clock tower with its moon face and jagged metal hands slicing off time, the grey slab of City Hall, and the prison's high outer walls. At the entrance to the prison, the parade falls silent. It takes a number of the Sirenese guards to drag the huge iron gates open. A tremendous roar goes up. The prisoners are pleased to see them.

Herb conducts his hands and struts through. In his wake come the pipers. They pump leather airskins under an arm and manipulate brass valves to produce their tinny folk music. The road underfoot is a slurry of salt edged with cobblestones. Prisoners crowd the sidewalk; wardens shocking them back with electro-batons.

The first wagon rolls in. It is pulled by clothhods, their splayed hooves beating up the salt path. The wagon is decorated with silver knot-work and mirrors, reflecting in, reflecting out. Up top ride the Scuttlers. They clatter about the rooftop, performing head stands and singing rhymes as children are prone. Most of the prisoners applaud. One or two throw stones.

The tall HawkEye comes next, and the prisoners like that. A warrior in their midst! One who sacrificed the freedom of his flesh – and one day soon no doubt, his mind – to fight. They knock elbows in common sentiment. Their crimes might keep them locked up beneath a harrowing sun, but that poor son of a gun would never rest easy again. Look at those tattoos, brand of the HawkEye, and the well-worn boots, and the uniform – that musta been smart once, they tell a neighbour. And what about the steel eye itself – the diametric revolutions of the metal ring stack around the amber lens – and above, the twin bone ridges that protect the inner wiring? The prisoners bow their heads as the HawkEye passes – instinctually respectful of he who fought to preserve society in spite of their enforced removal from it.

Their misplaced pride is replaced with intrigue as Wolf Girl's wagon rumbles by. Those on one side of the sidewalk are left to guess at the wagon's contents; they are presented with the closed-in decorative panel and it unnerves them. Why do those prisoners opposite jeer and whistle, yet fall back a little?

Inside the cage, Rust peers out at the savages enclosed in their own white walls. She stretches her underarm to her mouth, flicks out her tongue and wets the fur there. Coating the back of a hand with spit, she drags on an ear while Pig Heart snores under a mound of sage, Hellequin having been unable to persuade the wolf to part with her prize. She guards the pitchman now, squatting on her heels, spider eyes burning out from behind her raggedy mane.

The catcalls get louder as Rust's wagon gives way to Lulu. In high-waisted shorts and a tasselled bra, the ladyboy presses a palm to his lips and tosses out kisses. For an instant, the crowd are in love. Then Lulu's coquettishness bubbles over and there is a flash of realisation. Knuckles flex at the trickery.

But it is a rare day in Zan Prison that music fills the air. Let freaks be freaks, the men decide, their spirits bouncing.

And this next one is the real deal, they know that instinctually. Womanness pours off her like molasses. Seated in an extravagant carriage, Nim is a picture of allure. Her hair is scarlet, her eyes glassy red. The jacket of her riding suit is unbuttoned, providing a glimpse of décolletage. Her riding skirt is knee-length and teasingly modest. She rests a black parasol over one shoulder.

Only a keen observer – or a HawkEye – would notice the accelerated rise and fall of her chest. She breathes through the panic that threatens to break her ribs. *Too many bad souls crammed into that baking space, with its salt walls rising on all sides.* Nim fights to shut her demons out while the wardens electrocute the over-amorous. Grown men yelp like pups. The stench of hot meat rises.

But Nim needn't worry. Tantalising as she is, Herb saves the queerest for last. The largest wagon passes through the gate, a tremendous steel cage divided in two. The framework is adorned with grotesque figures boasting mirrored eyes, antennae, garish stripes and spines. And inside the cage? The men gasp, beat on a neighbour's shoulder, pat their breasts and shake their head. Hoppers! Two of them. Giant scraping creatures that twist awkwardly around inside the cramped quarters. Calcium deposits litter the floor like anthills.

"Get the buggers back!" The handler calls to the prison wardens. His whip cracks overhead as the wardens plunge their batons into soft sides and bellies. "Easy, gents," they coo, as if the words are a salve to counteract the wounds.

But it is too much for some prisoners. After the relentless white of their cells, they find it hard to process the strange sight. And it's worth the sting of the baton to nose closer to the beasts. *Hoppers*, they whisper, hands reaching for the bars.

"I'll cut you with my whip, gents!" The handler's voice is laden with alarm. He runs alongside the cage, yanks on a handle and tries to unfold a screen across the bars. "No more for you, gents. No more for you!" he hollers.

But the prisoners are having none of it. They want to peel off one of the hoppers' hoary scales, or secure themselves a tuft of the head filaments. Souvenirs like that'd be worth a dime on the prison's black market. Enough to buy a good few packs of smoke sticks, maybe even a poke with one of the street whores who trades their flesh for cash with the wardens.

"Just a glimpse, Jo," they say in sing-songy voices, appealing to the charitable nature of the warden nearest, every one of whom bears the nickname of 'Jo' on the inside. "I ain't had a turn to see," they argue, and "Just a gander. Just a stroke of it."

Electro-batons bite at the men. But there are more prisoners to replace those who fall. As the handler succeeds in dragging the screen halfway across the bars, the prisoners became a determined swarm.

"You gotta back up!" The handler flails his arms. "This is precious cargo."

He pushes to the front and steps up by the driver. "Herb!" he calls, and cracking his whip, catches prisoner and warden alike. "Herb, we gotta get these fellas off. The hoppers are getting choppy with each other!"

The wagon sways. The hoppers squeeze off loud chirrups. Their wing cases and hoary limbs clatter against the bars.

Climbing onto the roof of the wagon, the handler kneels, stretches a hand down and tries to shift the screen the rest of the way across. A shadow falls over him and he squints back over a shoulder.

A tall figure in silhouette blocks out the sun.

"What's the priority?"

The handler shielded his eyes with the flat of a hand.

"Blackout screen. It's jammed."

Hellequin indicated the man aside. He lay down in the handler's place, stretched a long arm over the edge and tried to grab the handle of the screen. It was impossible to get a good grip with the prisoners crowding close and rocking the wagon. Gaze whirring, he took in the action. Hands clustered at the bars of the cage. Flesh bruised like Black Fruit. Several wrists had gang tattoos, similar to the dark blue sickle blade he'd spied at Asenath's earlobe a day earlier. His amber lens revolved a few degrees in its socket and he stared into the cage. One of the hoppers was hurt; a front limb leaked a thin green gore where thieves had torn off fistfuls of the hessian-textured exoskeleton. The creature rubbed against the divider between the two pens and its neighbour responded in kind. Their chitinous bodies rasped off one another, like blunt saws juddering through petrified wood.

Hellequin noticed a hunk of calcified spit caught in the runner; a prisoner stretched eager fingers towards it, hopper chalk being quite the prize. Hellequin gripped the gilt piping that edged the roof with one hand. Retrieving his bowie knife from its sheath, he swung down, his legs dangling loosely just above the prisoners' heads. He drove the knife down into the runner, flicked out the calcium lump into the grateful hands and swung back up onto the roof – just as the screen shot across the cage on spring release, skinning any fingers in its path.

There was a roar of pain and disappointment. But with the freak show closed, the mob finally backed off. Wardens buzzed the prisoners nearest for good measure, but most inmates stood and stared up in awe. The HawkEye unfolded on top of the hoppers' wagon, bowie knife in hand, steel eye flashing under the fierce white sun.

TEN

The moon rose high and fat over the salt plains. At the edge of the desert, a cluster of yurts had been erected from poles of dark twisting petrified wood and draped in white canvas. Inside was carpeted in wool from the caravan's small herd of humpbacks. Incense smouldered in metal bowls. Pierced metal lanterns were strung up in the eaves and gave off a muted glow.

The chieftain nestled in oversized robes, peering out from his headscarf with a toothless grin and glistening eyes. Another elder piped a snaking melody from a cane flute while the women danced, laughed and flirted, grateful for the company of men who still had fat across their bones. Handsome women, they wore black robes cinched at the waist with braided gold, and more gold thread stitched into their hair. Charm bracelets chinked at their wrists. Bells jangled at their ankles. They wove in and out the men, offering up the stem of a hookah pipe or entwining themselves in a lap. A fistful of dollars had secured D'Angelus food and shelter for his men for the night, with the chieftain throwing these, his youngest wives, into the bargain.

Smoke off the hookah pipe fogged the air. The atmosphere inside the tent wavered. Jaxx felt hazy, a sensation which reminded him of the sweat huts favoured by Sirinese mystics. Around him, bodies coiled, mouths pressed. The ecstasy of it all filled his belly like rotten meat. He found his way to the doorway and stepped out into the night.

Leaving behind the pool of light off two large tar torches

and the slumbering humpbacks, he entered the twilit plains. Under the huge moon, the salt flats stretched to the horizon. Stars blazed; Jaxx navigated his way north by them. The further he got from camp, the quieter the desert became, until he grew aware of his own footsteps. Shapes ran across his path, roo rats scurrying back to their burrows. Otherwise, his only companion was the vast noiselessness.

The position of the heavens told him that it was the hour of Last Prayer and he stopped walking. Taking four small engraved brass discs from a purse at his waist, he laid them out to form a square on the ground. He knelt inside the square, raised his hands in invocation and began to chant. In his mind's eye, he thanked the spirits for the joy and bitterness of his day – in the case of the latter, recanting of the blood he had spilt and the pain he had caused. His voice flooded out into the illimitable dark. The prayer circled. His sins turned to dust, and blew away.

The footfall was whisper-soft.

"Enšā Dianāh." The conclusion of his prayer.

He was on his feet in seconds, fists tensed by his hips, the reflection of the moon captured across his brow bolt plate.

"Need company?" The boy cocked out a hip. One smooth brown leg protruded from the slit sarong. It hinted at the just hidden sex above.

"No," Hellequin snapped. "No, thank you," he appended in a softer tone, nose to his Jackogin glass.

"Sure, sah? I can nibble your pinto. Like a little mouse." The boy brought his hands to his mouth and gnawed some imaginary morsel. He went too far when his scrawny fingers reached for Hellequin's groin. The soldier gripped the boy's wrist.

"You're not my flavour, runt!"

"Oh, tish tish. No need to manhandle the locals, Hellequin." Lulu arrived alongside them at the bar, kohl-eyed and dripping sequins. He laid a delicate hand over Hellequin's. "The boy is a baby, not used to violence. Unless you pay extra."

Hellequin let go of the kid's wrist. His amber lens retracted inside the steel eye socket.

"How old are you, boy?"

The kid attempted to fondle Hellequin's ear. This time, Lulu chastised him with a slap to the jaw.

"I'm guessing not twelve years old yet and already acting like a jaded hag. Is it the salt in the air which sees you past your prime so soon in this neighbourhood?"

"Is the sad old queen jealous? Johns prefer to stick it to a dung brick than your wrinkled ass?"

While the frown was still forming at Lulu's brow, Hellequin had already drawn his bowie knife and pressed it up under the boy's chin. The blue blade reflected oilily in the gaslight.

It was warning enough. The kid melted back into the crowd.

Hellequin produced a rag from his waistcoat pocket and ran it smoothly along the blade.

"Gutter bug!" Lulu bit his thumb at the boy's disappearing back. Sidling onto a corroded steel stool, he raised a finger to the bartender, a Jeridian with red skin, oval eyes and a ladder of piercings down his throat. The man poured a measure of Jackogin into a metal beaker. Lulu slid coins across the bar.

Crossing his legs neatly, the ladyboy took a swig from the beaker, his Adam's Apple bobbing. He cradled his drink between painted fingers. "Good thing you addressed that situation in the prison this afternoon. Herb might like to crown himself king pin, but outside the walls of Cyber Circus, he's just a fat old man in an ugly hat."

Hellequin stared into his beaker of liquor; the glossy surface showed the opposing rotations of the twin rings as his steel eye focused in. The lens dulled to an ember glow. "It's what I was trained to do," he said.

"That's hardly accurate, is it?" Lulu waved a hand in front of his mouse eyes. "HawkEyes were created as look outs, *time travellers* whose job it was to glimpse the future and act on it before the enemy. This need of yours to protect the circus and all who sail in her, it's touching, my darling, but it's got nothing to do with your time as a soldier." The ladyboy bit his bottom lip. "Is it that we're all the family you got?"

"Yeah, that's it."

"Really?" Lulu stared intently at Hellequin and his pious expression broke into a frown. "You're teasing me." His hurt was quickly replaced with resignation. "Keep your reasons stitched up inside then. I've no use for them. All I know is I feel a whole lot safer with a HawkEye to watch over us."

"Nice to know someone does." Hellequin sipped from his beaker.

"Oh, if you're talking about Nim, she's been sliced, diced and prettied up with wires, and still there's not a soul in Humock can tame her." Lulu got a far away stare. "In some ways, she's even wilder than Rust."

"Shame she hasn't got Rust's claws."

"Yet despite your perceiving her as a creation of blown glass, she endures. And happily." Lulu gestured past the soldier's shoulder. Hellequin twisted around in his seat. The drinkers had parted to reveal Nim, perched on one of the large salt rocks that served as tables. She was talking with the Jeridian, Asenath. The women appeared to share a joke. Asenath laughed and Nim's eyes filled with warmth.

Jealousy curled like a snake inside Hellequin's gut. He chastised himself. Lulu was right. Nim had been sliced and diced and screwed with. Last thing she needed was another man making demands on her.

Lulu leant in. "Those two girls are having a good time. I bet that just eats you up inside, hmmm?" He gestured to Nim with his lace handkerchief. "Apart from the obvious, what is it that gets you so fired up about Miss Nim there?"

"They re-stitched her too." The statement was unexpectedly honest.

Lulu's tremulous eyes grew wide. "You're drawn to her out

of kinship? Oh my darling, Nim is never going to thank you for it. See, her…alterations." Lulu chose the word with care. "…were none consensual. And what do you know about Nim, Hellequin, aside from her public face or the shrew who shoos you from her dressing room? Do you know she was nine when she got sold into D'Angelus's whorehouse, or that it was a soldier who had snatched her from her parents' farm and tired of her days later, or that the reason she was chosen for the surgery was because she's part Jeridian? They heal better," Lulu supplied in answer to Hellequin's silent enquiry. He smiled sympathetically. "She's unusual. Most times Jeridian genes don't mix outside their own, but now and then, a Pinkie is made. That soft pink sparkle skin of hers, it's not down to synthetic light fibres alone. And the eyes, Hellequin. Those beautiful red teardrops? Jeridian-made."

"And you'd know this how?" Hellequin watched Nim place a hand against her neck as she smiled, almost as if she was afraid to let the happiness out.

"I was Nim's valet for a while." Lulu danced a fingertip around the rim of his beaker, allowing Hellequin time to absorb the fact. Not that it made anything except sense to hear that Nim and Lulu had once been connected so intimately, thought the HawkEye, raking a hand through his hair. He'd knowledge enough of brothels to know top earning girls were cared for at both a mercantile and medicinal level by ladyboys – individuals who posed no threat to the girls sexually and who came in handy as an additional resource for customers with a more eclectic palette. But why had Lulu kept the information secret until now?

"You noticed my absence when D'Angelus came knocking. Yes, I'm not the bravest of souls in a fight. Using one's fists can be very wearing on the nails." The ladyboy held up his painted talons to the gaslight. His lips trembled. "I'm nothing to D'Angelus – unlike Nim, he didn't notice if I lived or perished – but if Herb knew about me and Nim…" Lulu patted his moist eyes with his handkerchief. "I can hear Herb now. 'Too much baggage. Too much of D'Angelus's property stowed aboard.'"

"So you follow Nim around like botfly larva," said Hellequin harshly. His eye piece zoomed in on a bob of swallowed salvia in Lulu's throat. Fresh hurt.

Lulu stared over at Nim. "It's hard not to," he said softly.

Hellequin telescoped in on the soft pink light at Nim's bare shoulder. "Want to know why I fight for every member of this circus?"

Lulu didn't answer, perhaps afraid to interrupt the confession.

"Because the Zen monks say there's not a sin the Saints can't forgive."

The admission clearly disappointed the ladyboy.

"You don't think Religion sits well as my motivation? You're right." The twin bone ridges protruded at Hellequin's brow. "The Zen monks say that, but it isn't true. My sin *is* unforgiveable." He pushed up the sleeves of his faded frock coat. He might have been pushing back deeper layers. "You said Nim had her body modifications forced on her while I chose mine. The truth is I didn't have a choice either."

Lulu flicked his white gold dreads. "Yes, in so far as you didn't lose your sight on purpose. It's common knowledge the HawkEyes were gifted soldiers who'd developed tumours or got wounded out on field. You lot were given the choice to go blind, or carry a face full of metal and see. See better than almost every other living creature it turned out." The ladyboy frowned. "I feel for you, honey, I do. HawkEyes helped stamp out Soul Food. When farmers were blindsided by the crop yield, your kind saw through to its rotten roots. Literally as I understand it."

Images played across the inside of Hellequin's reengineered retina. Weevils, billions of them, invisible to the naked eye. Masticating Soul Food at a macular level. Transmogrifying the plant feed into poison.

Lulu continued talking. "HawkEyes opened our eyes to the truth then tried to stop us killing each other when the civil war broke out. For that, me…" Lulu circled his hand to indicate the others in the bar. "…we, are eternally grateful. But, my darling, you did choose this lifestyle, and yes, only the Saints know why…"

Hellequin brought his cyborgian face close to the ladyboy's. "Most soldiers did have a sight fault. But that's not my story. My choice, if it can be called such, was to undergo the procedure or face being court-martialled."

Lulu got the same tight-eyed look he'd had when slapping Pig Heart the previous evening, and Hellequin clammed up. Why risk his livelihood, the canvas over his head, his proximity to Nim by sharing any more information? But then he stared across the room and saw a flicker of neon at Nim's forehead. The short circuit barely registered with her and she continued to share her laughter with Asenath. She had a life aside from the modifications fostered on her, and that's what he wanted too.

The metal mass dominating his features, draining any true emotion from them, he confided, "My family owned Soul Food Farm. We flew over what was left of it this morning."

Lulu's mouth slackened. His painted gaze darted off to the corners of the bar. "Jeepers, Hellequin! That old skeleton? By the Saints, your kin have a lot of blood on their hands."

Hellequin let the machine in him lead the conversation. "My dad was the biological engineer responsible for splicing the genes that gave us Soul Food – or for poisoning the land as it turned out. I had no interest in the family business. I was a tactician, got a passion for military hardware, skills which led me to sign up to the Humock Guard. My father stuck by his farming methods. I stuck by my unit. Then I got wind of the intention to blitz the farms that had spread the diseased stock, Soul Food Farm being top of the list." The amber lens burned liquidly. "I guess you're right. I did have a choice at that stage. I chose to go against my country and warn my family. And it did buy them a little time. But not enough to protect their land long term against the Humock Guard, against me."

"You took down your own family?" Lulu shuffled in his

seat.

Hellequin experienced an echo of the pain he'd felt when ordering his men inside the boundary fence. It prickled his conscience, but only faintly. "By then, I'd already been hauled up before my superiors. There was no other way for my family to have prepared against previous assault attempts as they had without my feeding them data from the Humock Guard base. I received an ultimatum – give an eye or face being court marshalled and most likely shot by firing squad." He focused on the ladyboy, the concentric rings of his HawkEye whirring as they rotated.

"Two weeks later, I gave my first order as a HawkEye. From my lung basket, I saw a chink in the barricades at Soul Food Farm and despatched my platoon to move on in. The procedure eased the guilt. There are limiters built into my circuitry which inhibit my emotions. Also the imaging process of the HawkEye stores memories in a more compartmentalised format than the brain is capable of. Non-tactical memories are given less priority, their sharp edges blunted." Hellequin threw back the remainder of his Jackogin. He sighed and rubbed a hand up into his fleshy eye, muttering, "So, that's my history."

"Here. Let me buy you another." Lulu indicated to the bartender. The Jeridian nodded. Uncorking one of the dark blue apothecary bottles collecting dust on a shelf behind him, the man sluiced new measures into their beakers.

Lulu inclined his beaker towards Hellequin and smiled weakly. "So the poor darling is emotionally stunted. I knew there had to be a reason for the cold shoulder." His smile broke into a coy grin. "You and Nim make a good pair."

The Zen monk stood a short distance away. In the silvered twilight, the monk's habit appeared even more grotesque. The sackcloth hood was a scarecrowish thing brought to life by eyes that glittered while the belt of relics resembled the tools of a witch.

The monk's stillness unnerved Jaxx. Had the man come to see a Sirinese at prayer? To stand and watch and judge, the only form of condemnation available to a member of a silent order? Jaxx lowered his fists and stared at the monk, perplexed.

"What you doing here?" Eerie confusion settled over him. The monk couldn't have followed him from the camp. There was nowhere to hide out on the salt plains. There was only endless distance. The crunch of boots over the salt surface, the tug of air at a person's lungs, the quiet swallow of saliva... he would've noticed these things – and not only because he was attuned with the world, but because a man in his profession could not afford to let a stranger creep up.

The monk remained motionless beneath the huge desert moon.

"Sorry to disappoint, but I am a spirit man, father. No disrespect to you, your order, or your followers, but the Saints are too heavy-handed in their laws and precepts to lure me in. Any effort to unsettle me in my prayer will be futile." Jaxx instinctually brought his fists to his hips again. He felt the depth of the desert pressing in.

His mind swam as the monk untied the belt of horrors from around his waist and cast it aside. Jaxx tucked his fists beneath his armpits, unnerved and wary as the monk gathered up the folds of his robe at the thighs and pulled the garment over his head in one swift movement. In the process of doing so, the monk exposed smooth white thighs, a triangle of down, the concave run of flesh from the hip to the waist, the bud of breasts and nut-brown nipples, and, as the garment was cast aside, a young woman's face. She threw down the robe and stared at him. Her mouth was overgenerous, her eyes wide and knowing.

She walked over to him, her bare feet making small shushing noises on the salt. Jaxx tensed his fists tighter. Blood drove inside his eardrums. She was in front of him suddenly. Her scent, a mix of hops, sweat and the dark, sweet wine offered by the desert tribe. The young woman cupped his face, fingers touching the stitched flesh at his brow plate. She drew his face to hers.

Their lips touched, parted and remoulded. The hands slipped from his face, leaving heat there. Moving down to his waistband, they dug in and dragged the loose linen shirt up. Jaxx let his arms rise. The press of breasts against his chest made him chew the fat of his lower lip. He breathed heavily; it was as if the salt itself had crept inside his lungs. Her mouth was on him, wetting the eaves of his throat, the scarred clavicle where the knives and nails of others had fought back, the brass rings at his nipples.

"Harām." *Sanctity.* The word broke free of his lips. A prayer, or a statement of fact as the woman unclothed him, knelt down, and bid him join her?

"Do you speak?" he asked. She was tangling herself in his lap now, easing onto his sex and pressuring down. He gasped, eyes coruscated and drawn to the dome of stars overhead. He went to buck against her, but she pressed her heels to the ground behind, leant back on one hand and forced her own movement, a rhythmic rocking like a grain sheaver passing its blades over crops.

"Do you..?"

The nut of a nipple was crushed into his mouth. He wanted to bite down, feel the choke of its red heart inside his throat. Resisting, he lapped the dappled areole, felt the agonising, glorious tug and slide at his groin, and smashed his hands up beneath her buttocks, clutching her to him.

A name escaped her lips. It began with V, tailing off to a whisper. She broke his mouth feel of her breast and her tongue was a wisp of flavour at his inner cheek, a probe where his top lip met his teeth. He shivered as his mind flooded with snapshots: a huge gridded eye, tiny strands of sensilla at mouth parts, a chitinous thigh. More images came, torn and grainy like burnt-edged photographs. A fibrous wing taking out a slice of teeth. Crabbing insectile limbs that battered and suffocated. Bright blood sprayed against stone. He heard such screaming – the screaming of men – appalling, protracted, dying out. At that same instant, he clawed the soft skin beneath his fingers, felt the high blaze of release, tensed, and at last, softened.

The woman unsaddled. She stood awkwardly, legs cramped, and stretched out.

Jaxx was crying. As tears drained from his eyes, he found it hard to pinpoint why. He forced himself to stand and dress, then stagger over to the spot where her robe lay.

"Here." He offered it.

She gathered the robe to her but didn't attempt to put it on. Jaxx understood that once the mask was back in place, the silence would flow again between them. He rubbed the wetness from his eyes.

"Zen monks are eunuchs. You are not ordained into the order." His waist-length black hair had slipped free of its band. He bunched it back and retied it. When he got no reply, he stared at the woman with a new level of demand.

"Did you see the future?" she said in a rush of words. Softly though, as if the noise of them might cause the sky to fall.

"Future?" He was cautious. He had heard of men returned from the desert and lost to rambling incoherency. Men who claimed to have imbibed fantastic potions, or tasted the lips of seductresses, or bargained away their soul to a crone.

"Did you see him? Tall as a porch post, just as thin. Eyes like lead shot."

"I didn't see a man. I saw... death." The grotesque images were still laid across in his mind: the crisp fold of a wing case, the slash of flesh, chalk mess and shit across a rock face.

He refocused. "Lead shot? That's a rare breed of ammunition. Most folk rely on rock shot or the blade since the civil war. You're a stranger. That much is in your accent."

"The land changes but the dust is everywhere. And it breathes. You hear it?"

Jaxx listened. He could have sworn he heard the long ahhh

of air where there was no wind.

"Why the guise of a Zen monk?" His raised eyebrows pressured against his brow plate. "Silence is a dark undertaking. Just you alone with your mind." To Jaxx, the idea of squashing up inside the flesh case he walked around in was abhorrent.

She was more girl-like then. Generous mouth loose, her mind on other things. "Zen monks accompany the mining worms below ground, and that's where I lost him. So I search the bore tunnels and, one day, the caverns…"

"The caverns?" Jaxx was still haunted by the mess of images she had conjured in him. "Who'd take you there?" No one in their right mind navigated the caverns. Stories told of a warren of natural caves, otherworldly and bioluminescent. Home to dark things that crawled.

"Not many," she admitted. "There are places I haven't managed to explore yet. Wormholes where only a child would fit. A child without bones," she added eerily.

"Who are you looking for?"

He knew even before she answered that she searched for a lover. Her use of him had demonstrated her loss, alongside a need to remember the taste of masculine skin and feel another's pulse inside her belly.

"I suspect he's salt and ore and other minerals by now. The flesh will be gone," was all she managed on the subject before striding over to him. She touched a hand to his cheek.

"You and I, we're in the wrong place," she said softly.

Jaxx felt the world tip. His mind battened down. A great wind howled, dust blew against his skin and he drifted into blackness.

ELEVEN

A hand settled on the bar. Hellequin looked down to see red skin and the whorls of tribal scars across the knuckles.

"This is a good bar, ya?" said Asenath, the Jeridian who'd taken over from Pig Heart to head up the pitch crew. With that evening's performance concluded, it was she who suggested an expedition to one of the city's drinking holes. Hellequin had agreed to come once Nim had.

"It's an interesting choice." Hellequin eyed the Jeridian. In her buckskin vest and pale leather jeans, she looked no different to any other itinerant worker. Except she'd an edge that came from more than her Mohawk, scarification, piercings, red skin, or the gang tattoo at an ear lobe.

Asenath nodded to the bartender.

"Another shot, Solomon."

The bartender whipped his cloth up onto a shoulder and retrieved a bottle from the shelf. Uncorking it, he poured himself a measure.

"Let me guess. It was your idea to bring the HawkEye here, Asenath." He threw back his shot, slid the cup over to Asenath and poured her and Hellequin a shot each.

Hellequin regretted the heat of the liquor in his guts. The Jeridian woman had suggested the midnight jaunt to the bar, which indicated what? His eyepiece zoned in on the beads of sweat at her upper lip, her tongue moistening dry lips.

"What you got me into, Asenath?" he said with a dark tone.

"I've a score to settle," she admitted.

"And I'm gonna help out how?" Hellequin focused on the sickle tattoo at the woman's ear lobe again. The steel lens captured the image as a photo-plate. He shifted his gaze to the left ear lobe of the bartender; the photo-plate shifted angle to overlay the man's matching insignia. Hellequin also recognised the way the man's tongue flicked out to moisten his lips.

"Does all your family live in Zan City, Asenath?" he asked.

The two Jeridians exchanged a glance.

Asenath told him, "My brother and I are the last of our family. Zan City's blood worms took our parents and older sister when the Showmaniese sold us out. Sometimes I come back home to remind myself of the stink of those fuckers. Solomon abides their patronage. This bar is his living. I, however, am under no such restrictions."

Hellequin reeled in his gaze. He stared at Asenath. "And my role in this?"

"To help me add a Showmaniese head or two to my collection."

"And why would I break the bodies of men I don't know?"

"For love's sake," said the woman bleakly. She swallowed back the slug her brother had poured and indicated the far side of the bar with her empty cup. Nim was attempting to shrug off the wandering hands of a gang of drunks – suited Showmaniese with lemony skin, womanly hands and tight black shining eyes. They reminded Hellequin of large desert cats he'd seen sprawled over rocks, bellies to the sun. At the same time, Lulu returned from the shitting pit outside. His flushed face suggested either the Jackogin had addled his brain or he'd pressed flesh with another in the minutes he'd been gone.

The ladyboy settled back on the stool alongside Hellequin. His gaze went from Hellequin to Asenath to the bartender.

"What is it?" he demanded, mouse-like eyes wide.

"Asenath wants to know if I am going to defend Nim's honour again. I'm thinking that since Nim has proven less than grateful for my intervention previously, I may need to leave her to fight her own battles," said Hellequin. He kept the courtesan in his line of sight though.

The bartender, Solomon, pointed to the group of men. "One of you take the big one's head for me. He's got a mouth on him."

The 'big one' was a foot taller than the rest of the Showmaniese. All were tattooed under the throat with a fat 'V'. In the case of the largest man, the tattoo looked like a clothhod yoke. His face was fattened up like a baby's.

"And HawkEye, if the whore won't entice you to fight alongside my sister, here's added incentive," said Solomon – and while Hellequin could pre-empt physical impulses, he couldn't read minds. The bartender shouted up, "You're the son of Jackerie, purveyor of Soul Food, you say? Well, there's an interesting thing."

Hellequin swung around on his stool, taking in the reactions of those surrounding him – rage tucked into creased foreheads, sneering lips, the pinch of muscle between eyes.

The Showmaniese were first to react.

"Son of Jackerie? In this hell hole?" hollered the largest. He approached the bar, the crowd parting either side.

"You the spawn of the bastard farmer who killed the land 'n' pocketed our dollar and left us to choke on the dust?" The giant did not direct his gaze to Hellequin. Instead it appeared that Lulu had been taken as the devil's offspring.

"Lulu'll never survive. You've stitched me up, Asenath," Hellequin muttered as the Jeridian reached over a shoulder and drew her scimitar from its harness.

"Maybe. It's written into your Daxware to protect your platoon. You've admitted that much. Which means you're stuck protecting Cyber Circus and all who sail in her, which includes me." Asenath glanced at Hellequin. Her face was ablaze, not with fear but anticipation of the fight.

So be it, Hellequin told himself. The steel eyepiece

interacted with the wires in his brain to map the arrangement of bodies in the room. Directly ahead was the largest Showmaniese. Over by the rock tables, Nim had closed in on herself. Crowded either side were the rest of the Showmaniese, nine men with fight stars, tin swords and wooden handled blunt blocks. To the right of the room were the whores of both sexes and their liquor-pinked Johns. Nothing to fear from those lilies and their overlords. To the left though – and all this taken in by Hellequin's lens inside the millisecond – a figure in the shadows as well as five Jeridians – three female, two male. Mohawks caked in green reed sap and baked hard. Piercings at the throat. Sickle tattoo at every ear lobe. Friend or foe? Hellequin caught a snarl at one woman's lips, her gaze bearing down on the Showmaniese in the centre of the room. Friends, he concluded.

Drawing his bowie knife as the largest Showmaniese powered forward, he sliced in front of him and cut the stub of the man's nose clean off.

His attack acted as a clanger to start the fight. Lulu slid across the bar and ducked under it. Solomon stayed put while Asenath stood her ground.

The giant ignored the spill of blood from his nose to career head-on into Hellequin. An outsized fist mashed Hellequin's wrist; the HawkEye dropped the Bowie knife, an instinctual reflex to the crush of pain. At the same time, Asenath drove her scimitar towards the giant's neck. His forearm blocked her attack, the power behind the blow forcing Asenath down. She pivoted on the ball of a foot to avoid slicing into her belly with her own blade.

Dodging blows, Hellequin was distracted by the figure in the shadows. What was it about the silhouette that seemed so hauntingly familiar? Regardless, the figure chose to remain incognito, unlike the remaining Showmaniese who muscled in on the fight against the five Jeridians.

Hellequin refocused. The neuro-feed off his HawkEye enabled him to take in the movements of his attacker and those of his companions. He dodged a slug from the giant, spine arching back. Meanwhile, Asenath sliced the heads from the shoulders of two Showmaniese. Each body crumpled to its knees and collapsed. Blood ran out the newly separated necks like sewage from a spurting drain.

He landed a blow to his opponent's mouth. The Showmaniese hacked and spat a tooth aside.

"Let me alone, HawkEye," he hollered, discharging spittle. "It's the pansy I've issue with. Stand aside and let me strangle the rat."

"Past's dead," shot back Hellequin, weaving between the giant's punches; he saw the trajectory of each blow milliseconds before it landed. "Leave the lad alone. This ain't his fight. And it ain't yours."

"The hell it ain't!" the man spat against the blood pouring off his nose.

Hellequin went to drop to the floor to retrieve his knife. He was restricted by the time it took for him to bend at the knees and extend a hand. It was warning enough for the giant to step on the blade and secure it underfoot with his entire body weight.

"Leave it be, HawkEye. Maybe your kind did this world a service, but that one good deed ain't enough to let you cut me more than once." The giant brought his face to the HawkEye's, bending at the knees as he did so. Few men matched the soldier's seven foot stature let alone were forced to stoop to look the soldier in his one natural eye. "Now back off and let me do for Jackerie's pansy son in a manner that'll satisfy the revenge needs of all Humock," he spat.

"The pansy ain't no son of Jackerie!" Hellequin had enough sentiment left in the knotwork of his mind to want to admit his lineage. He owed his family that much.

"You want to settle a beef with a family member, start with me."

His words carried through the room like dust swept up and carried by the wind. Time slowed. In the briefest instant before the Showmaniese giant brought his fist crashing down, Hellequin saw the reactions of those around him. How the Jeridian braves looked to Asenath for confirmation they were fighting on the right side. How the Showmaniese faltered, mid-brawl, their black eyes pinned wide. How Nim stared across the emotional miles that separated them. Newly distanced.

It was an instant of distraction, but it was enough to let the giant land a colossal blow to Hellequin's head. His circuitry misfired, half his world thrown into pitch black as his steel eye failed. He experienced a queerly powerful blaze of emotion. Dread lined his stomach like quicksilver.

Again, the distraction worked in his enemy's favour. The Showmaniese launched three hooks to the soldier's stomach. Hellequin wheezed and doubled over, aiding the delivery of a fourth hook to his chin.

His neck snapped back. The HawkEye whirred into violent motion. Hellequin got a grip on his compound sight and forced his body to negate the pain.

He struck back, the tight knots of his fists striking the giant up under the ribs with force. The man gasped. Hellequin didn't falter in his attack, raining blows. He pictured his father – tall as a hang man, lips that had pursed so many times when he was deep in thought that they had settled permanently into that position. Hellequin recalled his family's homestead as it had stood before he despatched his neutralising platoon; it had looked like any other home on the plains, paint faintly peeling but with clean curtains at the windows, a creaking rocker on the porch, fingerprints of the dead and living imprinted on the door handle. He remembered trace emotions of love and fear and searing loss. And as the giant stumbled backwards, he dipped to the floor, retrieved his bowie knife and started to drive it towards the man's throat.

Before the blade cut in, he saw a curve of silver whip across and back at the giant's neck. He stared into the dead man's eyes, forever startled, and leapt aside as the head toppled forward. It struck the floor heavily. A pound of flesh.

The body collapsed, pumping blood. Behind stood Asenath, her scimitar held towards the gaslight and greased red.

"Moj nagradu!" she growled. "My prize," she told him, hard about the eye.

Hellequin didn't dwell on the Jeridian's victory. His eyepiece refracted to take in events across the room. Nim had been grabbed by one sharp-suited Showmaniese. The man had a blunt block resting on her skull; one tap and Nim's brains would spill. Apparently the hostage taker had lost faith in making it out of there alive. Hellequin understood the man's panic. The Jeridian gang seemed newly invigorated now the giant had fallen. As Asenath took out the ribs of one with a swish of her scimitar, the other three female Jeridians formed a lethal collective. Back to back, the women joined in the fray. Fight stars whirred in from the Showmaniese contingent; as one mass, the three Jeridians bowed back at the spine, the blur of lethal metal passing millimetres from their faces. In a deadly dance, they bent, wove and sidestepped as one. Three scimitars whipped high, down then up again. Blood glossed each blade. Showmaniese heads rolled.

"Mi smo victorios!" cried the women and they knelt down, washed their hands in the blood of their enemy and smeared it in streaks down their cheeks.

"Slice another head, bitches, and I'll do for the whore here!" yelled the Showmaniese holding Nim hostage. It was distraction enough for one of his fellows to smash a blunt block into the chest of one male Jeridian. The man said "Oumph!" with the sickly tone of one who is shocked to greet death so quickly. He crumpled, choking on blood-filled lungs. No one intervened when the Showmaniese brought down the blunt block a second time. Better to finish it, even as the Jeridian women used the pain of loss to fuel their high-pitched eerie war cries.

"Shut it, you fucking red bitches! What say you, Solomon? Gonna let these jackasses slice your customers?" demanded the man with the block at Nim's skull, his black eyes buzzing every which way.

Hellequin wondered the same thing. While Lulu poked his nose over the lip of the counter, the bartender took his time, wiping up gore from the same surface. "I'm more neutral than most in this nest of blood worms. Your kind wanna sell mine out. Well, I reckon it's fair to slice a few heads in return." He glanced up from his macabre housecleaning. "Want my advice? You and your buddies should ease on out of here for the night."

"Screw that! Ain't no guarantee any of us Showmaniese are escaping this joint in one piece tonight if these red bitches have their way. I say let's even up the odds." The man raised his arm. "Seems this whore means something to some of you." He started to bring the blunt block down, Nim cringing in his foul embrace.

A hand broke the descent of the blunt block. Fingers gripped the handle, yanking it aside. Hellequin had seen the way of things at the exact same instant the man had taken action. Soft as a sidewinder, he'd slunk over. By the time the Showmaniese had sensed the HawkEye by his shoulder, he was already in the process of slamming down the blunt block. Now the soldier's hand forced the block back up at force. The Shomaniese took a face full of the weapon, nose shattering on impact. He wasn't going down without a fight though and drove his teeth into Nim's neck. She gave a sharp cry.

Hellequin backed off, hands raised. The Showmaniese stumbled back towards the door, passing between the terrified whores and Johns, his teeth dug in just short of Nim's jugular. The surviving Showmaniese fell in step with him. Weapons poised, they backed up to the exit.

None noticed Asenath slink the whores and Johns in and out. She stepped up, scimitar raised, and slid the blade in at the back of the hostage taker's neck. The man fell away from Nim like a dried up tic. Inside seconds, Asenath had withdrawn the blade and swept it around on a descending trajectory. The remaining Showmaniese lost their heads. Their corpses hit the ground and the bar fell silent.

Asenath drew Nim up from the floor. The courtesan was gasping, a hand pressed to her neck in an effort to staunch the wound.

The Jeridian delivered Nim to Hellequin, passing her into his embrace with insistence. She walked across the blood-slicked floor, interwove her fingers in the hair belonging to the giant and held up the severed head.

"Moj nagradu!" she cried. *My prize.*

Solomon and the rest of the Jeridians opened their throats and offered up the same strange prayer.

TWELVE

“I’m not extravagantly shy and when a nice young man is nigh, for his heart I have a try, and faint away with tearful eye!” sang Lulu.

“Are you trying to wake all the blood rats of Zan City?” Hellequin muttered.

Lulu giggled and fussed at the HawkEye’s coat sleeve as they walked.

“Word’s out by now. Cyber Circus boasts some of the finest brawlers in all of Humock.” The ladyboy stumbled into Hellequin, who pushed him up.

“How much Jackogin you had back there?” Hellequin went to take his arm away. When Lulu started to fall again, he was forced to hold the ladyboy upright.

“Oh, ain’t no Jackogin, my pretty soldier boy. Remember when I slipped outside a while back at the bar? Well, I encountered a lovely gentlemen, robust and more than a little rabid.” The ladyboy floated his hand before his mouth in mock alarm. “He slipped me a little Dazzle dust,” Lulu confessed, his strung out eyes confirming the fact.

“You don’t say,” said Hellequin dryly.

“You okay back there, Lulu?” Nim called from where she walked alongside Asenath ten metres or so out in front.

“I’m peachy.” The reply came out as slurred, accompanied by a fresh stumble.

Hellequin pulled the ladyboy back up. “He’s jacked up on

Dazzle Dust," he called.

"Ahhh, don't tell her," Lulu groaned. He put his forehead in his hand.

"That old poison, hey, Lulu?" Nim shook her head and gave her attention back to the uneven path of salt bricks. They were passing through one of the medina's unlit spots, an alley thick with shadows.

"She's pissed now." Lulu muttered something about the HawkEye wanting Nim and sacrificing all others. His chin dropped onto his chest, the weight of his head a burden.

"I'm a soldier. I deal with facts," Hellequin offered half-heartedly. He could wish Lulu's soul to Hell and the ladyboy would still cuddle closer.

But Lulu surprised him. Peering up into Hellequin's face, he looked freshly earnest.

"Ask me, you're more fond of us freaks than you'd like to admit. This whole 'Daxware makes me protect you' argument is just a way to stop us guessing the truth. That while you're wired with electrical conductors, a small part of you remembers the man you once were." Lulu poked Hellequin's stomach, the other man tensing at the contact. "You're just a soft belly when it comes down to it."

Hellequin exhaled heavily. He put his hand to the back of the ladyboy's neck, steering him. Staring up at the great cavern of starry sky, he muttered, "Maybe you're right." He felt no different inside though, only filled to the brim with nothingness.

"How's your neck?" asked Asenath.

Nim kept the makeshift bandage of Lulu's handkerchief applied to the spot. "Not as bad as it looked. Bleeding has eased up."

"Why'd you let men paw you like that, like they did back at the bar?"

Nim stared over, struck by how the woman at her side seemed to take on all sorts of angles in the darkness. The

Jeridian's eyes sparkled. She'd the look of a devil.

"I'm more likely to keep on breathing that way," she shot back.

"You could fight back. I'd teach you." The Jeridian tapped the neck of the hessian bag she carried over one shoulder. "Plenty of men have learnt the hard way *I* don't play like that."

"And plenty of whores I've known have ended up buried in the dust for complaining." Nim jutted her chin. "Could be I've had enough violence forced on me that I've learnt it's easier just to take it."

"That's a bad way of living." The Jeridian shook her head. "Might as well hold up a sign that says 'I was born pretty. That's my fault.'"

Nim laughed sourly. She liked the Jeridian in spite of her vile hobby of collecting heads. But it was difficult not to resent the way Asenath made her feel – as if she'd a duty to her sex to fight back against the tongues, hands and genitals. And hadn't she fought in the beginning! With nails and teeth and bucking hips and spit. Nothing had spared her. In fact, it had only made them ride her harder.

"Born pretty is a better state of being than born bad." The Jeridian inclined her head towards the blooded bag at her back, her wide mouth grimly set.

"Are you referring to you or the folk you behead?"

Asenath's lips parted. Her teeth were white as fresh clothhod milk. "I suppose I came out the womb pure as any other. The Showmaniese spoiled me when they picked off my family and sold them to the blood worms."

Nim couldn't imagine a nastier fate. The blood worms operated mainly in Zan City, selling out their fellow men to those in need of a fresh body or two.

"I didn't lose family to one of those devils, but I do know what its like to have my flesh re-stitched against my will. Troubles like ours harden the heart over time." She didn't want to dwell on the bad times. Glancing back down the path, she stopped walking and said, "Where's Lulu and the HawkEye slink off to?"

"Maybe Lulu has finally persuaded your soldier boy to try a different flavour." Asenath snorted. She slung her sack of flesh down onto the salt brick path and arched her spine, bones cracking.

"More likely the HawkEye has lost patience with my old valet and gone back to the bar. Now we've had a glimpse into his lineage, it's not like he's the type to stick around those in need. We'd best go back and look for whatever hole Lulu crawled into." Nim glinted softly in the darkness of the alley. Neon pulsed around the contours of her lips, crackled and shorted out.

"You know, it doesn't have to be like this. *You* don't have to be like this." Asenath drew closer. She laid a hand on Nim's shoulder. Warmth flooded Nim's skin. "In Jeridia, we are taught to honour our enemies by preserving them. The heads? They attest to my victories. More importantly, they ensure I never forget the faces of those I have murdered. It saves me from dreaming of those same faces, turning the guilt and terror of each death over in my mind. You should find a spark of bravery inside yourself, Desirous Nim. Learn to burn the flesh from your enemies."

A hand slipped behind Nim's neck, prompting her cheeks to glow faintly. Threads of neon lit up either side of her throat. Asenath moved in, her hard lips, hips and ribs moulded to Nim's softness. The Jeridian's mouth was a spiced taste against Nim's lips. Asenath's tongue whipped up behind Nim's teeth, a long muscle that fed on her... Images penetrated Nim's mind. Hands that massaged her windpipe as she bucked. The digging into her by countless fingers, cocks and every other instrument they found to probe her with. The savagest of rapes in their turning out her natural light when implanting their own beneath her virginal skin.

She pulled away.

"I am no one's," she said firmly. The beaded light across her bare shoulders went out. "I'm broken," she added more softly.

"Think about what I've said." Asenath retrieved her sack and swung it back up onto her shoulder. She fixed Nim with glassy black eyes. "Think about me."

Nim bit her lower lip. There was a residual trace of Asenath's taste there. Spice of a red-skinned Jeridian. Smokiness of a woman.

She stared back down the alley. "We should look for Lulu."

The Jeridian nodded sharply. She strode off back the way they had come, the gore-soaked sack knocking against her lower back.

Nim raised her eyes to the heavens. She felt the sting of tears at her eyes. So much damage was ravelled up inside her. But she wanted to exist beyond her failing circuits sometime. Not now though, she thought, overwhelmed by tiredness suddenly. She let her eyes drop and prepared to follow in Asenath's footsteps.

Large masculine hands grasped her from behind. Her gasp was smothered by a stinking, soaked rag applied to her mouth and nose. The world kaleidoscoped.

Asenath dropped her sack and raced back towards Nim, swift footed over the jagged salt bricks.

"Krvi črvi!" *Blood worms.*

Her cry woke the jackals from their slumber near the fire pits. As the dogs lifted their snouts and howled, Asenath leapt into the air and drove both heels into one man's back. The blood worm matched the dogs with his own howling.

Nim was hiked up over one man's shoulder. Her neon network faintly illuminated her assaulters. Showmaniese, junked up on Dazzle Dust by the look of their wide, bloodshot eyes and jerking movements. The man carrying Nim wore an old duster coat – military in origin, Asenath surmised. The emblem had been torn off one sleeve. Misjudging his step, the man tripped and fell forward onto his knees, cursing as the jolt re-sparkled Nim's circuitry. Her body blazed into life even as she lay across the man's shoulders like a bag of bones. Asenath blinked against the light, and made out the shape of the HawkEye, arms draped over the shoulders of two Showmaniese, head lolling, heels dragging. She went to pull her scimitar from the sheath at her back when a blunt block swung in and connected with her temple.

Consciousness returned in a prickling of awareness accompanied by searing pain. Asenath blinked several times. She became aware of the rough texture of bricks against one cheek and pushed herself up. She sat a moment, temple pulsing, rubbing the dirt and salt from her palms.

A voice came to her, small and uncertain. She rose shakily to her feet.

"Asenath? Is that you?" Lulu staggered up. He collapsed onto the sand brick path, curled into himself and let out a sob. "Those blood worms took Hellequin." The ladyboy tried to dab his nose and eyes but seemed unable to keep his hand steady at his face.

"You're high on Dazzle Dust, ya?" Asenath didn't need a reply. Even as the ladyboy cringed into a ball of self-loathing then burst out laughing in a pitch to match the jackal dogs, she'd already guessed it.

"You'd better sober up, boy, and get yourself back to Cyber Circus with me," she said sharply.

"Aye. Time to go night night." Lulu giggled but clawed his way to stand. As Asenath took up the burden of her bloody sack, Lulu glanced around blearily.

"Where's Nim?" he asked.

THIRTEEN

"Tali! Tali! We did it, gal. We got the deal done. Look here."

Jackerie Rongun waved the document up under his wife's nose. She took it for herself, held it off a little and focused in.

"Jackerie Rongun... provision of Soul Food Plant Food to the Humock National Farmers Guild... under statute 69 of Humock's Biogrowth Law... ninety dollars a quart." Tali Rongun glanced up. Her eyes shone in part-disbelief, part-wonderment.

"You hear that, Hellequin? Deal's done and dusted. Bet you're not so eager to sign up with the military now, son." Jackerie's face had the same snub-nosed look it always did when referring to his eldest son's rogue ambitions. "Makes you think, huh? A bit of knowhow mixed in with a whole lot of effort can bring home one helluva prize."

Hellequin watched his father crow, heard his mother praise the Saints and start planning her spending – new apron material, beading for his youngest sister Lily-Anne's Sunday Best dress, a flock of peckers to lay enough those delicious lemony eggs of theirs, plus a book of Southern Plain Ornithology for her bedridden momma in the room next door. All the while, Hellequin's siblings had joined in with the mood of triumph. Twin boys clambered out their boots and bounced on the low divan. Second eldest, Hellequin's sister, Lu-Georgia, held onto her curls and sucked her fingers, wild-eyed at the family's nonsense, but lit up on the inside no doubt by the thought of ninety dollars a quart. Hellequin was sure she joined their mother in thoughts of all they could buy – the dresses, the scents, the smart jackets, the jacquard curtains, not to mention a Sirinese man servant to shine the silver and wind the clocks.

"What about the crops that died out at the west hill?" Hellequin asked softly. His statement swept the room silent.

"Faulty batch. Test crop from early on in the season." Jackerie got narrow-eyed. "You want to brawl with me again over that? Today, boy?" He snatched the document back from his wife and shook it close to Hellequin's face, forcing his son to blink. "This piece of paper makes a world of difference to your mother and I, to this family and to this homestead."

"I'm just asking you to analyse the soil up on the west field. It's dry and grey, more dust that dirt. And the greenbacks? Yesterday I saw one grown as big as a man's fist. Creature like that could feed on a hundred times the quantity of crops as its ancestors." Hellequin felt his own voice scattering like dust in the wind. None of his family wanted his sourness to ruin their good fortune. Every one of them stared at him with distaste and one wish. Just go away.

Only Jackerie voiced the sentiment. "I think that's the barracks I hear calling your name, son. Time to suit up and boot up. And let me tell you, once you step outside this house, you'd best keep on walking. 'Cause in our memories you'll be no more alive anymore than the sloughed skin of a rattler."

Half an hour later, Hellequin had arrived downstairs with his pack and best boots on. His mother and sisters cried and moaned at his departure. His twin brothers lay asleep on the divan, sucking thumbs like liquorice sticks. His father rocked backwards and forwards on his heels as if to use up the minutes remaining.

"On your way, son." Jackerie opened the door. Beyond the world was on fire beneath a sunset.

Hellequin stepped out onto the porch. The wind whipped up, driving dust into his eyes. He heard the beat of hoppers' wings, Nim's cry of suffering, the sorrowful pipe of the calliope, and Herb's cry of "Come one, come all!"

The dream fractured. He swam back to the surface.

Slowly he focused in on a gas lamp swinging overhead.

"Hello Lieutenant Rongun. Pleasant dreams?"

A face interrupted the blaze of light. The pale green eyes were familiar, as was the scar at one eyebrow where a skirmish early on in the civil war had seen the man take a slice of flint courtesy of a well-aimed rock rifle.

"Corporeal Lars." Hellequin didn't need to test the restraints which bound him to the table; an ex soldier like Lars was capable of securing an unconscious man. He also understood how he had been brought down. It was only when attacked from multiple vantage points that his Daxware had lost perspective, and, with it, the advantage of advanced defence systems. It would take a soldier in the know to hijack a HawkEye.

"How you been, Lieutenant? Good? Yeah, I can see that. You've got a sweet deal with the carnie crew. Stand up and tell a tale or two? Bet they got you shooting holes in bits of paper they shower down too, hey? Yeah, I heard about your gig on the grapevine, but I never thought you'd hawk it here in Zan City. My lucky day, huh?"

Hellequin swallowed. His throat was dry as baked clay. That face! It had haunted him over the years, belonging to Corporal Jay Lars – the soldier he had left behind in Zan City all those years before.

"I see you carved yourself a new life in Zan City, Corporal."

"Carved is the right word." The man sneered, showing two great holes in his cheeks. He poked his tongue through one, wiggled it and sneered again. "Took a bullet clean through my face that first night. Whaddya make to that, Lieutenant?"

"There was protocol to follow," Hellequin embarked but Lars interrupted, keen to tell his tale.

"I was left for dead in a ditch for three nights. Swept out the very bar I saw you in this evening. No more significant that a pan full of dust."

Hellequin remembered the figure who had occupied the shadows at Solomon's bar that evening. Now he understood why the silhouette of the man had seemed so familiar. The distinctive angles of the Humock Guard duster coat had struck a chord, once worn by the hundreds of foot soldiers who'd fought tooth and nail on the government's behalf. His own faded blue frockcoat had been part of a uniform peculiar to the HawkEye – as if the aim had been to despatch his kind to the heavens in their lung baskets and have them blend with the blue skies. Sometimes it made the HawkEye too clear a target. Just like that evening.

"Ah, the dreams I had in that ditch," continued the Corporal. He braced his hands either side of the table and leant over Hellequin, his pale green eyes hard with the lust for vengeance. "I dreamt about my wife believing I was dead and shacking up with another man. I dreamt about my young son being raised by my replacement – a red-skinned Jeridian bastard with his hands on everything I owned."

Lars grimaced. He appeared to ride a wave of untenable grief. "When I woke, I was left to the squalor of Zan City's residential district. The coat, see." Lars pinched the lapel of his duster coat and gave it a disgruntled tug. "There's folk here who still respect the guard for winning the war. There's folk who'll still pick a soldier up out of the gutter, pack his shot-out cheeks with herb-mix and minister to him 'til the flesh heals. And there's others who'll leave a man to die when he gets jumped and can't get back to his platoon on time."

"Protocol," Hellequin repeated. He was still soggy with the fumes off the rag that had been applied to his mouth and nose earlier.

"Protocol? Bloody mindedness more like." The ex-soldier's hand loomed large over Hellequin's face. It poked at the HawkEye implant; the lens telescoped out to focus on the whorled fingertip then retracted. "All this vision and you still couldn't see your way to rescuing me."

The hand disappeared. Lar brought his face back close to Hellequin's. "Fortunately for me, I'm the resourceful type. The old maid who fixed me up had these tales of how she'd rescued me from blood worms who traded in living flesh. Demand was high thanks to the biomorph specialist in residence just a few short streets away. Didn't take me long to realise there's only one way to protect yourself against blood worms in this city. Become one."

The ex-soldier smiled, showing off the great lacerations in his cheeks. "Let me introduce my boss, Miss Yalda Danan."

He stepped out of Hellequin's sightline, allowing a new figure to move into view. The woman was Sirinese, her hair tucked up under a blood-stained bandana. Wisps of it escaped to frame her face, like shreds of clothhod fleece caught on barbed wire. Her nose was hooked, the nostrils large and flared – holes into her soul. She was crumpled with age, the necklace of small, bird-like bones around her neck betraying witch doctor inclinations. Smiling, she showed off the dull black stubs of her teeth.

"Good morning, Sir. Yes, it is indeed morning, although an hour or so short of sunrise. Never mind though, you and I, we have our work to do, wouldn't you say?" She tried for familiarity and kindness; the range of surgical instruments she examined under the weak gaslight as she spoke suggested she was anything but.

Hellequin bucked against his restraints. His heart pulsed behind his ribs. "I've been rearranged enough for one lifetime," he muttered and thrashed his head side to side... Only to be terrified anew when he saw another figure stretchered on a second table. Nim's luxuriant red hair flowed around a steaming gas mask. Her entire face was covered by the mask, a black rubber and glass arrangement with a protruding snout and a great many mechanical buckles fastening it in place. Hellequin could hear the bubble of steam, alongside the draw and ebb of gas fed into the mask. Nim was anaesthetised – at least he prayed she was with every last trace of religious principle he possessed. She had been disrobed and cut open, a mess of bloody wires protruding from one arm.

"I will tear out your throat, bitch," he told the surgeon through gritted teeth.

"Oh, there now. No need to be unpleasant. We each have our jobs to do and, well, since your Daxware requires you to protect those you serve with, it seems you didn't do your job very well when it comes to the little lady. Then again, as Lars tells it, you never were quite wired right in that regard." The wizen witch shook her head as she held up the long needle of a surgical suture. "Leaving a soldier behind? It's a sin the Saints themselves could not forgive. And all that talk of protocol? Just a glitch in your Daxware. I'd stake my professional reputation on it."

"What are you hurting Nim for?" Hellequin fought against the leather straps securing him, his knuckles going white.

"I'm not hurting her. I'm fixing her. After all, I was the one responsible for installing her wiring in the first place. Mister D'Angelus thought it would make her a unique proposition for his clientèle. As it turned out, that same difference made her such an unusual act with the circus. But any fool can see her wiring needs a little attention. Added to which, the dust handlers who pass through here have suggested D'Angelus wants his main attraction back." The surgeon squinted at the needle. "Quite the generous financial settlement for whoever returns her in one fully-functioning piece. And I'm not just going to repair her. I'm going to improve her."

"Without her permission!" Hellequin lifted his head as much as he was able. His vision swam until he focused on the restraints holding him down. The belted straps restrained him at the wrist, upper arms, hips and ankles. His head dropped back again.

"Well, I'm inclined to think the least of my worries is whether the whore gives permission. No, I am concerned purely with restoring her biomorph functions and pleasing Mister

D'Angelus, who is one of my very best customers." The surgeon knocked against her black front teeth with the tip of a scalpel. "A sweet tooth for sugar root ensured Mister D'Angelus had a mouthful of rotters. Luckily we encountered one another and I was able to form him a new set." Miss Yalda Danan looked pleased with herself, adding, "The teeth are bolted into the jaw, you know."

"And pulled from the mouths of dead men as the dust handlers tell it."

The woman shrugged. "Most of them were dead when I embarked on the extractions." Her eyes grew wide like a child's in wonderment. "And now I have my own HawkEye to study into the bargain. A live one this time." Over a shoulder, she said, "Well done, Lars. Very well done indeed."

"My pleasure," Hellequin heard his ex-comrade mutter from the far side of the room.

"Two hundred dollars I believe we agreed," murmured the surgeon, bringing the scalpel to bear on the amber lens of Hellequin's eyepiece. She placed the tip onto the uppermost ring; the eye tried to retract in on itself, whirring like an angry fly as it was prevented from doing so. "You'll find the money roll on the table. Under the spare parts cabinet."

She left his eyepiece alone and gave her attention to the tray of surgical instruments. Hellequin twisted his head to one side and stared over at the cabinet. His HawkEye focused in on jars of organs pickled in formaldehyde – a pair of pink lungs gilled like an unusual fungus, a heart pinned in place to form a fleshy pincushion, myriad eyes crammed into one large bottle, and numerous other horrors. Boxes were stacked on top of one another and labelled with such macabre titles as 'fingers', 'tongues', 'horns', 'marsupial tails', 'assorted scales' and 'wings.'

Hellequin shifted his head to stare the other way. The opposite side of the room resembled a tinker's workshop. Spools of wiring nestled between circuit boards, transformers, brackets and a great many stainless steel mechanisms.

Bile washed up into Hellequin's mouth. The decision to leave Lars behind all those years before had been a dark one, even with his emotions stilted by his implant. But now it struck him as an even greater imposition on the world since he had abandoned a soldier and, in so doing, unleashed a monster. How many men, women and children had Lars lured to that sterile torture chamber? And while he had to admit Nim was all the more exquisite for her light system, how many abominations had the surgeon created alongside?

"Aren't you going to stitch her up?" he shot sideways at the surgeon.

"Dust. It gets everywhere," murmured the woman distractedly. She breathed on the blade of a small hacksaw and rubbed it carefully against the sleeve of her dark grey pinafore. She laid it down again, and, seeming to remember Lar's presence, twisted around on what Hellequin took to be the stool she perched on. "You can leave us now, Lars, if you like. I'm just going to have a poke around the thing." She used a fine metal skewer to gesture loosely towards Hellequin's eyepiece.

"If it's all the same with you, I'd like to stay and watch you gouge out that unnatural eye," Lars shot back. Hellequin lifted his head. Lars stood over by the door, one leg resting up against the frame, hands in his pockets.

The ex-soldier batted a hand off his eyebrow in salute.

"Oh, it's not so much a question of removing it as establishing its make up," said the surgeon, pulling on a pair of thin clothhod leather gloves. "I am eager to dissect the arrangement of wires into the brain. The memory is affected some say while, of course, it's common knowledge the emotions get short-circuited." She fitted a circle of magnified glass to her eye and leant in, examining Hellequin's steel attachment with intensity. "The funny thing is that this particular individual seems to have emotional attachment to the whore. Which could be the first signs of the cognitive weakening which eventually drove all HawkEye quite mad. Or it could indicate a reduction in the efficiency of the Daxware hardwiring. In which case, if we are to say this specimen *feels* as any other intact being, we must also accept that he chose to leave you behind all those years ago, Lars." Miss Yalda Danan showed her squat black teeth. "The Lieutenant here must have really despised you."

"Yeah, well the feeling's definitely mutual," said Lars from his spot over by the door.

Hellequin was in no way defensive of his actions or offended. All he knew was Nim was broken, and properly so, and needed putting back together.

"Finish your work on Nim first," he hissed as the surgeon hovered a second gas mask near his face.

"You see, Lars. Real affection. Or at least an admirable attempt at it. Notice how the natural eye is teary, how the skin strains over the bone ridges at the brow. Talking of which, I may begin with those. Slice back the skin and dig around a little. The pioneers of Daxware made two incisions in the skull, fed the wires in through the brain that way, then re-grafted the bone. These horn-like growths are the result." The surgeon shook her head in amused amazement.

Hellequin swallowed a mouthful of bile. His flesh ran hot then cold. "I'm not going to ask you again," he whispered so quietly the surgeon was forced to bring her ear close to his mouth. "Put Nim back together again or I shall rip your heart out."

"Scary little soldier." Miss Yalda Danan laughed, her face a leathered knot.

Hellequin saw sweat at the surgeon's forehead though. He'd worried her; any second she would go for the gas mask and seal him in. Sensing Lars move slightly, alerted to some noise beyond the room, he butted his eyepiece up into the surgeon's face. There was a millisecond of a different view – of skin cells pressing through to honeycombed dermis – then he pulled away. The doctor was screaming now, hands to her face and cursing up a storm. Hellequin manipulated a wrist bone and wrenched one arm free of his restraints.

Lars was already on his way across the room, blade readied. Hellequin grabbed a chopper off the tray of operating equipment and sliced through the bonds at his other arm. It took him precious seconds to unbuckle the strap at his waist and sit up. There wasn't time to attack the restraints at his ankles. Lars was on him, hacking out with his knife. Hellequin forgot the use of his legs, concentrating instead on each fall of the blade. His own knife was missing; he spotted it on top of a steel cabinet at the far end of the makeshift operating theatre. The mechanism of his HawkEye was soaked in the surgeon's blood and kept cutting out. In snapshots, Hellequin saw the slash of Lars' blade and the surgeon moving in with the second gas mask.

"I don't want you to kill the bastard, Lars. I want you to pin him down again," she insisted, blood streaming from her cheekbone, voice tight with hysteria.

Lars' face shone with triumph as he drove the blade into Hellequin's shoulder. "This fucker ain't breaking free of me a second time."

Hellequin bucked. His view through the HawkEye lens spattered like a lit candle stub. He tried to focus, stomach clawing as the gas mask closed over his face.

"Hold him, blood worm, or I'll have my men outside slice and dice you without aid of anaesthetic."

Lars heeded the surgeon. Struggling to make sense of his bearings with his natural eye, Hellequin found his arms pinned behind him. The pain from his stab wound was excruciating but he fought against Lars' iron grip even as the doctor lowered the gas mask over his face. Hot bursts of steam escaped the sides. Wind mechanisms crunched and wheezed, automatically pulling the straps tight. Hellequin heard the eerie whoosh of gas and tried to keep from breathing. Lars tightened his grip, antagonising the stab wound. Hellequin gasped in spite of himself and choked down a mouthful of the drug. In seconds, he was on the precipice of blacking out.

The door splintered under Asenath's shoulder. Having torn out the throat of the last sentry with her claws, Rust bounded over. Pig Heart brought up the rear, panting heavily, tusks bared against the pain he laboured under.

"Motherfuckers!" A scarecrow of a man wearing a Humock Guard duster coat leapt away from one of two stretcher beds in the centre of the room. The man wielded a bloodstained knife.

"Move away from the HawkEye," said Asenath slowly.

The man juggled the hilt of his blade between his hands. Behind him cowered a second scarecrow, a woman once was. Now she resembled a mummified child – skin baked down into wrinkles, bird-bright black eyes – and wore a wreath of tiny bones around her neck.

"Get out!" The old woman grabbed a small hacksaw off the surgical tray. "Get out, get out, filthy street rats!"

The three carnie folk saw Hellequin and Nim on stretchers. Both wore large steaming gas masks. Nim appeared unravelled at one arm. Wires and unbolted circuits spilled out from her over a metal tray on a high table alongside her. Hellequin was bleeding through his faded frockcoat, the HawkEye lens gored.

Having made short work of the men on guard outside the room, the new arrivals took on Lars. He was agile, weaving in and out of Asenath's attack with her scimitar while delivering a boot to Rust's collarbone when the wolf girl sprang at him.

Pig Heart watched the fight from the sidelines initially. He'd been warned to lead the way to the surgeon then take the lead no more, his wounds making it difficult enough for him to stay upright let alone fight. But it was hard to watch the slap of the ex-soldier's fists into Rust's bare flesh as she ran at him again.

"Bite the bugger, gal!" he called from the sidelines.

Rust craned her mouth, revealing sharp incisors. She tore a chunk from the man's cheek, reopening one of the two old wounds. He knocked her sideways with an elbow and drove his blade hard at Asenath's chest. Rust ducked to avoid the surgeon's hacksaw. She slashed out at the old woman, who fell back awkwardly, sending the tray of surgical instruments clattering down onto the floor.

Pig Heart lumbered over to where Hellequin lay prone on one stretcher. He tried to make sense of the gas mask then forced a stopcock on the cylinder stored beneath. Batting at the straps that secured it, he must have released something; there was a hiss of steam–driven mechanics and the mask's straps un-popped.

"HawkEye!"

Hellequin didn't reply. Pig Heart slapped him a couple of times around the jaw.

"Pig... Heart?" said the HawkEye soldier woozily.

"Yeah. I may not be a pretty sight to wake up to, but at least that crazy bitch surgeon didn't get her hooks into you." Pig Heart squinted over to where Nim lay unconscious. "Unlike your beau, Nim. She's mauled and then some. Rust'll make the doc pay though. She'll gut that bitch good and proper."

Hellequin tried to form words. They came out as a soft pop–pop.

"What's that?" Pig Heart lent in. He listened and looked up.

"Rust! Incapacitate but don't kill that doc bitch. We need her to stitch Nim up again!"

Rust's response was immediate. She drove her claws up under the surgeon's ribs and stopped just short of tearing the skin there. The woman froze.

"Move and I gut it," said Rust by the woman's ear.

On the far side of the room, Asenath was floored by a fist. Lars squatted and lent over her, blade at her throat.

"I did for your kin, Jeridian. Got that great clot of a Shomaniese to show me where the weak ones holed up. I just had to reach in and pick them off. Miss Yalda Danan was kind enough to pay me a hundred dollars a hide and, my my, the work she did with them red skins. Prettied the fuckers right up with wires under flesh and re-bolted bones and animal organs."

"And I for one am mighty grateful." Pig Heart inclined his head towards the surgeon. Rust kept her claws at the woman's ribs.

"Hello there, Miss Dannan. Thought we'd find you here. Same address, same love of dabbling with what's natural and what ain't." Pig Heart tapped his chest. "Ticker's kept me up right these past few years. But there's been a price. You see that about me, doncha?" Pig Heart showed his tusks. Savageness crept into his voice. "You saved me and re-made me, and the price I paid was to become less man than swine." He honked in his throat. It came out as a loud grunt. "So I thank you, Miss Dannan, for the life I got given by your fair hands, and I curse you just the same."

Pig Heart stared at Asenath. "Just gonna lie there or take that bastard's head?"

"She's gonna lie…"

Corporal Lars never finished his sentence. He fell over to one side, the grip on his knife slack. It clattered onto the floor and he clutched his hand to his chest. The handle of Asenath's scimitar protruded from his left set of ribs.

Asenath stood up. She grabbed the man's hair in one hand, put a foot to one of his shoulders and dragged her blade out his body. The ex-soldier gasped in reaction. It was his last breath. He collapsed forward. Blood seeped around him in a smooth reflective pool.

Pig Heart turned back to Miss Yalda Danan who had the look of a frightened roo rat about to be readied for the stew pot. "Now, Miss Danan. I'm going need you to put my two friends right." He picked a scalpel off the tray and gestured to the wall with its bank of bottled oddities. "Else I may have to get creative."

FOURTEEN

Jaxx awoke. He was lying on the sand, curled up like a child, hands pressed into a prayer against his face. The air was crisp. But he sensed the voracious heat that was to come.

He swallowed against a dry throat and pushed up onto an elbow. His head swam, a faint sense of nauseous suggesting he had been more directly affected by the drug fumes inside the nomads' tent than he'd supposed at the time. Nonetheless, he struggled to his feet.

The rising sun flamed at the horizon. Jaxx was grateful not to have missed Dawn Prayer. Having emptied his bladder in a hot tight spill of urine, he strode off a short way and knelt down in the sand.

His voice was strong, his devotion faultless. The events of a few hours earlier preyed on his mind though, in particular thoughts of the monk – or as he knew her now, the girl who *did* speak. He retained a sense of her in the small relaxing of his shoulders, the release of sex having eased the burden of everyday living some. He could still smell her too. Perfume of sweat and womanness layered him.

Jaxx concluded his prayers and stood. The sun was molten, risen clear of the horizon. He started to walk, measuring out the advance of dawn with every step.

The camp was busy by the time he got back. Men sluiced themselves down with the contents of clothhod water bladders. Others sat around, devouring flatbread or a bowl full of the starch porridge the wives had cooked up over a charcoal pit.

Jaxx saw D'Angelus duck out from beneath the flap of one of the smaller tents. The pimp positioned his trekker's hat on his head and strode over to the cooking pot. In his wake, a couple of the wives emerged from the same tent, blinking against the day and tidying their hair and garments.

D'Angelus spotted Jaxx.

"Hi! Hi! Over here, Jaxx!"

The pimp beat his hands and shrugged his shoulders, shaking off the exertions of his night-time pursuits. He'd a manic glaze to him that morning, prompting Jaxx to wonder if it really paid him to stay in the man's service. Sure, he'd a better standing in D'Angelus's little army than most – even more so since D'Angelus's right-hand man lost his life to the wing of a hopper. But Jaxx felt no personal desire to pursue Herb or any other in Cyber Circus. Even the swine man was just another face in a long list of those Jaxx would murder one day. When the fates prescribed it.

You and I, we're in the wrong place. The girl's words haunted him.

"You Sirinese and your prayer rituals! Dawn, dusk, and probably all hours in-between." D'Angelus accepted a small bowl of steaming tea, gesturing to the woman who brought it to bring another for Jaxx. "Well, I'm hoping your prayers will keep us on the right side of the Saints – and, yeah, I know they're not the recipients of your praise. But it's the will that matters, ain't it? Either way, it's all we got now the monk's gone."

"Gone?" Jaxx recalled the terrible visions he'd seen when the girl had lain with him. His ears played tricks. There was the small murmur of a breeze. Dust seemed to coat his tongue suddenly.

"When did the monk go?" he asked, careful not to betray the true sex of the monk while uncertain who he was protecting. He suspected himself. The tears that had flowed after she'd finished with him were born of some great sorrow which wasn't his own. He suspected their coupling had brought about a queer osmosis of emotion – one which both sated and drained him.

"Wouldn't know. Must've taken to the desert before dawn because there's no sign of the bastard now. He was a lousy conversationalist anyway." D'Angelus slapped Jaxx on the arm. He screwed up his eyes as the sun grew in strength, reflecting fiercely off the Sirinese's metal butting plate.

Jaxx liked how the pimp was blinded by the light coming off of him. Partly, he wanted the sun to keep beating down and burn up the pimp. But he'd no reason to feel so. Other than a dull headache, a dry throat, and the stench of sweat over his body.

One of the women brought him a bowl of tea. Jaxx raised it to his lips. The tea was sweet and laced with hot mint. His mind freshened.

"We'll drill a shallow trench from here today to Deralisee east of Zan City," he said between mouthfuls.

D'Angelus got animated. "Good man, Jaxx. You got the scent of those carney bastards, huh?"

Not really, Jaxx wanted to say. They weren't far enough from Zan City yet for him to track the dirigible based on scent alone. But he'd a hunch the troop was on the move again. It was akin to a physical tug, as if some invisible thread connected him with the movement of the ship.

D'Angelus fed a smoke stick between his lips. "Since we've lost the Zen monk, I guess you'll serve as our good luck charm. Watch you steer us right now, Jaxx." The pimp cracked a smile. Smoke oozed between the tics of his teeth.

"I'll check Das has stoked the boiler with dung cakes and water. Then the men can board."

"You do that," said D'Angelus dreamily, staring out at the expanse of desert. "Stupid bastard monk. If the jackal dogs don't get him, the dust storm will."

Jaxx glanced over his shoulder. A thin brown line had appeared at the horizon.

"We need to get on our way," he said.

"Dust's getting up," said Herb, staring out the grimy glass on the bridge.

Asenath signalled one of the pitch crew to relieve her from the frilled ship's wheel. She joined Herb inside the viewing pit. Framed by gilt pipes and lumpen green matter, the window gave out onto the endless dustbowl of the Garenga Stretch, south of Zan City. The area was vast and barren. When the Hamatan hit, it blew in hardest over the Stretch.

"I see it." Asenath felt a dark space open up beneath her ribs. Herb would never turn around, not with D'Angelus pursuing them anywhere north of the Stretch, not when there was money to be made across the desert in the township of Deralisee.

"Want me to turn her around?" asked the crewman at the ship's wheel.

You haven't been with the circus long, thought Asenath. She noted the man's dust handler stoop. He'd worked that thankless job longer than most, hauling great quantities of dust out of the mines, only to have the storms sweep the mess back in inside the week. If future generations dug up the man's remains, they'd find his backbone a perfect curve.

"Try it and I'll have you keelhauled," replied Herb succinctly. "Turn Cyber Circus around?" He gave a short, sour laugh. "Like she'd let you anyways."

"It might be prudent to set the ship down though." Asenath didn't like the look of that dust cloud. She known the circus buffered by some mighty storms. But they'd never flown directly into the Hamatan over the Stretch before. She suspected a storm that fierce would sweep clean everything in its path.

"Maybe. Maybe." It was always Herb's standard answer to the suggestion they delay their arrival to a destination any. Asenath knew it meant diddley squat.

She felt the first small buffer of swirling air. Herb was right, she thought. The dust was getting up. And pretty soon they'd be in the heart of it.

Installed in the cockpit of Wanda-Sue, the glass hood left up to provide airflow, Jaxx concentrated on tracking Cyber Circus. Having shaken off the haze of his strange slumber, he felt newly invigorated. Loudest of all was the flight path of Cyber Circus. He could taste it on the air – rancid, caramelised.

"Take us south-east," he told Das.

"Yes suree." The navigator pressed the steering rod away from him and, reaching to flip a couple of valve switches, enveloped the cab in steam. Wanda-Sue got hot under the collar and bucked as if straining against a dropped anchor.

Das glanced back. D'Angelus slumbered under his trekker's hat. He glanced over the other shoulder at Jaxx.

"You know the dusts getting up, dontcha?" The navigator's voice sounded anxious. "We wanna dive below when we can, but this part of the Stretch is the crust above the old Rongun mines. Tales of swarms aplenty around these parts."

"Just keep her steady," said Jaxx, adding softly, "Where the prayers fall, the spirits lead." A Sirinese proverb. Because just then he'd got the strongest whiff of their prey. And, yes, there it was, floating in the sky off to the west! The circus blip, candy coloured lights streaming from it like a welcome flag.

The stowaway climbed the steps to Herb's private quarters. Of all of the circus's interior she had encountered so far, the pustule was the most fantastical. Composed of the same fibrous green as the bulk of Cyber Circus, the pustule sat in its own egg cup of brass filigree, with five ornate steps leading up to a circular door. A pumpkin palace, she decided, hollowed out to house a fairy or a shrivelled nimblejack.

She knocked gently – and was relieved when the sound went unanswered. The handle was a brass gnarl. She tried it. The door clicked open. She stepped inside, and instantly imagined this was how it would feel to step inside an emerald. Pendulous gas lamps hung about walls, exuding a rich green glow. In the centre of the room stood a brass bath. Pipes wreathed around it, concluding in four flower-shaped spouts. A rustic patchwork of clothhod hides lined the floor.

To one side of the room stood a desk with a thick brass writing slab, numerous drawers and letter slots, and an inkwell. The accompanying chair seemed to grow up out of the floor, plush and faintly tumour-like.

On the opposite side of the room was a second round door – leading to a water closet perhaps – and a small stove in one corner, the chimney of which rose up and through a hole in the upper storey and presumably kept on rising. In between these main fixtures, one wall was decorated with tiny clockwork counters, a brace of heavy iron levers, and a large glass globe. Inside floated a rubbery green organ with flesh tubes running off of it. It reminded her of a specimen kept in a jar. She peered in at the thing, mesmerised, leaping back as a thin covering retracted in the centre of the organ, revealing a great eye of dull green glass.

A sound – like something rolling over the metal floor grid outside – caught her attention. She froze. Waited. Nothing intruded.

Relaxing, she felt a new awareness of her filthy skin under the sackcloth robe. She'd sweated in the act of coupling with the Sirinese, kept up that heat while crossing the salt plains to Zan City. Arriving just ahead of dawn, she'd come upon the circus in its last half-hour of slumber and slipped inside. Traversing the huge circus ring, she'd seen the rigs and unlit spotlights craning overhead like long thin birds and, way up, a trapeze, the swing of which seemed to keep time with some underlying rise and fall of breath.

Backstage had been curtained off by a large steel screen. She'd laid her hands then ear against it. Had she heard a faint heartbeat? Unable to progress further, she'd wandered the circus ring once more, only to hear the hushed arrival of strangers at the tent's entrance. They had come in, strange elfin folk. A pig man and a red-skinned Jeridian woman, doing their best to carry a girl who sparkled with living colour. In their wake came a HawkEye soldier. Thin as a reed. Magnificently tall. He appeared worn out in every way, from the faded frockcoat he wore to the angry adjustments of his bloody eyepiece. His emotions too – she sensed those were awkward and weary.

Approaching the steel screen, the Jeridian had left the girl in the pig's care to work a key into the lock. The screen drew back on well-oiled runners and the small gang made their way backstage.

She'd followed at a distance, through the mess of props and stage flats to a drop of flimsy fabric serving as a wall along one side. She'd watched them slip behind the gauze, their outlines dancing behind the curtain like outsized shadow puppets.

As dawn broke, and the crew began to yawn and scratch and rise, she'd been the first to use the lift rig. No one noticed her step out onto the second level where Herb's private quarters were housed, or when, finding the ringmaster already risen and absent from home, she'd slipped up the brass stairs and through the circular door.

Now she took a long deep breath, inhaling the scent of brewing coffee from the canteen below. It wide-eyed her slightly. But her shoulders and feet still felt world-weary from her travels. It didn't seem so very strange then to twist the stopcock and have steaming, greenish water glug out of the flower faucets. The temperature inside the room rose a few degrees; she luxuriated in the noise and feel of the piping water. When the tub was full, she closed off the stopcock and undressed, her robe and grotesque mask things to be shed.

She fed a toe into the bath, stepped in and lowered herself down with a pleasurable gasp. The green water immersed her. She slid below the surface.

"A mermaid." Rind nosed at the tiny window. The glass was thick and densely entwined with brass piping, restricting the view.

"Nah, a nimblejack fresh out the grave." Tib's eyes were bright buttons. "I seen it moving. Smooth it goes. Not rumble tumble like me and she and thee."

The second girl, Ol, made a queer pop-pop sound as she crept down the roof, beetle-like. "It's a Saint. Come to catch sinners and chew down on their bones."

"We're good 'uns. Let's leave it be," whispered Rind. She clattered away from the window and rolled off a short way. Unfolding, she snouted the air for any indication of danger.

Ol was less timid. "I ain't hiding in my shell. I got a blessing owed me since them up in the heavens let Papa breed us this way. The Saint needs to say he'll take my soul on up when I die. Other two of yous as well if he's willing."

"You's gonna roll on in there and ask it of the one that's bathing?" Tib became edgy, tipping back onto the base of his shell, segmented limbs waggling. He lifted his face, jabbed out a stubby pink tongue and nodded. "Steam's in there and the stink of soap shavings." Fascination drew him to the steps towards the circular door. He stretched a pincer towards the handle.

"Mermaid'll dazzle you with her shine," Rind hissed. She put one leathery foot onto the first step however.

"First sin you'll be judged on is prying where bogey noses ain't wanted," chimed in Ol. She followed his lead though, pushing ahead of Rind.

Tib turned the handle and pushed open the door. Each child blinked, grew accustomed to the light and hobbled forward.

"Hello, my beautiful boneless children." The woman soaped her naked breasts with Herb's washcloth, bathing in the ringmaster's tub as if she was no less of a fixture in the house than the stove, desk, or mechanical motherboard.

FIFTEEN

The sleep of a HawkEye was a ragged, bruising experience. To the government who had commissioned the thirty HawkEye, each in charge of their own platoon, it seemed wise to keep their metalmorphosed soldiers on constant alert. With no facility to close down the implant, the HawkEyes entered a world of endless sight – something only the Saints should be blessed with, so the religious element of Humock had complained. And certainly it did seem the HawkEye acquired the perspective of gods; the eyepiece granted them the ability to process visuals in seconds, to zoom into 1000° degree magnification, and to access multiple views on impulse. But hardwiring the soldiers' brains into a state of eternal visual stimuli was not without consequence. Far from retaining their elite status beyond the Civil War, HawkEyes turned drunkard, addict, lunatic and suicidal. In the past three years since he'd joined Cyber Circus, Hellequin had never encountered another like him, and he was glad of the fact. The mess of hardwiring in his brain might dull his emotions, but it never entirely erased the suffering. Meanwhile, the resultant sleep deprivation served to exasperate the condition.

Slumped in a chair alongside the bed where Nim lay sleeping, Hellequin dipped in and out of consciousness. He dreamt of his parents' farmstead, his family out on the porch. The land around the house was desolate, but the family smiled and waved. Hellequin felt a rush of half-emotions as his mind played snapshots from his past. Collecting peckers' eggs as a child, hand-in-hand with his mother. Soothing his twin brothers with spoonfuls of clothhod curd. Tearing the ribbons from the sisters' hair ahead of church. Feeling his father's disappointment like a gob of spit to the face.

And he was in his lung basket suddenly, staring down at the farmstead as he shot the flare to give the order. Soldiers spilt in from all sides and they brought with them the great lime dust guns designed to raze the Soul Food crops to the ground in minutes. Except, the dust drifted on a sudden, freakish gust of wind. He saw his family wave on, flesh melting off their bones like dripping wax.

" Mi smo victorios!" he cried. Asenath's cry of victory.

"Hellequin." The voice was soft. It bled inside his mind, closing off the fantastical nightmares and bringing him back around. While his natural eye blinked, the HawkEye implant fed in its compound spread of images – the fold of Nim's knees as she sat up, legs slung over the edge of the bed; the tentative placement of one of her hands over the fabric which bandaged her rewired arm.

She put her hand to her throat. "Is there water here?"

He was already handing her a metal cup. His shoulder pulsed angrily where the ex-soldier, Lars, had stabbed him. Asenath had stitched the wound then charged him with the role of acting bodyguard to Nim. It had made sense. No one could alter his permanent wakefulness. He might as well make use of the condition.

Nim's hand shook as she sipped from the cup. She stared at Hellequin. "You called out. I thought you were asleep." She narrowed her beautiful red eyes, scrutinising him. "Asleep is the wrong word, I suppose. But you didn't seem quite conscious."

"I have waking dreams sometimes." Hellequin didn't care to expand. He gestured to her arm. "That bitch scientist took your arm apart. We made her put you back together again."

"And then what?"

"Then I cut her throat."

Nim's chin jutted. "Good."

If she was bloodthirsty, Hellequin understood. Nim had been made to feel like a foreign body squatting inside her own flesh.

"We were hoping the only good to come might be if she'd gone and fixed your shorting circuits. That'd help with your act and such." Hellequin trailed off. He'd no ability to judge the right or the wrong thing to do when it came to Nim. But Asenath had also acted in Nim's defence, so the crime of having saved her again should prove forgivable.

"We?" Nim went to put down the cup. Hellequin took it from her, placed it down on the side table.

"Asenath, Pig Heart, Rust. Pig Heart got his ticker thanks to that blood worms' witch. He led the others to us. Good thing too. I wasn't exactly on track to play hero before they came along."

"You tried though, I bet." Nim flexed her hand, a dancer's movement. Light rippled across her forehead. From beneath her loose blouse and satin bloomers, a neon glow bloomed. She seemed to notice her attire.

"Did you assist me into these?" It was a question without weight. Nim was used to sharing her nakedness.

"Asenath," Hellequin clarified.

Nim shrugged. Her mouth slanted, almost playfully. "So what's the story, son of Jackerie, purveyor of Soul Food?"

Hellequin leant forward in his chair. He put his hands together and looked down. For a moment, he could picture himself strapped into his lung basket again a hundred metres or so up. Across the wilting acres, he saw his parents' homestead and his platoon, invading the territory like termites. As they ran, the soldiers hosed the land with the red counter-agent powder pumped from backpacks. The atmosphere had clouded with the discharge until there'd been nothing to see but blood red miasma.

Hellequin pushed the memory away. "I betrayed my family," he said stiffly. "For the good of Humock some might say."

"And what do *you* say?"

Hellequin stared up, the concentric rings of his eyepiece magnifying her face. He saw a patch of raw flesh at Nim's lower lip, the concentrated brown pigmentation of a small mole at one cheek.

"I say my father was an idiotic dreamer. Too selfish to see the pain he'd inflict on other folk and on the land, too greedy to care. But he didn't deserve that switch in the wind that blew the neutraliser over the house and killed him. I lost my momma too that day. Same with my grandmama, sisters and kid brothers."

Nim's playfulness evaporated. She nodded slowly. "It hardens the wet parts of you after a time. The tongue, the heart."

The soldier frowned, twin bone ridges exaggerated like horns.

"Watching your family die," Nim explained. Her skin glowed with a gentle incandescence. "D'Angelus and his men did for mine."

Hellequin sucked in his cheeks. That didn't surprise him given the pimp's line in disposing of others' flesh as he saw fit. There was little difference between D'Angelus and Zan City's blood worms, he thought with dulled anger.

He watched the interplay of light nodes under the skin at Nim's throat.

"You're glorious," he said on impulse.

She laughed then, in spite of herself. "Not a biomorphed freak?"

"No more so than the rest of us."

Nim cocked her head and stared at him. Really stared, as if studying a still life.

"Why'd you let the bastards fit you up like that? That tick-tocking eye and Saints only knows what stitched into your brain? What made you do it?"

Different angles of Nim overlaid Hellequin's left cornea. He focused on a wide angle of her face.

"Pig Heart betrayed Cyber Circus and you and Rust. Some might say he betrayed the only family he'd got. In defending the pitchman, everyone thought I'd joined the ranks of the mad HawkEyes who'd gone before me. You included."

He got to his feet, towering over Nim, and started to pace. Aware of the throb of his newly stitched shoulder, he rested his hands on the back of the chair. "I know what it's like to betray family, both blood and platoon. I tried to warn my father ahead of the assault. He wouldn't let me set one foot on the porch. The Guard though, they heard of my attempt to play both sides, and they had their own unique punishment for the crime of being Jackerie's son." He tapped the HawkEye implant with a fingertip. The amber lens flinched.

"You mean you didn't choose to become a HawkEye?" Nim looked aghast.

"Twenty years hard labour at Zan City Prison or submit to the biomorph procedure. So there was a choice, yeah. A lousy one."

"Did it hurt?" Nim stood and reached a hand towards him. Hellequin clutched her wrist on instinct. He released her. As if working out the planes and angles of him, she felt about the steel HawkEye. "Like acid on a wound, I imagine," she answered for him.

"What about the madness? Do you know when that will come?" Her hand traced the bone ridge above each eyebrow. Hellequin tensed at the sensations she stirred in him.

"Approximately fifteen years after the Daxware's activation. The weaker soldiers went first. The stronger ones held out a year or two beyond that."

"So you must be one of the stronger ones." Her hand was at his hairline, fingers teasing in. His eyepiece stole small pieces of her – her tongue's tip at a corner of her mouth, the swell and ebb of breath across her ribcage, heat at her temples.

"I'm strong enough to protect you from further pain." Hellequin spoke like a soldier. And he meant it that way, in part.

"Without pain, there would be nothing left for me." Nim's hands went to her hips. Neon blazed from the heart of her. She softened though as he stayed silent, applied both hands to his face, and worked its angles with the caress of each thumb.

"Death will be a friend to both of us," she said wistfully.

"Not I." Hellequin saw her small capture of breath as he disagreed. "I've witnessed enough death in all its fine and nasty detail. Layers upon layers, a great stinking jigsaw taking up my mind. I want to see light, masses of the stuff, until it's all that fills my eyes."

The clutching in the pit of his stomach was as close to real rage as Hellequin could muster. Rage at D'Angelus for his pursuit of them. Rage at the surgeon at her attempts to manipulate their flesh. Rage at Nim for making him so enthralled by her.

She reached for him then, pushing up onto tiptoes, her hand sliding around his neck. He allowed himself to be guided and lowered his face to hers. Their mouths met, pressed and parted. He moulded his tongue into the soft wet of her inner cheeks. The HawkEye mechanism was a slow pulse of movement. He pulled away and fed on every frame of her – the river of colour beneath her blouse, her pupils blossoming. She sat down on the bed. Her fingers opened the tie at the neck of her blouse. She eased the garment up and over her head in one well practised movement.

"I told you, I do not intend to collect on your debt," Hellequin told her, though the hardness at his groin told him otherwise.

"Am I to take you against your will?" Nim moved awkwardly into the centre of the bed. Her bandaged arm restricted her ability to ease down the pantaloons she wore.

"Help a girl out, can't you?" she shot on the cusp of angry tears.

Hellequin sat on the edge of the bed. He took his bowie knife from his belt and laid it on the small table. Moving gently, a tin man in fear of rusting, he helped Nim out of her clothes.

"Look at me," Nim demanded. Hellequin had retracted his eye's zoom to give Nim her modesty. "See me now," she told him, and he glanced up, taking in the creamy skin, the spill of breasts, each long thigh, the triangle of down in-between.

She grasped one of his hands and guided it over her like a wash rag. Under her will, his hand passed from the bud of each nipple to her secret, swollen places.

"I'm underneath the lights," she told him.

He unbuckled and stooped over her, arms braced either side of her head. His frock coat had been discarded, bathed in his blood. The wound to his shoulder was an angry web of stitches. Beneath it, the regimental tattoo of the HawkEye branded him like any other member of a flock.

He eased inside Nim, his breath stolen by the encompassing heat of her sex around his. "Is this where you are?" he asked, wrapping his arms around her shoulders and tugging her down, and himself further in. "Are you in the darkness?"

She caught his mouth to hers. He bucked, a match to the rhythm of her hips. The coarse fabric of his loosened pants rubbed his lower spine. His boots were an awkward weight on the mattress.

He gasped and felt the sweet, metallic flow as he came.

The light worked up beneath their sweat and static. Nim began to burn with a saintly purity of light. Hellequin shut his natural eye against it. The HawkEye implant filled with brilliance.

Tension filtered through the zoo platform. Hidden in their city of pipes, the roo rats whittled at one another in their soft strange mews. The wrinklenecks kept their heads tucked under their wings and stayed still as carved sandstone. Usually impassive and lumbering, the clothhods were restless. They pawed at the sage that carpeted their stall, interwove their long necks and tossed their heads.

The disturbance woke Rust. Her eyes widened, pupils

retracting to slits. She raised up onto her fingertips and listened. Just as any other animal in the zoo, she sensed something off kilter in her surroundings. The motion of the circus in flight was more exaggerated than usual; her stomach rose and fell away on waves of movement. But that wasn't what put the animals on alert. A new scent was detectable – dry and toasted like beet chips – and she had an instinctual impression of danger.

"Lie down, Rust. If I'm to heal, I need to sleep some," mumbled Pig Heart from his nest.

She hissed to hush him. Her eyes glinted in the half-light.

"Moody dog." Pig Heart eased back in his sleep. The pig genes from his borrowed heart hadn't heightened his awareness.

Rust moved to the front bars of her cage. She peered out into the gloom, breath heavy in her lungs. Listening past the distress of the roo rats and the clothhods pacing in their stall, she heard the sound of something being dragged. Also a dry click-clack, and in reply, a rasping. Two voices, thought Rust. Communicating with alien mouthpieces in sucks and whistles of breath.

"There's blood in the air," she whispered.

"What's that?" Pig Heart grumbled, not quite conscious.

"If not now, soon will be." Rust cocked her head. Who else would see what was afoot? Not the pig with his keelhauled spine. Not the roo rats in their tunnels, not the stone-still wrinklenecks or the dull-brained clothhods. There was only she – a lone wolf sent ahead of the pack.

Picking her way over the sage, she slipped out of the door. She slid the bolt across, less to cage Pig Heart in than to protect him from what lay without.

The sounds were coming from the hoppers' wagon, parked a few metres to the right of Rust's. Slowly she approached the cage, which was shuttered up behind its ornate screens. She flinched at a small swish of movement from inside and, again, the long drag of something pulled across the floor. Crouched in front of the screen, Rust listened intently. The click-clack utterances from inside definitely suggesting some level of communication.

Her hands and feet grew cold as the blood channelled to her heart, preparing for fight or flight. A dribble of calcified spit oozed under the screen. It teased down to the ground in a long drip.

Blood is in the air. Rust uncurled to stand on her two feet, her posture stooped and unnatural. She fed a filthy hand around the handle of the screen. Her heartbeat quickened. In one swift motion, she dragged the screen sideways.

The cage inside was in semi-darkness. Rust returned her hands to the floor to assume her preferred position. Her nose twitched. She stuck out a tongue and tasted the air. The scent of the nymphs lingered in their droppings and calcified bedding. Otherwise they might as well have been shipped out and replaced with very different beasts – which, in effect, they had.

A lone gas lamp hung off a nail alongside the clothhod stable. By its dim glow, Rust made out two great hulking shadows that traipsed and swayed about the cage. She brought her face closer.

Down below, the lift rig suddenly ground into motion. The sound tore through the tight atmosphere like a knife. A huge black wing razored out from the semi-dark of the cage, clattering against the bars. Rust leapt back. Crouched on all fours, she retracted her lips and snarled. She knew about self-preservation and all of her senses told her that there were bad things coming out of that cage.

The wing whipped out again, smooth like a beetle's wing case, but with a jagged outer edge tipped with a long thin barb. Rust glimpsed purple webbing at the underside of the wing. Then came the head of the thing, solidifying out of the dark as it moved closer to the bars. While the hopper nymphs had oval-shaped heads, this new form had protracted skulls and a large neck-frill the texture of calcified bone. A 'cap' of iridescent purple exoskeleton fed down between the eyes – which were the same black pustules that belonged to the nymph form, but greatly enlarged. Head feathers spiked out from the neck-frill, exotically pinkish. Mother Nature's poison signifier. Filamentous antennae fluttered through the bars. The pincers were bowed tusks of shimmering black.

A second head loomed alongside the first. Rust kept her fangs on display. She backed slowly away from the cage. What had happened to the divide bars that separated the cage in two and kept the hoppers apart? Rust's gaze zigzagged between the ooze at the rim of the cage and the stumps of the dividing bars, wilted like wax. Her brow swelled. Were the front bars also thinning at their base, liquidised by the new drip of mucous?

Below, the elevator rig started up again. The huge bugs rounded on their surroundings, kicking out with tremendous long hind legs that thwacked the floor so the whole wagon vibrated.

"Nasty crawlers." Rust maintained eye contact while making her retreat. Passing out of view, she scampered noiselessly back to her cage.

Hauling back the bolt, she bounded inside.

"Pig!" She pawed the robust shape of the sleeping man.

"Let me sleep some, woman!" Pig Heart adjusted his position and fell back asleep, snores breaking out one side of his mouth in spit bubbles.

"The shitter must drag itself out my stink bed now." She kicked him. "Hoppers have grown big and black. Real ugly."

Pig Heart's watery weak eyes shot wide. "Hoppers gone black, you say?" He struggled to sit upright, face twisting against the pain, and rested his elbows on his knees. He stayed still and appeared to listen. The noises came again – the distinctive click-clack accompanied by the heavy drag of razored wings through the sage.

"We gotta warn the others," he said in a sharp whisper.

"Bring us in real quiet, Das." D'Angelus shifted his trekker's hat further back on his head. He squinted up at the huge circus tent billowing in the air overhead. His lips tucked back.

But Jaxx caught the sense of something dangerous. He'd tracked Cyber Circus on instinct, but now he detected a new scent – fustiness which reminded him of animals in close quarters.

"Something's amiss." His gaze snatched every which way. The desert was empty except for the dirigible, the strengthening dust cloud and the burrower, which sledged on, spraying dust either side and leaving a deep trench in its wake.

"Time to shoot that bird from the sky!" exclaimed D'Angelus, all smiles.

"Stretch string's all out, plus we're better off maintaining speed to keep up with the circus rather than offloading the men to work the cannons," Das offered. He kept a tight hold on the burrower's steering rod, the red-lensed goggles he wore giving him an insectile appearance.

"Gotta use the Duster in the nose of this old gal then." D'Angelus unbuckled his harness and reached up to yank on the roof hatch, drawing it down and sealing them in.

"If we're gonna stand a chance of aiming the thing right, we've gotta dive. But it can't be deep, else we risk striking down into the Rongun mines." Das took a hand off the wheel and scrubbed the base of his neck nervously.

D'Angelus shrugged. "We don't need to dive deep. Just enough to get a steep trajectory on the upturn so we can fire into the sky when we surface."

"We're not alone," said Jaxx suddenly. He hadn't known the fact before he said it aloud.

His words went unheeded. D'Angelus clipped back into his harness. He glanced at Jaxx, flashing his customary dead man's grin.

"May your spirits bring us luck, Siriense!"

Up front, Das stretched a hand to the bank of variegated mechanisms and revolved a large dial by its short brass handle. With a colossal engine roar, Wanda Sue tipped and started to burrow under.

Descending on the lift rig, Pig Heart hollered down at the lower platforms.

"For the love of the Saints, we need a handler up here! Hoppers have gone locust on us!"

He'd devised a more sophisticated plan originally, one which had involved bargaining the information with Herb in exchange for his reinstatement as chief pitchman. But then Rust had directed his attention to the wilting bars at the front of the hoppers' cage and that had clinched it for him. The nymphs had shed their passive skin and metamorphosed into a more violent life form – Black Locusts. Which meant one thing to Pig Heart. The two locusts were attempting to break out of their cage in search of a swarm.

His cry filtered through the decks like nerve gas. Panicked voices arose as the lift rig arrived at the canteen level, where the creatures' handler stood waiting. The man had collected two whips and indicated Pig Heart and the wolf girl aside.

"You may as well stay down here." He gestured to the crowded canteen. "Once hoppers go locust, we ain't got much hope except to gas and dump 'em." Throwing back his shoulders as if steeling himself to the task, the man pressed the 'Up' lever on the rig. "I got a can of gas stored with the roos' feed," he shouted down as the lift started its ascent.

"Bare man's gonna need more than a can of gas to kill those crawlers," hissed Rust. "There's blood to be shed. Its stink lies in the air."

"Shut your yapping, Rust." Pig Heart glared at her. "Talk like that'll as good as curse us." He shivered though, in spite of the swelling heat inside the circus tent.

"Where's Herb?" he shot across the canteen. His question was met with coughed bursts of 'traitor' and mumbled curses. Pig Heart's old pitch crew hadn't forgiven him for selling Nim out. "Aw, come on you shitters!" he cried, exasperated. "Ain't there one of you on board who remembers the way it went ten years ago, huh? What it was like to lose so many good folk to the creatures once they turned?" Pig Heart dragged a hand across his glistening nostrils. His weak eyes turned glassy. "One of you motherfuckers needs to fetch Herb while Rust and me head on up and help the handler to gas 'em before a swarm gets wind of their scent."

He froze as a man's wail sounded from the zoo level. The sound visibly cut through every person below. The canteen darkened a moment as a huge black shape swept down and around the vast expanse of the circus tent. A second beast swooped down, the remains of the handler's torso suspended from its bloody claws. The hind femora clutched and lengthened. Wings – black, glossy and speckled with calcified spit – beat achingly slowly.

"By the Saints, we need to get those fuckers out of the tent!" Pig Heart glared at Rust. She was trembling – the wolf in her having a better idea of the danger they were in than all the men on the pitch crew.

Cyber Circus understood the violent potential of the two black locusts in its belly. The tent shuddered and tipped sideways on a steep axis as if trying to shake the locusts out the open bottom of the tent.

But now the locusts had shaken off their peaceable nymph sensibilities, they were ravenous. One swept in and around the living quarters and the platforms. The handler's torso landed alongside Pig Heart, discarded in preference for softer meat. Screams filled the hull as the second locust slipstreamed in behind the first, the rabid pair tearing chunks out of the rails, floor grids, tables and integral structure of Cyber Circus. An eerie whine escaped the calliope as the tent pendulumed. Pitch crew clung to the fixtures, lay flat on the gangways up in the Gods, tucked children into their arms, and held onto the circus for dead life. Some lost their footings, tumbling out into the ether with terrible, pitiful cries. Others were picked off by the voracious locusts.

"Blood in the air," moaned Rust, cowering at one end of a fixed trestle table.

Clinging to a table leg alongside, Pig Heart told her, "Don't worry, gal. Cyber Circus'll shake them out."

Do it soon, he prayed. Before a swarm comes.

"Something's amiss." Beyond the gauze curtains of the dressing rooms, Hellequin could hear the circus in turmoil.

Nim didn't stir. Her breathing quietened though, which suggested she was conscious.

"Nim?" he said louder.

"Yes..." She sighed – a bitter sound that suggested peace had been all too fleeting. "I know."

"I'm heading up to the bridge. You ought to stay put. Avoid whatever mayhem's occurring out there."

But Nim was already sitting up. "Last time I stayed here, D'Angelus's men broke in." She started to roll up her stockings, wincing against the pain from her arm, which had to be considerable. "Asenath's right. Its time I had more say over the uses I'm put to." She stood and tugged on a high-collared field vest with a great many pockets and brass fastenings. Her hair fell about her shoulders, loose, long, the colour of jewel fruit.

"Okay." Hellequin slid off the bed and fastened his pants.

They slipped out through the gauze curtains. Backstage was littered with broken scenery and a sort of caustic white dung which sizzled as it ate into the floor. Hellequin and Nim stared up in time to see one of the black locusts smash through the rail onto Herb's private platform then take to the air again.

"Saints almighty, the nymphs have become locusts." Hellequin got a grip on Nim's hand. "You remember at the prison when the inmates rocked their wagon? I'd a hunch the beasts had been rubbing up against each other. They can't do that, you see. After a while, it brings about the metamorphosis. But the handler was sure there'd be no fallout after the prison visit."

At that instant, a deep drone arose from somewhere far below the tent. It made Nim's blood run cold.

"Swarm," she said softly,

Hellequin let go of her hand. He stared at her and asked, "Can you use a firearm?"

"Locusts are terrible creatures. They'll strip a farm in a day." Dressed in her monk robes, the woman stood at the open door and watched the huge bug investigate the platform. The creature froze when it saw her. She stared into the black mirrors of its eyes and saw the ringmaster's pod reflected there, the narrow stairs, the open door. Her reflection was absent. As if she didn't exist in that world.

In a great puff of chitinous material, the creature powered off its hind legs and swept back out into the air space.

The woman closed the door. She turned around to find the Scuttlers cowering at the back of the room. Their wrinkled faces peeped out from their toughened shells.

"I've shut them out," she told the children – or so she presumed them to be. They were, after all, what had drawn her to Cyber Circus. 'A child without bones' was the way she had put it to the Sirinese, Jaxx, describing the one who would search the nooks and crannies of the mines for the lover she had lost. The Scuttlers were the closest match she had found.

They blinked at her through the steamy air, their soft bodies – the turtle meat of them – cocooned in keratin. In the case of all three, one of the front claws would snap on occasion, a spasmodic action. Their wrinkled old faces retained a sense of youth in the snub noses, blue-blue eyes and plump neck folds.

One of the girls shuffled forward and prodded the Zen monk mask on the floor.

"Nasty ugly," she said sourly.

The woman tied the belt of dried relics around her waist over the top of the rough cassock. "It's dress up. Nothing more. A peepo thing to scare off witches and other creepers in the dark."

"I's try it on," said the boy. He slunk forward on his belly. His claws were nimble as he worked the cloth mask onto his face. He stared at his sisters then the woman, a grotesque too horrible even for a circus.

"Take it off, Tib," hissed his other sister, shyer and keeping to the back of the room.

Cyber Circus lurched. The woman laughed as she stumbled. The children rolled with the movement of the ship, limbs tucked up into their nutshells.

The boy, Tib, took off the mask, cheeks puffing as if he was frightened by the fit of it. "Zen monks don't have titties," he shot, and all three rolled and snorted at his daredevilry.

"Zen monks don't talk," added the shyer, more incisive sister, a squint to one blue eye.

"I'm playing make believe, that's all." The woman smiled softly. Wearing the rough dress with its belt of dead things, she looked like a devil from the neck down.

"And your name is?"

"Rind, and 'tuther one's Ol."

"You an angel? One of the Saints' kin?" asked the bolder sister, Ol.

All three stared at the woman with want in their child eyes.

She sat cross-legged on the floor to match their skilful balance.

"Tell me where you came from?"

The three shortened their necks.

"The father bred us," said Rind.

"He was a bio-mor-pher." Ol sounded out the adult word. "Blood worms brought him the bits and pieces he worked with most of the time."

Tib added, "But we was special. Bred not made."

"Crossbred. Like the hoppers." The woman sucked her bottom lip and looked quite the child herself. "Oh, this is some world," she marvelled.

Her expression grew shrewder. "How did your father come to place you in a circus?"

"Law took him for breeding us. We weren't the way of what was natural said the government's man. Herb, he hears and comes and takes us in." Rind kept a shrewd eye on the woman. "We thought you a Saint come to bless me, he and she." She used her front pincers like opposable thumbs, indicating herself and her siblings.

"Ah, I do have a gift for stirring the souls of men. And agitating the lay of the land," said the woman absentmindedly. She took the mask from Tib and wore it over one hand like a puppet. "My gift is a blessing and a curse. I'm sure curiosities like yourselves understand the burden. And the thing I'd like is for us to help one another out." The woman looked fragile then. Her wide mouth trembled.

The Scuttlers didn't know how they felt about this mood shift. They were suspicious of the woman's suggestion they work in some mutual alliance – hadn't they always been put to work in that manner, by their father, by Herb? But they also appreciated the soft appeal of the woman, how she spoke to them like they had some significance in the world.

"What do you want from us?" asked the shrewd Rind.

SIXTEEN

The swarm rode in on the dust cloud, materialising through it like Hell's own demons.

D'Angelus and his crew had no knowledge of the strength of the storm or the arrival of the swarm. Wanda-Sue wormed through the dirt twenty metres down; any lower and they would have broken through into the old, unstable mine tunnels. D'Angelus tucked his fear inside. He couldn't understand why anyone enjoyed tunnelling underground when there was a perfectly respectable quality of life to be had up top. What he did appreciate was how valuable it was to suck the nutrients out of the dirt – gold, silver, and other precious ores. And to be able to burst free of the ground directly below an airborne enemy, weapon primed.

"Nearly there," he said, squeezing one hand with the other to reassure himself of the fact. Through the windshield, he saw a hurricane of spraying water, churned soil and noise – and all he could think was how much the land was like a woman. She could be ploughed, but any moment her stability could fail, burying him alive.

"How much further?" he snapped.

"Coming up for air now, boss." Das drew the steering rod towards him, between his knees. "You ready to fire soon as we surface, Mr D'Angelus?"

"Uh-huh." D'Angelus put a hand on the fat release switch.

"Aim true," said Jaxx, seated alongside D'Angelus. "Cyber

Circus is a cunning creature. Miss the shot and we'll lose the advantage of a surprise attack."

"I hear ya." D'Angelus's brow hooked. "I hear ya."

Nim didn't have much call to visit the living quarters of the pitch crew and the other stage acts. She'd chosen to make her home in the airier maze of the dressing rooms, taking comfort in their light atmosphere, how the flowing white curtains enfolded her. In contrast, the living quarters underneath the canteen platform formed a honeycomb of dark confined little rooms.

She heard the voices of children bundled into the tight spaces by their parents and was thankful.

Standing at the door to Hellequin's private space, arms bracing the doorframe as the ship seesawed, she saw a room woven from the same tough green fibre and gilt as the rest of the ship. There was a series of vertical nooks into which were tucked the few clothes the soldier owned, including a clothhod suede poncho she'd seen him wear when the air turned cool. The bed was against one wall, a fibrous bulge with a gaze canopy suspended overhead. It surprised her to see her old valet spread-eagled on the bed. Lulu snored in fitful bursts, nosing down into the sage pillow.

Crouched besides a small ammunitions chest, Hellequin followed Nim's line of sight to the sleeping ladyboy. He gave his attention back to the chest.

"Kid gets nightmares," he said gruffly. "I let him sleep on my floor when he asks. But he got high on Dazzle Dust last night. I figured he'd be nursing a thick head once he woke so I let him kip in here."

As if in anticipation of the hangover that awaited him, Lulu whimpered, "No, Sir. Not the rod… hurts… hurts." He sobbed and tucked himself into a ball of sweaty bedcovers and limbs.

Hellequin scowled as he collected his weapons. "As I said, nightmares."

Lulu opened his eyes. He cringed against what little light

there was inside the dank cabin, lay still a moment then let out a pitiful moan.

"Ah, sweet Saints! My head." He blinked at Nim. "Mistress Nim? I've had such bad dreams. I dreamt blood worms came and took Hellequin." His gaze moved to the soldier. "But here he is so I guess that was just the Dazzle Dust playing tricks."

"Yup, just another nightmare." Hellequin glanced at Nim and they made a secret pact to keep their kidnap secret.

"You gotta get up, Lulu." Hellequin threw the ladyboy a rock pistol. Lulu jumped when the weapon landed alongside him, but he gripped it firmly and forced himself to sit up.

"Who's attacking us today?" he asked, shaking back his mane of white-gold dreadlocks. His vanity was marred by a trail of dried spit running from his mouth to his chin.

Hellequin threw a small rock gun over to Nim. He packed a couple of pistols into the back pockets of his pants and hung a rifle off one shoulder by its strap.

The ship lurched. The drone that came from somewhere beyond grew ever louder.

"I don't know what I'm hearing out there, but it's not easing my poor sweet head any." Lulu stood cautiously and brushed down the chemise and pantaloons he wore, his biceps incongruous with his girlish attire.

Hellequin threw him two cloth packs of ammo. The soldier passed Nim packets of smaller grade rock shot.

"Only hope we got is to take the locusts out while they're flying over the open hull. That way, they'll fall into the ether below, taking their scent with them. Swarm'll let us be then."

"And if the swarm get inside the hold first?" asked Nim, feeding shot into her handgun.

Hellequin stared at her, his steel eye whirring in minute adjustment.

"They won't," he said.

"Ain't those suckerloops put the locusts down yet?" Herb

brushed a sleeve over his sweaty forehead, immediately returning the hand to the frilled steering wheel. He blinked lots, as if to clear the dust beyond the viewing pane.

Standing alongside, Asenath sharpened her focus on the swirling grey. She made out a black clot coming gradually into focus.

"Swarm's coming." She swallowed. Two-legged enemies she could intimidate and slaughter. But the ways of the black locusts were restricted to eating, shitting and reproduction. And they were arriving en masse.

"This ain't the best use to put me to." Asenath glared at Herb, her black eyes brilliant with defiance.

Herb gritted his teeth against the force of the storm, manhandling the ship's wheel until their flight path evened out. "Okay, okay. Take to the blasted warpath if you must, Jeridian. And you, man!" he barked in the direction of a pitch crew member working to manipulate the great score of levers and switches to the rear of the bridge. "Cook up a great fart of steam. We need to garner strength to power through this storm."

Calling out to the Jeridian's retreating back, he added, "You fighting sorts better have the skill and luck to put those locusts down. Otherwise, me, you, the whole darn circus is done for."

Asenath was holed up in the Gods wearing the stretch string harness that had saved Lulu from many a deadly fall back in the early days of his act. Crouching at the far end of a walkway, she stared down at the circling locusts. The bugs swept around the open hull, their flight choreographed to bring them within millimetres of one another's wingspan but never touching.

Her gaze fell on the HawkEye soldier who was riding the ascending lift rig. The others in their makeshift gang were newly armed and slotting into position at the canteen platform. The exquisite whore, Nim, tucked in behind a stack of boxes. Lulu knelt nearby, back to the wall. Rust trotted back and forth in front of the table Pig Heart crouched behind. Asenath saw the pitch man indicate Rust aside with a jab of his rifle. Rust was having none of it and carried on weaving in front of her man, a mother protecting her cub.

Asenath prayed to the souls of her kin that these strangers, these carnie folk, would have her back. "Ahoj na vás, Mama Sunstar." It was the prayer offered by every Jeridian warrior who was about to engage in a battle they'd small chance of winning.

She took a deep breath and, drawing both scimitars, ran halfway along the gangway and leapt off.

Air roared in her ears as she fell. Her stomach rearranged beneath her ribs. One of the giant bugs whirred near. Asenath drew her legs into her belly, condensing herself. She brought one blade down hard on a passing wing. There was a sickening crunch as the keratin armour gave a little – and a sharp ping as a rock slug took out one of the creature's feelers.

Asenath cursed the pitch crew shooters, muttering, "Pozorný." *Careful.*

Her descent was rapid, the stretch string pulling her up just short of the roaring, dust-filled expanse below. She catapulted back up as the string retracted. Chitinous material dusted down as the second locust passed overhead. Seconds later, she rose up level with the bug, lashing out with both scimitars and putting two great rips in one wing.

Momentum carried her back up past the gangways and Asenath found herself looking down. She had a sensation of floating near the roof of the tent; in that moment she saw the HawkEye peel off shots at the two bugs in rapid succession and Pig Heart manhandle Rust aside to fire at the insects, who dipped and skidded in and out the platforms.

She was tumbling again. Asenath saw a spurt of shot tear up the first bug's wingspan as she fell towards it. The creature reared and caught her up on its back. Her repetitive lift and drop was substituted for a swooping buckaroo. Asenath took hold of the leathered neck frill and used it as a means to grip on. Her thighs pressed in and rubbed painfully over the bug's slick scales.

Still the bullets came. Asenath rode the locust while hacking into its neck frill with her blade. Blood welled where she worked, gluppy and pus-yellow. Glancing up, she saw the HawkEye, standing tall on the lift rig as it ascended to the zoo platform. The bug seemed intent on the same destination. Asenath threw herself forward so that she was protected from the soldier's fire by the armoured neck frill. Blood dashed into her face as she drove both scimitars around to the throat and in at the fibrous flesh there. All the while, a barrage of shots assaulted the locust.

The creature kept flying – except now Asenath realised the trajectory of the bug's flight was off. It headed hard at the lift rig. She saw Hellequin squat as the bug's undercarriage skimmed over him. The bug hit the deck and skidded on, propelled forward by the sheen of its body armour. Asenath took to her feet and rode the back of it. The dead insect slid between the stables of livestock to slam hard into the destroyed wagon that had once been its home – just before it did so, Asenath felt the breath torn from her lungs as she jerked back, the string of her harness having reached its maximum stretch. But as she travelled towards the upper reaches of the tent again, Asenath felt a blow to her back, followed by the whip of something soft and stinging to her face. The second locust dropped away, head feathers billowing out from its head crest in a poisonous halo.

The Jeridian was in trouble, Hellequin realised as he watched her gasp and writhe on the stretch string. There was fight in her yet, the scimitars driving out now and again to catch the locust a slicing glance.

"Asenath's hurt!" he called down to the others. "We gotta take the last one out before it makes mincemeat of her."

Volleys of rock ammo rang out. Hellequin zoned in on the flashes of black spark powder, the trails of blasted shot. The rocks pierced the insect's undercarriage, releasing great sprays of yellow blood. He telescoped in on the microfibers of the locust's keratin armour, the hair that fibrillated at each huge ham of a thigh. Zooming out, he saw the soft parts revealed when the insect breathed and armour plates moved apart a little.

He applied his HawkEye to his rifle sight; the implant laid a grid across the view, plotting the vulnerable chinks, and he fired ten shots in rapid succession. Each ripped into the exposed belly meat and wing sinews. Yellow blood exploded out in starbursts.

His sub-natural sight redirected to Asenath inside milliseconds, but he wasn't quick enough to see who fired the shot that cut the stretch string – and for that he was later thankful. Asenath careered down, landing between the wings of the shot-up insect.

"Mi smo victorios!" The cry rang out, vitreous yet tremulous.

There would be no collecting and preserving the heads of the vanquished on this occasion, thought Hellequin with a tinge of bitterness. The locust carcass tumbled away into the swirling ether, the Jeridian brave splayed across its back.

For a few seconds, not a single voice could be heard through the entire tent. In the hush, the carnie folk listened to the swell and exhale of the circus in flight, a mechanical scraping noise that appeared to originate far below, and the thunderous drone of the swarm.

"The body of the first bug's still in the zoo!" Hellequin hollered down from the lift rig. He leapt off so the others could make use of it and ran towards the broken mass of the locust at the far end of the platform. His steel eye scanned and processed the weight of it, and he knew by imprinted instinct that he couldn't shift the cadaver alone.

"Hurry!" he thundered into the echoing space at his back. The noise of the swarm provoked in him the closest thing to fear he'd felt in a long time. He heard the stiff grind and punch as the lift rig ascended. No time, he panicked silently. No time.

But figures started to crawl over the edge of the zoo platform. The ladyboy, flipping into a handstand and back around onto his feet. The wolf girl, who tumbled over in a rush of awkward limbs. Pig Heart, levering his bulk up via the wires of the lift rig, colossal muscles tensed. Nim, who arrived in a silent, pink-faced effort and fell off to one side just as soon as she was safely on the platform. Hellequin zoned in on the clamminess of her skin, how her eyes rolled back to show the whites. Only her strength of will kept her conscious.

Together, the group dragged the carcass between the stables, the beasts either side silent now as if out of respect for their fallen fellow. Arriving at the edge of the platform, they worked to tip the carcass over. The group watched it drop in that loose-limbed manner of the dead. It was swallowed up by the dust storm below – just as the first few scouts from the swarm crawled in at the base of the tent. Hellequin watched them scuttle up the inside walls, mandibles chittering. They paused now and then to scrape their tremendous back limbs and signal back to the swarm with a reedy solo.

"We're done for," said Pig Heart.

The HawkEye's steel eyepiece took in a sectionalised grid of images: the crawling horrors, the mass of insects burgeoning at the opening to the hull, and Nim, terrified, beautiful, and pulsing with pure white light that made her an angel.

When the sonic wave off the rocket launcher struck, it wavered up and then throughout the tent, invisible to all but Hellequin's sensitive lens. The others were flung back by the power of it. Hellequin alone stayed grounded, crouching at the edge of the platform, hands woven into the gridded floor. A great burst of flaming shot burrowed up through the layers of insects, exploding out into the hull. Bright red rays streamed in all directions, punching holes in the wings and exoskeletons of the twenty or so scouts circling in the circus. At the same time, the rays pierced the fibrous walls of the tent in many places.

"Volcanon shot," Hellequin shouted to his companions. He arched his spine at a dramatic angle; the millisecond he gained from his advanced sight enabled him to avoid a red hot rock that skimmed past his shoulder. He dodged a second rock and stood up, hands to his hips. Firepower like that had to originate from a costly war machine – a burrower enabled for underground mining explorations as well as military engagements.

"D'Angelus." Hellequin stared at the smoking carcasses of the locust scouts, twitching and tumbling down to join the ashes of a good number of their kin below. The remainder of the swarm must have taken to the wing again, their drone definitely receding. Peering down through the dust and fallen locusts, he made out the nose cone of D'Angelus's burrowing machine.

Retracting his telescopic sight, he concentrated on the state of Cyber Circus. Fires had broken out where the interior walls had been punctured. The dirigible was listing heavily to the left. Hellequin knew with certainty that the airship was losing pressure and, with it, buoyancy. The ship was heading down.

The body parts of blown-apart insects littered the ground nearby, but otherwise all D'Angelus saw through the dust was Cyber Circus, coming closer at alarming speed.

"Dive, you motherfucker, Das! Dive!"

Das stayed gormless, his eyes wild behind his goggles.

"No time," said Jaxx, as calmly as if death was just another segment to his evolving life.

D'Angelus gasped. Dampness spread out across his lap as the enormous circus settled fully over the top of the burrower. For a brief instant, the dust storm ceased and the atmosphere became fantastically still. D'Angelus found himself staring out of the burrower's windshield at the flaming interior of Cyber Circus, and the HawkEye, hands on hips, at the uppermost platform. Then the circus was rising again and Wanda-Sue was back out amongst the roaring dust.

D'Angelus watched the dirigible drift away into the dust cloud, a lame animal retreating to lick its wounds.

"The fucker looked at me," he whispered.

"Who?" The Sirinese stared over.

"The HawkEye." It came out as a gasp, followed by tight, hysterical laughter.

"You believe the soldier's genuine?" Jaxx's tone suggested he had never doubted the fact.

"Stared right at me with his twitchy metal eye." D'Angelus laughed, as if finding the notion incongruous, before stabbing a finger at Das's shoulder. "What're we sitting here for, man? We got them wounded and on the run."

Das scrubbed a hand around his chin. He glanced back over a shoulder. "There's nowhere for the circus to go if it keeps on south-east like that. Unless it means to dip into the caverns to escape the storm a while."

"Go into the old mineshafts?" D'Angelus inhaled deeply. "Screw it, I ain't no lemon-belly gonna miss out on a kill this close. Take us down, Dax." He gave the navigator's arm another jab. "And you'd better deliver me safe above ground again or, by the Saints, I'll skin your hide, even if I have to come back from the afterlife to do so."

Hellequin replayed the snapshot of D'Angelus peering up from behind toughened glass, his Daxware having stored the captured image. He zoomed in on the figure in incremental degrees until he saw the pimp's expression in detail: the arched brows and pupils, liquid with fear.

"Need you working alongside me, soldier. There'll be time to stand and stare once we're free of the storm and have put the fires out." Pig Heart nodded towards the mayhem of the circus in flame. "Rust's staying put here to soothe the beasts."

"You in charge of the pitch crew again now Asenath's dead?" Hellequin asked brutally.

"For the time being, if the men'll have me. Got to save the circus from burning up then they can jack me out on my ear again."

"What do you say, Lulu, Nim?"

The courtesan swung her rifle up onto a shoulder. Her red

eyes were wet. "I say Asenath was a fierce and loyal friend. I wish she was still with us. Since she's not, let the pig do his job." Tears brimmed over. Her face did not crumple though.

Hellequin maintained her gaze. He nodded.

"Enough with the tears and make ups," snapped Lulu. "Can we get on with putting out the fires before this whole damn circus burns down around our ears?" He stamped a foot and stared accusingly at the others.

"Sure thing." Walking past the ladyboy, Pig Heart stopped suddenly and delivered a right hook to Lulu's jaw.

The ladyboy hit the deck.

Pig Heart directed a spit gob alongside him. "That's for slapping me around so enthusiastically when I got tied up a day or two back. And for expecting us to forget one of our own inside minutes of them expiring."

Nim strode past Lulu in the direction of the lift rig. Hellequin adjusted the rifle on his shoulder and followed after.

Herb strutted along the gangway, pink-faced with rage and concern.

"Put out these fires quick smart!" he barked at the pitch crew, and superfluously since Pig Heart had already arranged them into fire fighting squads. Buckets of water were being winched up on makeshift rigs, then passed hand-to-hand until the final man in the line sent the contents sloshing out. Some buckets steamed with water siphoned off the fat-bottomed boiler.

"Cyber Circus is weak enough without draining her," Herb muttered, chin on his chest, sweat pouring off him.

"Who's got the wheel?" demanded Pig Heart, striding up to the ringmaster. He swiped an arm across his brow, adding to the soot already smeared there.

He and Herb stared at one another.

"I hadda put you through it." Herb sniffed with that awkward way of a man under pressure to make right but with no intention of appearing wrong.

Pig Heart clucked in his throat. "You near on did for me, Herb. Good job I got a tendency to heal tough as a ham hock and quicker than most. Back full of scars will give a man jip forever though." His small watery eyes widened. But the anger died back and he sighed. "I got greedy, Herb, and I got a hiding for it. Now, how's about you let me get on organising the patching of this craft so we've any kind of hope of staying airborne. Plus, I say again, who's got the ship's wheel?"

"Some fool off the pitch crew. I hadda come see how the old gal was fixed." The ringmaster stared around him, gave a low whistle and shook his head. He put his hands on one of the brass rails running either side the gangway and stroked the metal gently. "I'll have you fixed up real fast." He nodded, lips pursed. "Real fast."

He got a steely look then, and bounced his hands off his pot belly. "I've given the order to take us into the caverns. You more than anyone else here understand why that decision weighs heavy on me."

Pig Heart nodded. Both Herb and he carried the burden of their last trip to the caverns years earlier, how they'd been unprepared for the destruction a swarm could wreak on an airship full of soft meaty bodies. It went without saying that neither man wished to return – just as it went without saying that the gale outside the tent was strengthening by the minute. Sooner or later, Cyber Circus would be torn limb-from-limb by the storm. Their only option was to risk it underground.

Rooting around at his hairline, Pig Heart muttered, "If we're gonna risk it in the caverns again, lets set our best man to the task of navigating the ship. One who's got the need to protect his fellows embedded in his skull and who's got sight that'll pierce the dark and then some."

Herb nodded slowly. He stepped to one side of the reinstated pitchman and hollered down at the HawkEye soldier, who was patching a rent in the wall at the zoo level. "Get up to the bridge, Hellequin. I'm trusting you to steer us through the pits of Hell to paradise."

The caverns burrowed deep into the Fathenora mountains dividing Humock from Siria. Border control was non-existent either across the mountain range or beneath it. Any fool enough to cross to Siria was welcome to its barren sheets of rock while those who would journey to Humock had already done so – or else been lost to starvation in that waterless, stony land. Meanwhile, anyone choosing to enter the old mine caverns was a danger to himself and the rest of the world – best he wander inside and be swallowed up by the devilled dark.

Hellequin stood on the bridge, staring out the view-pane at the ever-shifting grey.

"I can't see anything," said Nim. She had followed him up there. Although as she pressed her hands to the viewing pane and remained intent on the view beyond, it seemed she was there less to support him than for her own reasons.

"I see enough," he answered gruffly, with a hunch she'd been talking to herself. And he could see. Just. The concentric rings of his eyepiece whirled, making sense of the distorted landscape. Cyber Circus was floating no more than fifteen metres above the ground. The float bladders were the only things keeping the craft aloft now that the integrity of the hull had been compromised. With the water in the boiler drained dangerously low, it was impossible to work up a fresh bloat of steam. The last dregs of power were being channelled to the pendulous root mass at the rudder so he could steer the ship at least.

Hellequin checked the chart coil to the left of the ship's wheel, using the foot peddle to scroll the thin cloth between the brass winders. There were no townships marked this far south-east. They were headed straight for the vast mountain range.

"We aren't far from the entrance to the caverns," he told Nim. She might not be listening but it gave him a sense of comfort to be in her company.

Nim looked at him suddenly from her spot slunk down

amongst the cushions and rag-rugs in the viewing pit. She looked fragile.

"So many folk have died or been injured just so we could outrun D'Angelus. I ain't accustomed to thinking of others. Always been some fucker ready to paw me or rub me sore. Asenath might have encouraged me to fight back but did she really mean to go and sacrifice herself while I was getting round to it?" She was crying again, but with no suggestion of needing to be comforted. Hers were bitter tears which washed away the numbness and left vengeance in its place.

She sighed raggedly. "So much blood spilt just so D'Angelus could try to get a bolted horse back in his stable."

"Pig Heart invited the pimp in. Rust attracted the suckerloop's attention. Asenath died by her own code of decimate or be decimated." Hellequin's voice was sharp. His hold on normal emotions was always more tentative in combination with adrenaline. "Yes, there are members of the pitch crew who've fallen and I suspect their families will share a savage whisper regarding you… and me, no doubt."

He scowled, the twin bone ridges at his brow more pronounced. "Ask me though, there's only one soul you oughta say sorry to for this upset."

"Who's that?" Nim asked, swiping the tears from her cheeks and chin in irritation, as if surprised to find them wet.

Hellequin patted the ship's wheel, the frilled matter rippling beneath his touch. "Cyber Circus," he said softly.

"Old gal's the forgiving sort." Herb waddled out onto the bridge. He nodded at the viewing pane. "That the entrance?"

Hellequin nodded. A vast rock formation was materialising through the dust. Rugged black folds towered over them where the ground had split and poured out its guts. A gaping chasm ran up the mountainside. The hole was lined with sharp crags; to all appearances they might well have been delivering themselves into the mouth of Hell. Hellequin glanced up as Cyber Circus was slowly swallowed by creeping, almost tangible darkness. Seconds later, the fibrous green cell-structure of the circus started to glow with bioluminescence.

As the dark threatened to seep though the glass, Nim abandoning the viewing pit to come and stand alongside Herb and Hellequin.

"You got enough light to steer by?"

Hellequin nodded. He was operating on a neural-macular level, retuning the circuitry that wormed into his brain. The amber lens in the centre of the HawkEye became red, providing night-vision.

"I see the truth of it," he said, guiding the ship between two great slices of rock and into a cavern that dwarfed the dirigible. Hellequin parted his lips in wonder; the cavern might have been built to house the Saints. Fat columns of calcified stone spiralled up to a ceiling too high to glimpse. The ground was carpeted in stalagmite needles a few short metres below. Now and then a colossal rock sculpture would rear up through the darkness, formed by water long evaporated. Then the rock would fashion itself into waves, like broiled tongue, or take on the face of a crone hunkered down amongst that vast subterranea.

"And what is the truth?" asked Nim at last as if she had been wrestling with herself not to ask for fear of the answer.

"Rock mostly. And dust." Clouds of the stuff had swept in over the years, banking against the sides of the cavern in soft grey hills.

Herb asked, "And the locusts?"

"They like it warm. The swarm will have holed up further in." Hellequin's eyepiece revolved in measured clicks. The red lens flicked up and side-to-side.

"How's the re-patching going?" he asked. Herb needed to remember that the swarm wasn't their only worry. The circus itself could expire at any moment.

Slotting his thumbs into his waistcoat pockets, Herb rocked onto his toes and back onto his heels. "Flames are all out. We got the methane pipes hooked up to the gas lamps quickly re-rooted. Thankfully our propellant gas isn't flammable, plus the old gal's skin don't burn up easily. She's hurt though. Time we travelled the caverns before we didn't have no HawkEye to see through the blackness. Then we were reliant on the blaze offa Cyber Circus. Today though, this glow" – he held his arms out from his sides to indicate the twilight – "is as much as she can manage."

He rocked back onto his heels again. "Pig Heart's doing a fine job of putting my boys to work down there. We got skin grafts off the polyps out back by the boiler. We should be able to heat up the hull again before long. Just so long as we can find a water source and let my old gal drink her fill."

"Easier said than done." Hellequin took a sharp breath as he manoeuvred the ship over the tallest spikes in the cavern floor with what he guessed were centimetres to spare. Herb and Nim were oblivious of course, being blessed with natural sight.

"What about the Black Lake?" Nim bit a corner of her mouth.

Hellequin had spent enough time around a campfire to have heard just about every folk tale bandied around. As far as the tale went, it was claimed that the Black Lake was a piece of ocean trapped inside the Fathenora mountains. Still as black ink, the lake was home to the heart of the swarm. Nest place of the Black Locust queen.

"I'd always thought that was just a dust trail myth," he muttered.

Herb piped up, "No sign of the place last time we negotiated the caverns. Don't mean it don't exist though." He sucked in his cheeks. "Don't mean we want to go looking for the place either."

"Except, maybe we don't have a choice." Hellequin indicated a large glass gauge in the rack to his right. The waterline was very low. "I'm going to get us across these spikes then find a place to put down."

"What spikes?" said Nim anxiously.

"Exactly." Hellequin reeled himself back in so as not to disclose any more information about the truth of their situation.

Herb scratched his bald head with fat little fingers. "I'm not saying I'm against it. So long as we keep the flaps laced tight any crawlers out there should find it hard to get inside. But my problem's this. It'd take our last slurp of water to get airborne again. And what then, when we run outta steam in the belly of this place?"

"I'm suggesting we send out scouts to look for water before it gets to that." Hellequin eased the dirigible over the last of the jagged spikes and into a second smaller cavern. Something about the way the rock formed here gave it an obsidian sheen. Reflected in its element, Cyber Circus's luminescence magnified. Now Nim and Herb saw out into the cavern, a goblin hall of crystals and glossy rock folds.

Nim slid back down into the viewing pit and pressed her hands to the glass. Herb huffed and puffed like an old tin kettle.

"Scouts? Out there? Where you gonna find folk willing?"

Hellequin noticed a flat outcrop of rock. He snapped a lock bar to the wheel to hold them steady and worked a series of pulley straps located above his head. They set down in a soft puff of dust.

The soldier wiggled his wrists, cracked a couple of finger bones. "We got to look to those most suited to the task. Those who can protect themselves from the swarm, who can look through cracks in places normal folk can't reach. I'm thinking we send the Scuttlers."

Nim broke away from the glass and stared at both men, appalled. "You want to send children out to do our dirty work?"

Herb narrowed his eyes. "It's not a bad idea." When Nim attempted to interrupt, he held up his hands in appeal. "Whaddya wanna go against the say so of a trained soldier for, Nim? HawkEye to boot. This guy has got more strategy going on behind that clockwork eye of his than I could hope for in a lifetime! And it ain't like the Scuttlers are your average rug rats.

Hides like rhinohorns. Great sharp pincers. And a way of manipulating themselves into any nook and cranny. The HawkEye's right. We gotta send them out."

Nim gave her attention back to the weird world beyond the glass. "And hope that they come back again," she whispered.

"Where are those scab balls?" Herb strutted across the bare rock surface in the centre of the tent, kicking up dust as he went. "Any of you slackers seen the Scuttlers?" he hollered out to the pitch crew who had crawled down off the bones of the circus to explore the peculiar ground underfoot.

"Little fuckers got a habit of tucking themselves away," Herb muttered. "You!" He pointed a stubby finger at a young boy who was employed in smoothing oil over a freshly patched area of the tent wall. "Go peek behind the calliope. They hide away there sometimes."

The kid ran off to the gilt staircase spiralling up to the calliope.

"Craggy little blighters," Herb muttered.

"Another hour should see the canvas patched," Pig Heart shouted down from one of the gangways overhead.

"Dirty warthog. Scragglewort children." Herb kept up his huffing until a cry of "No sign here, boss!" came from the balcony of the calliope. The boy shimmied down the brass banister of the staircase and landed roughly. He smirked as he slumped back off to his oiling task.

"No Scuttlers means no scouts." Herb put his hands behind his head and circled on the spot, a spinning top in the form of a fat little man. As he did so, he glimpsed something out of step with the circus – a grotesque figure to the fore of the platform dedicated to his own living quarters. The vision brought bile to his throat, it was so unexpected. But the ringmaster in him shouted, "Hi there! What's that devil?" He pointed, directing the pitch crew's attention just as the figure scrabbled down the wires of the lift rig and disappeared onto the scaffold behind the dressing rooms.

"Get me that motherfucker!" screeched Herb, spinning on the spot again.

No longer required at the ship's wheel, Hellequin was stepping out onto the gangway above the calliope when he saw the stranger. The ghoulish appearance of the figure aroused instinctual revulsion in the soldier. The feeling was fleeting; his Daxware kicked in and rationalised the enemy. A Zen monk aboard Cyber Circus? The notion was nonsensical, but Hellequin didn't question the fact, or delay his pursuit. With fluid strides, he ran to the far end of the gangway and leapt off, using his long arms to propel his flight. He landed in a crouch at the edge of the canteen platform; the gridded floor rattled at the impact. Pushing off, he charged across the empty room, passing the spot where the monk had stood seconds earlier.

Scaffolding branched off either side. Hellequin levered up onto the bars to the left of the canteen where they disappeared behind the dressing rooms. The last time he'd navigated the narrow bars was to observe Nim's assault by D'Angelus's men and quite literally leap to her defence. Now he pursued a different, unquantifiable threat in the form of the figure threading between the crisscrossed bars. Hellequin did not have the acrobatic skills of Lulu or Nim, but he was highly adept at using his own assets. His legs were fatless but muscular; he cramped them to step under the scaffold braces then lengthened out. His HawkEye clicked in sharp rotation, focusing on the monk at the same time that it allowed him to see where to scramble next.

He drew up suddenly. The monk had stopped in between two upright bars, a wilted thing in a gilded cage. Hellequin magnified the finer details of the figure. The sackcloth mask with its slashed mouth, running stitch nose and eyeholes. Small hands that protruded from the long sleeves of the cassock... a young man's? No, a woman's, Hellequin rationalised, and felt no less committed in his pursuit of her.

She leapt then, clearing the scaffold and dropping down to the kited silk of the dressing rooms below. Unlike when Hellequin had tried the same trick, the fabric held under the woman's lesser weight. She slid down; Hellequin used the grid across his steel eye to plot her trajectory. Calculating the drop off point, he shinned down the nearest vertical pole, hit the floor backstage, ran forward and plucked the woman out of the air as she skidded off the roof.

His arm locked in around her waist. His bowie knife sat tight to her throat. She gulped in air. Hellequin felt the quick pace of her heart where his upper arm grazed her ribs.

"Queer how that Zen monk up and abandoned us in the middle of the doggone dessert!" D'Angelus sucked his cheeks against his teeth and looked even more sharp-boned. The burrower rattled in its ribs and gave off occasional spurts of thick smoke. It unnerved D'Angelus. He tugged at his neck tie, loosening it in an effort to ward off the sweat. His palms were clammy and he couldn't help wishing the monk was back in the cab with them, a charm as crucial to the miners as a song bird in a cage.

"Whaddya you say, Jaxx? You think its queer how that monk went about it?"

The Sirinese nodded. He didn't speak though. D'Angelus wondered if the man was not a fan of journeying below ground either and said, "Not natural for men to be poking about in the dark like this." But Jaxx gave no indication that he believed it unnatural, but just stayed inert, eyes fixed on the plethora of grit, streaming water and rock fragments assaulting the windscreen.

"Nope, nothin' right about a man being this far underground." D'Angelus' gaze darted about the cab. The confined space reverberated while the apparatus in the dash became increasingly complex to his eyes. A single kerosene lantern lent his surroundings a spectral green glow.

"We're almost through to the caverns." The mechanic glanced back at D'Angelus, eyes magnified by his goggles as if he belonged out amongst the swarm rather than riding in the cab. "I'm bringing us in at an angle. If we wanna avoid the locusts, we've got to use common sense. They're gonna want heat, which means bedding down in one of the deeper caverns. They're gonna want water. Steam off one of the underground hot springs. Throwback to that whole air plant genesis. My thinking is we tunnel in clear of any water source. Thing is…" Das lent forward and rapped one of the large brass dials in the dash. "I got a way of avoiding the wet stuff thanks to this here Diviner gauge."

"Hold up, fella!" D'Angelus took off his hat and laid it on his lap. Without the hat, he looked older. "What's the one thing we can guarantee the circus will have to seek out? What makes that flying freak pit stay up in the sky?" D'Angelus smiled, tic teeth dazzling in the gloom of the cab. "Hot air! And they generate it with steam-driven apparatus. Without water, Cyber Circus is just a big old tent stuck underground."

"If we seek out water, we're going to have to deal with the swarm too." Jaxx's butting plate reflected the sickly glow off the kerosene lantern.

D'Angelus gestured sharply over one shoulder with a thumb. "You're forgetting we got a whole load of muscle back there in Wanda-Sue's backend?" He kept up his dead man's smile. "Plus, there's nothing like upping the stakes when it comes to trophy hunting now, is there?"

SEVENTEEN

The children crept along the narrow passageway on their soft bellies. Tunnelled out by the water flow millennia before, the passage curved and spiralled; only the Scuttlers with their flexible shells and tiny bodies could have attempted to negotiate it. The dark was punctured by beams off the headlamps each child wore, tied in place by the lady monk who'd produced special ribbons for the purpose.

"Lazurite blue," she'd said to Rind, adding, "For the queenly one." Ol got "Red as jewel fruit. For the spicy one." And for Tib. "The warrior. Green, like the eyes of a rattler." She'd shown them how to wind the clockwork generators inside each lamp. Then she'd shown them the way. Up into the gods of the tent, to one of the two points where the circus roof steepled. She'd lifted each in turn and they'd scrabbled out the canvas trapdoor there.

"Look for my love in the crags and the black spots," she'd told them. "Do this for me and I promise you each a free pass to Heaven."

So they'd crawled through the passage in the rock like worms through dirt, front pincers elbowing forward. The roof of the tunnel was centimetres above their heads. Every so often an insect would be caught in the glow off the headlamps, beautiful weird things in metallic shades.

"Hello, mister beetle. Where you scurrying?" Ol poked the bug, a many legged oddity with huge opalescent eyes. The weight of her pincer crushed it.

Rind was out in front, her little old woman face shrewd as she led her siblings through the chasm. "Shadows can be big. Shadows can be small. Me's thinking the lady's love might have tucked further in, where it's chapel quiet." She stopped and nosed backwards, "What do he and she reckon?"

"I's reckon the lady's a nutcase. Brain gone mushed," shot Tib from the backend of their procession.

"I's think she's an angel," said Ol, her voice sweet with hope. Underneath her, the bones of tiny dead things crumbled.

"I's think she's dangerous. A creeping thing that knows too many secrets and keeps magic in her itty bitty fingers." Rind poured herself out of the tunnel. Like any other insect, she ran up the wall where the passageway came out, followed by her sister and brother. They climbed the fleshy folds of the rock face, limbs clattering beneath their beetle backs. In and out and over the craggy surface they climbed, spread out to investigate at greater speed. Potato noses poked in at crevices. Claws scooped in at cracks. Dust billowed out into the black world at their backs.

"Nuthin?" Tib called.

"Nuthin," agreed Rind and Ol in unison.

They entered another fissure and scurried out onto the walls of a new cavern. Their small weak eyes blinked. Bioluminescence coated the distant roof-space and dripped down the walls in great thick loops. Shadows roamed the walls or clustered in at the honeycombed rock. Mandibles dripped. Wing cases chaffed.

"Nasty creepy things," whispered Tib. He pop-popped his mouth in delight.

They'd seen the one giant locust back at the circus. Landing on Herb's private platform, it had spied the monk woman and taken to the air again. Now, the Scuttlers were hemmed in by hundreds of the creatures.

"Don't like it," muttered Ol.

The children backed towards one another. One of the

colossal insects moved in close, its movement impeded by the keratin wing cases and hugely powerful yet overlarge back limbs. Head feathers waved at its neck frill. Cold black eyes switched focus from Rust to Ol to Tib. With the tip of its antennae, the creature felt about Ol, the child closest. The head feathers shivered and the locust returned its attention to processing some stinking matter inside its jaws.

Slowly the children unbuttoned from one another and began to move amongst the swarm. Head feathers brushed against their hoary hides; the stings did not penetrate. Integrating with the herd, the Scuttlers grew in confidence. They took to investigating the pocked rock, where hoppers raised their plated skulls and lazily looked away.

The atmosphere grew increasingly humid as they journeyed down the walls. Below were two great banks of rock and accumulated dust. Between the banks was a wide stretch of water. The surface was phenomenally smooth and shining like black ink. Steam rose up from rock pools in the banks either side. Condensation left a greasy layer over the walls.

This was a proper crawling brew, a witch cave, said Rind.

Ol was more accepting. "Nimble sucky mouths. No different to coyotes at the teat. Lovely damp air too." She leapt down onto the nearest bank and tipped back to seesaw in her shell, buffering it in the layered dust. Locusts whirled overhead.

"Oh, oh!" cried Tib, the beam from his headlamp dancing over the flying insects like a spotlight. "They're pretty when they fly."

Rind, though, hadn't quite given over her heart to the monsters. Instead she stared at a shimmering slice of rock at one end of the lake. Inside the rock moved a shadow. Tall, man-like, with a long spread of limbs.

"Listen!" she snapped.

All three hushed and listened beyond the click-clack of jaws and whir of looping flight.

"Ca-ca," said the voice, low and resonant. "Ca-ca... Carrie-

Anne."

The crew of Cyber Circus stood on the dusty rock surface in the centre of the tent. At the heart of them stood the HawkEye and the Zen monk.

"Move it, move it!" Herb bustled through the onlookers, egg belly leading the way. He stopped abruptly in front of the intruder. Resting his hands on his hips, he rocked back onto his heels and pulled a face.

"Well, ain't that just the butt-ugliest outfit you ever saw, folk? Mask like that? Sheesh, its gotta turn the milk sour in a clothhod's udders. And that belt? What ya got dangling there, fella? All that dead stuff hanging about your person? Ask me, it's unsaintly."

The carnie folk stayed hushed. Only Herb had the nerve to bad mouth the extremist ways of the Zen brotherhood.

Herb peered at the mask, getting in close as if the more he examined the nature of the thing, the greater the chance he'd find it less despicable. "Way I understand it, you Zen monks make yourselves as hideous and death-riddled as possible so if a Saint just happens to be in the neighbourhood, they'll judge you a worthless abomination. Now *that*, my fellow carnies, is self-flagellation!"

He shook his head and rocked back onto his heels. "Not one iota of it makes sense to a Saints fearing man like myself. But enough about the perverse ways of your order." His eyes grew tight. "What the hell are you doing here inside my circus?"

The monk didn't reply.

"Silent order." Herb nodded. "Ain't that friggin' convenient." He held out his hands to include all. "Whaddaya say, folks? Do we keelhaul him some until he learns to use his tongue, same way we chastised our chief pitch man."

Herb gestured to Pig Heart, who stiffened at the reminder. "And he's a fella I've trusted the care of my circus to for many a year." He got in close to the mask again. "Want to start flapping those gums now, sonny?"

"He's no sonny, Herb," Hellequin said quietly. "You'll trust me when I say I've got a way of seeing things differently and there's a woman inside that garb."

The Zen monk turned to the HawkEye in apparent surprise. Rather than suffer the indignity of being forced to do so, the monk removed the hideous headdress.

"You were looking for the Scuttlers? They are on an errand for me and will no doubt discover any other secrets the caverns have to offer in the process." The woman spoke softly. Her mouth was just a little too wide, but there was sensuality in the face. And sadness to the eyes.

Nim stepped forward. "Where did you send those children?"

"And what makes you think they will come back?" Lulu rubbed a hand about his collar bones, mouth budded. "They ain't the brightest."

"Because we made a pact." The woman knelt. She scooped up fistfuls of dust. Her head cocked as she let the dust sift from her fingers. The motes fell strangely, curling in and around her body, spiralling down.

Herb shuffled back. "Where'd you come from, lady?"

"The big old house where the corn grows plump and sweet and Indian Blanket spreads either side the porch." Her eyes got wild. Tears ebbed. "The dust wrapped me in its soft grey material, and this strange underworld opened up to me." She pointed at the floor. Her eyes flitted all around the metal-and-fibre circus tent.

Herb arched one eyebrow at the woman, clearly unsure of her sanity. "What do you want with Cyber Circus?"

"I can't fit into the caverns' tight spots. If I can just find the shadow of my beloved, I can use it as a template. I can mould him back out of the land." The woman held up her greyed palms. "The dust told me so."

"The dust told you, did it? Well, ain't that hunky-dory."

Herb's mouth had a sour slant. "And you just thought you'd creep in here and fill the Scuttlers' tiny minds with your madness? Saints almighty, Hellequin!" Herb threw up his hands. "We've gone and bagged us a lunatic. Meanwhile, the only freaks in this company who stood a chance of scouting ahead for us are long gone." He knitted his fingers and hooked them behind his head, cheeks puffing. "So what now, soldier? What the hell do we do next?"

Hellequin stared up at the gloomy upper reaches of the tent. "We ask the Scuttlers what they've found."

It was a few seconds before everyone else saw the three beetle-backed children come clattering down the inner walls of the tent.

Just at that moment, Cyber Circus gave a tremendous shudder. The weak luminescence inside the ship went out.

Voices. A great tumbling of panicked voices coming from all directions at once. From somewhere off inside the living quarters, the cries of the young sounded, like screeching baby birds.

"Nim." Hellequin spoke by her ear. "I can see still. Now listen to me. I need you to come with me now."

It hurt Nim's ears and heart, this cacophony of fear. Hadn't the circus suffered enough, she wondered bleakly while feeling Hellequin's hand slip into hers. He led her away from the chaos. They moved over the alien surface of the rock, boots swishing through dust. Nim allowed herself to be led blindly on.

She heard the approach of the Scuttlers.

"Children. Did you find water on your travels?" she heard Hellequin ask and three high, reverberant voices answer in turn.

"Oh yesee."

"So black, so stink hot."

"Where the lady's ghostman sits, walled up behind rock."

"Did you find a route that would let this ship get close to the water?" Hellequin cut in.

"We found holes in walls."

"Nooks and cranies."

"Spots no bigger than a roo rat. One passageway's large enough to fit this giant through."

"I need you to guide us there," Hellequin told the children.

"Hick pick, would if we could, but circus ain't lit up anymore," answered one youngster.

"Nim is about to change that." Hellequin made as if to stride off, dragging Nim in his wake.

"What now, HawkEye? You gonna act like you own me just because you got to go there with me for free?" Nim yanked her hand free and seethed in the darkness.

Hellequin leant in. Flesh and metal brushed against her cheek. "Trust me, Nim. I wanna see you safe. I wanna see you free. But first I gotta see you."

His voice was needful and perplexingly genuine. Nim could think of no reason to not allow herself to be led.

After a time, Hellequin stopped and led her hand to a strip of warm metal. "You go up the stairs first."

Nim felt for the first rise of the steps. She climbed, sensing the stairs spiral around and up, and finally level out onto a narrow platform.

Hellequin stepped up behind her and secured her hand on the rail, his lean frame moulding against hers.

"Nim," he whispered. "I need you to shine now. Shine with all that rage you got tucked up inside at the men who've hurt and torn and choked the fight from you. I need you to hear me when I say I'm a broken man, literally broken because the day the authorities put this biomorph implant in me, they nerve-blocked my emotions. But you light me up, Nim, and I can't begin to explain how. All I do know is if you shine now with every bit of rage inside you, I will bring you back from that darkness."

Nim heard the words. They cut her deeply. She'd no desire whatsoever to open up her mind and body to the savageness exacted on her over the years. But one thing she did know incontestably – she was the only light source on board Cyber

Circus.

"Fine," she said, a throb in her voice. "Now back off or I'll burn out your eyes. Both of them."

"On past the booger rock." Ol indicated a huge stalactite to one side of the passage and beat her tremendous front claws in rapture. A smile broke over her shrunken face.

"He and me and she cut marks in the grot they smeared there," piped up Rind with enthusiasm.

The man with the stitched metal eye was less elated. "They?" he asked in that bleak tone the Scuttlers recognised from the times Herb or some harder hand had beat them when they got clumsy in their act.

"Crawlers," ventured Tib.

"And they let you live?" The soldier wrestled with the wheel while the ship shook and listed on its last dregs of steam.

"We likes their tickly feather heads," giggled Ol. The three shared in the fact, laughing like snorting piglets.

The soldier gripped the wheel and got a lock on it. "So the locusts can't sting you. Nor do they see you as other than themselves. As food." He steered around the stalactite while the children beat their claws in merriment and tumbled in and out of the viewing pit.

"How much further?"

"A skip and a bit," said Rind.

"Let's hope so." The soldier's eye whirred. "I'd say we got a few drops of water in the boiler then we're grounded for good."

Rind rubbed one of her large red claws over the warm brass surround of the viewing pane. "Poor circus."

Ol copied her, cooing, "Poor, poor circus."

"Would you like to help the circus?" said the soldier. His metal eye switched and shifted.

The ship drifted into the cavern on silent wings. Glowing softly, it passed over the black slick of the lake. Pitch men waited up on the gangways near the roof, their young locked in the chambered living quarters. Seeing by the neon light feeding off Nim on the calliope balcony, the crew clutched their limited firearms and barely dared breathe. Below, hundreds of black locusts crawled.

Without the smell of dead kin to attract them, Cyber Circus was just another creature in that vast hive. Men were the fodder and, so far, they were staying in the shadows. Moulding with the ship.

The closer they drifted to the shoreline, the sparser the number of insects. Cyber Circus set down with a soft displacing of dust.

Inside his private pod, Herb put a hand on the door handle and told his unexpected house guest, "My boys know their knots, lady, so don't go rubbing your wrists raw trying to get those loose."

He stared back into the opulent gloom. The woman was seated in the chair at his desk, wrists trussed.

"I'm sorry to treat you so, but ain't a thing known about a hair on your head. Except that you sent those kids out there on some mischief, and I ain't entirely sure you're sane." The ringmaster tapped his large forehead. He closed the door behind him and, this time, he locked it.

Descending the lift rig, Herb marched through the backstage area and out into the ring. The HawkEye and the Scuttlers joined him. Behind the calliope balcony, Nim remained aglow.

"Okay, so let's see if you kids understand the way of it?" Herb pointed to the huge boiler, located beneath the calliope. Thick ropes of ornate brass looped around and back on themselves, decorating the boiler's base. "Whaddya do with that lot?"

"Drag it, drag it," the boy offered.

"Where'd you drag it to?"

One of the girls said, "To the black water where we slip it in."

"Good," said Herb, and the girl looked pleased. She danced her great limbs, clattering dreadfully.

"Sssh! You gotta keep it down." Herb brushed a hand over his forehead which was shiny with sweat. "Whaddya do next?"

"Come back here and say 'start it pumping!'" said the second girl.

"Start it pumping!" parroted her siblings.

"Good kids. And then you reel them hoses in again once the boiler's full and we can scat." Herb glanced at Hellequin. "They'll have to go out the main flap. Hose won't reach otherwise."

The HawkEye nodded. "I'll let them out. Keep an eye on them too."

Herb bustled off to the brass staircase and climbed up and out onto the balcony alongside Nim. He squinted against the blaze of her, laid a hand on one of the girl's which gripped the rail tightly, and felt her jump.

"Time to turn your light off now, gal," he told her softly. "We're about to open the floodgates."

EIGHTEEN

The circus was silent but for slight eddies of air through the pipes of the calliope. Drawing the heavy material of the tent flap aside a crack, Hellequin waved the Scuttlers out. The children rattled away into the weird twilight, pulling the hose like the body of a giant worm.

Hellequin kept the flap open a small degree and peered out. His steel eye piece ticked in small revolutions, the red lens burning out. The cavern teemed with locusts; they crawled over one another, forming ant hills of squirming brittle bodies. Others crisscrossed the roof of the cavern, wings reverberating with a low, woody whisper, or clung to the walls, mandibles dripping luminescent bile.

He tried to dismiss the swarm as no more significant than a savannah full of clothhods and concentrated instead on the lake and the Scuttlers, just another breed of insect drawn to the water's edge. Hellequin half expected enormous arms to solidify out of the black fluid, grasp each child and pull them under. Certainly the lake struck him as an entity that attracted worship and demanded sacrifice.

"Hush little children," he said under his breath. The hose unravelled off the framework of hooks beneath the calliope, dragging out of the tent with a small 'slush' of sound. Hellequin mapped the quadrants of the cavern in his mind, the whirring insects overhead and those milking bile on the honeycombed walls. Nothing reacted. The children were mites to be tolerated.

What couldn't be relied on was the randomness of the insects' movements. One of those in flight came in to land nearby, clamping down on top of the hose and forcing the Scuttlers to come to an abrupt stop a couple of metres short of the lake. The children rolled in their shells, instinctually defensive.

Hellequin collated the movements of the swarm, his circuitry working to make sense of the options. They had to get the hose to the water as soon as possible. Sooner or later, the flesh-eating locusts would nose their way into the crevices of the circus tent and, with just one kill, bring their brethren swarming.

The soldier drew his bowie knife. It would be nonsensical to openly kill the beast since spilling its inner fluid would attract the interests of the swarm. But it went against his programming to leave the circus in danger. Rifle hanging off his shoulder, a fistful of ammunition in a top pocket of his combats, he slowed his breathing and slipped out of the tent. His steps were hushed by the dust underfoot. The further he got from the circus tent, the more he was engulfed by the illumined gloom. Locusts hauled their bodies over the rocks in all directions. The humid air was punctuated by weird sounds: creaking long limbs, p'ffing exoskeletons that lifted and sucked around soft meat, and the cack-cack of mauling jaws. Hellequin walked softly, but the children spotted him and called out him.

"Hi! Hi!"

Hellequin cursed their stupidity. He put a finger to his lips and motioned to the three to take hold of the hose again, which they did. Now it was his turn to act.

The colossal locust nestled on top of the hose, churning its mandibles like a clothhod chewing the cud. Hellequin crept closer. The Scuttlers waited.

Kneeling slowly, the solider fed his hands around the ribbed brass hose. It was lukewarm and surprisingly soft to the touch. He attempted to lift it, encouraging the bug to take flight of its own accord. The creature stayed rooted, rubbing its hind legs off one another and producing a long, sonorous note.

Dulled panic set in beneath Hellequin's ribs; he was programmed to use the emotional stimulus as a fresh shot of adrenaline. Muscles tightened and pulsed. His only option was to kill the creature swiftly, silently, and without spilling its inner fluids.

He ran at the thing with swift strides, pulling up last second to stare into its roaming eyes. *See me now?* The locust answered with a toss of its head, spraying acidic matter. Its voice was a soft cack-cack. For an instant, Hellequin feared the insect might zone in on his hardware and dismiss him as fleshless. But then the great back limbs powered down and the locust sprung forward, displacing dust.

Hellequin had seen the response a precious millisecond in advance. His eyepiece gridded and calculated the trajectory of the creature's spring. He leapt up, rolling and going into a crouch an instant before one of the locust's vast wings swept above his head, unsettling his hair. Hellequin grabbed for the wing, propelling himself up and onto it. The sinew and fibre mass rippled as the creature tried to shake him off. Hellequin kept low, desperate to stay incognito to the rest of the hive. When he was assured of his balance, he ran along the wing and leapt onto the beast's back. The lethal head feathers washed dangerously close; he registered their stretch and concluded that he was safe.

Snatching a glance backwards, he saw that the hose had been freed and the Scuttlers were dragging it the last few metres to the lake. Positioning his bowie knife at the base of the locust's neck collar, Hellequin drove it in. He gave the blade a sharp twist. While unsure of the exact biology of the species, he'd enough desert experience to know he could kill a hand-sized spindleweb with that same method.

The locust collapsed under him, exciting a small dust storm. Hellequin glanced up and around him. *Had the swarm been alerted to his presence by the tussle?*

Nothing altered in the atmosphere. The trills and reedy notes of the insects still coloured the air. Their shadows continued to crisscross overhead.

The bowie knife was abandoned in the meat of the carcass; Hellequin knew he couldn't pull it free since the slightest trace of death in the air would attract the creatures. Instead he jumped down, readjusted the rock rifle strap on his shoulder and stared out to the lake's edge. Having fed the hose into the water, one of the three siblings was in the process of toddling back to the tent. Hellequin followed after.

When it came, the shot rebounded off the cavern walls with the sound of a tremendous whip crack. Rock ammo pierced Hellequin's shoulder blade near his newly stitched stab wound. Feeling pain flash-fire inside him, Hellequin wheeled around. His HawkEye took in many different angles to form a cohesive panorama – the two Scuttlers by the shore of the lake, balling up inside their hard shells and rolling back towards the circus, the new twitchy awareness of the locusts, the barrel of a rock pistol in D'Angelus's hand as he stood in the open cockpit of the burrower, and men pouring out the backend of that surfaced conveyance like a second swarm.

Hellequin refocused on D'Angelus's aim. The pistol was trained on his heart.

Seconds stretched. The burrower coasted forward, D'Angelus riding high in the cockpit like the eye of the machine while his men jogged either side, rock rifles primed. Hellequin breathed long and slow. He couldn't move since risking his life might mean abandoning Nim to the pimp.

As the disturbed nest came to life, the burrower seesawed over uneven ground. Hellequin took his chance and began to charge back towards the circus. Ammo fire bit at his heels. *These are my final moments*, he told himself. His one consolation was the fattened hose that led inside the tent and the knowledge that Cyber Circus was slating her thirst.

He was nearly at the tent flap when a colossal shadow passed overhead. The lens of his eyepiece brightened, taking in a black mass of locusts. One creature landed a few short metres in front, blocking the tent entrance. Hellequin threw himself down into the dust as D'Angelus's men discharged their rock rifles. Shot pierced the insect's hoary shell. With no understanding of its true attacker, the locust thrust its tremendous head at Hellequin. The mandibles yawned, spit-gummed and pop-popping.

The soldier zoomed in on the goo and knew that in spite of his advanced sight, he couldn't shuffle back in time. Drops splattered his chest, burning through fabric and flesh below. Hellequin showed his gums and cried out. He struggled to reach his rifle. At his back, he heard the burrower sledging in. His steel eye focused on the face of the locust, moving closer.

He freed his rifle and pointed it up at the last second. Before he could pull the trigger, the locust's jaw exploded seemingly from within. He shuffled back on his hands, clearing the locust's mammoth body just before it flopped into the dust. Riding the spine of the thing was Nim, rock pistol drawn, balance impeccable. She leapt down nimbly. The courtesan's red eyes were livid with emotion.

"Herb says we have to keep D'Angelus and the shitters with him outside the tent. We can't close the flap until the boiler's full. Anyway, that burrower could just tunnel in under us."

"So what are we meant to do?" panted Hellequin, joining Nim as she crouched behind one of the splayed wings belonging to the dead locust. Rock shot whistled past their ears.

"We've got to kill them." Nim thrust a hand into her hair and bit her lower lip. "There's also the hive to worry about now."

Indeed there was. Hellequin scanned the air and here they came, hundreds of the creatures, tumbling in and over one another like the plague they were.

"By the Saints," whispered Nim, glowing faintly in the twilight as if in a bid to make sense of the whirring above.

"Shit me!" Pig Heart appeared alongside, rock pistol tearing hunks off the next locust to zone in. Lulu brought up the rear, touting an unusual yet effective weapon. During one of his acts, he made use of two exceptionally long whips. He wielded them now with skill and a boldness Hellequin had not recognised in the ladyboy before that time. Whether the drive came from a desire to protect Nim, or rage at the kinds of men who would take what they wanted, no matter the damage, Hellequin had no idea. But Lulu slashed out at the bugs, taking out eyes and head feathers and wing scales and slices of neck frill.

All the while, D'Angelus was riding closer in the burrower, his men taking out their share of the locusts with the sweet burnt scent of fired rock shot.

Hellequin heard a new wave of artillery. He stared back over a shoulder. A great number of the pitch crew were assembled at the mouth of the circus tent, rifles and pistols raised and firing off into the half-light.

"Guess you were right all along HawkEye," Pig Heart snorted, sending a blaze of shot into the chattering skies, reloading in a clink-clunk and rip of action, and taking out one of D'Angelus's men.

"About what?" Hellequin peeled off a shot from his own rifle and dripped back down below the dead locust's tattered wing.

"Guess we carnie folk do support our own when the squeeze is put on us." Pig Heart inclined his head towards the pitch crew. He stared Hellequin hard in the face. "Any idea how we're gonna wrangle our way out of here alive?"

Before Hellequin could answer, Pig Heart stood up and aimed for another of the pimp's men. Hellequin tracked the bullet; before it had time to home in on its target, the pimp's man was twisted chest from limb by the mangling jaws of a locust. The instant the man fell, he was left behind by the burrower. In the wake of the machine, the creatures clustered in, shredding the flesh of the man most likely while the breath was still working in his lungs.

"We gotta beat off the locusts, we gotta punch D'Angelus's brains from his skull, and we gotta fire up Herb's gasbag and get us the hell out of here." Hellequin exhaled sharply. "Simple as that."

Except it wasn't simple, he thought. It was the most outnumbered fight he had been embroiled in. Locusts streamed towards them from all directions and would keep up their assault long after D'Angelus and his men had succumbed.

"Alright then," said Pig Heart, sounding as unconvinced as Hellequin that they'd the slightest hope of survival. "How long 'til the boiler's full?" he shouted back at the wall of pitch crew.

One man disappeared inside the tent. He returned a few seconds later and yawped, "Got a way to go yet!"

Pig Heart cursed. The fire off the pitch crews' guns was taking out the first wave of locusts. But in the chaos of battle, D'Angelus and his men were forgotten. The burrower dipped and arched over a difficult terrain of calcified boulders. Meanwhile, its hired thugs tucked in amongst the stones and launched an attack on both the swarm and the pitch crew.

Hellequin was glad of the cover provided by the dead locust as he saw five of the pitch crew taken out or badly wounded inside a minute.

What to do, he demanded of his natural mind and its cyber circuitry. He was the only one with the eyesight capable of taking out D'Angelus's snipers.

"Concentrate on the swarm!" he cried, yanking his bowie knife free of the dead insect's neck collar.

"Deserting me?" said Nim quietly.

Even through the storm of rock shot and rustling wings, he heard her.

"I'm doing what I'm programmed to do," he shot back.

A moment later, he was running towards the nest of boulders. Rock sliced by within centimetres. His eyepiece whirred, the concentric rings zoning in, and in again, mapping the locale of each of the pimp's men amongst the burgeoning stones. His Daxware tracked the trajectory of fire from each man's weapon. Hellequin weaved through the flesh-slicing shot, pausing now and then to defend himself against the jaws or weighty limbs of a locust.

Fortunately the swarm appeared confused by him for the most part. Insects zoomed in half a metre from his head, but most seemed to see him as a box of wires and unpalatable metal.

He didn't stop to argue. Sliding in alongside the first of D'Angelus's heavies, he put his blade to the soft throat and ripped. The man's gargle was lost to the engine noise of the idling burrower. A second man occupied a pockmark in the stone. Hellequin slid the bowie knife into his ribcage. Guzzling for air, the man collapsed. Hellequin dragged him clear of the machine. Moments later, there was a great chattering of wings as the locusts descended to strip the carcass.

Hellequin went to work on a third man wedged between two slabs of rock like a meat filling. But the blood spill had attracted the locusts in number now. Hellequin fired his gun up at the brittle black mass – just as a fourth man launched a shot at him. The HawkEye dodged the fire which broke open the skull of a locust at his back. Before the man could take another shot, Hellequin speared him up under the chin with his blade. Dragging the knife free, he prompted his eyepiece to assemble a number of views across his retina – insects coming in to land among the boulders, the burrower reigniting its engines and ploughing head on at the circus tent, the pimp riding in the open cockpit alongside a driver and the Sirinese fighter, Nim shooting a locust an instant before its jaws struck and being showered with the poisonous head feathers...

Hellequin was already on his feet and speeding towards her. At his back, the remainder of D'Angelus's ground crew fell victim to the honey trap he had set – the bodies of their fallen colleagues arousing the gore sensors of the hundreds of locusts. The men's screams echoed through the cavern, sharp and terrible and phenomenally lonely. Hellequin shut out the noise and raced back towards the tent.

The majority of the pitch crew had retreated inside. He saw Nim collapse, the burrower sledging towards her while Pig Heart and Lulu drove back the scoreless locusts that hovered and dived overhead. Battling against the agony from his freshly wounded shoulder, Hellequin brought up his rock rifle as he ran and tried to keep the flesh feeders at bay.

Two figures leapt free of the burrower as it struck an extra large boulder a few metres short of Nim. The huge machine idled; the HawkEye lens pierced the dense glass of the windshield, which had been slid back into place. He saw a man's head, not D'Anglus and not the Sirinese. The driver, he concluded. No doubt the fellow had been instructed to hold steady while the pimp retrieved his precious runaway – who happened to be lying prone in front of the circus tent. Hellequin saw the pimp kneel down, slip a hand around Nim's neck and bring her lips to his.

The HawkEye cried out in unfamiliar rage. His voice was lost to a harsher, wilder sound.

"Caa-ri!" said the voice. Rough-edged. Locust-like. "Caaree-caa-ahn!"

Hellequin whirled round, his magnifying lens drilling into the honeycombed cells among the walls, off to the inky lake, up to the canopy of great black clattering insects. He came full circle and stopped short of D'Angelus, that sour devil of a man. The pimp had reeled around on the spot, his eyes frantic, rock pistol shaking in his grip.

"What the fuck?" D'Angelus wrestled Nim up in his arms and started to drag her back towards the burrower, all the while staring out at the shadows all around him. Pig Heart and Lulu were too distracted to come to Nim's aid. The Sirinese had launched an attack against them, oddly controlled in his disposition, as if the strange new voice was just another piece in the mystery that led to Desirous Nim.

Hellequin was raising his rock rifle when the voice got louder, then louder again, beating up the dust so that the atmosphere clouded.

The woman stepped out from the heavy canvas flap. She knelt down and felt for the hose. The fat worm pulsed beneath her fingertips.

"Almost done drinking?" she said softly and patted the hose affectionately. Standing, she stared out at the luminescent cavern. She'd heard the call from inside Herb's cabin and shrugged off the ropes which bound her wrists. The carnie folk could bind her to that world no more successfully than a Zen monk mask could make her truly holy. She'd made her way through the blacked-out tent, steps soft as the whispering air through the caverns. No one saw her. She was ghost-like, a shadow out of step with all that surrounded her.

"Go to the lake," the Scuttlers had said. The shadow you asked for dwells there behind a great rock slab. The voice too – she had recognised her lover's cadence. His low sweet rumble as he spoke her name.

Dust reacted to her every step. A locust drove at her through the gloom, its jaw blooded. The woman raised her hand. Dust sprang up before her like a wall of hot grey glass. The insect was shredded inside its element.

She moved oddly, in tight little rushes of steps. Not quite in time with time itself but a millisecond ahead so that she sidestepped the bullets skimming by. She held up her hands and the insects were stopped short in their attack by a squall of dust that built and towered around her,

The two fighting factions slowed in their motion by the smallest degree. Only the HawkEye soldier appeared to follow her advancement to the lake with precision; his steel eye flicked between her and the unconscious courtesan in D'Angelus's embrace.

She forgot him, concentrating on the shadow behind the crystal wall – long and thin, with soft wavy hair in silhouette, and holding up a lantern.

"Virgil!" She cried and wadded into the black water.

"Ca-ca," replied the shape of her lover, making its way to

the side of the crystal wall, lantern waving to seek her out.

"What the shitting Saints is that?"

She heard the rough cry of the swine man, glanced back and saw him duck to prevent the butting plate of the Sirinese from caving in his skull. Others among the circus crew gasped – the male acrobat with the pretty girl face, the pimp, even the HawkEye – and it seemed for an instant that time had shifted again and they could see the way of things before her.

The woman stared back out across the lake, heart enraptured as the shape of her angular lover extended from behind the crystal wall, the lantern emerging first as a huge black obelisk of a head, two vast orbs protruding either side. The body followed – a colossal slug of a thorax that took several seconds to finish materialising. The creature was wingless, its undercarriage looped into many small udders and terminating with a long, clear ovipositor which squeezed off eggs now and then, like glossy white sausage meat.

The queen ca-ca'ed in the woman's direction, and the sound bounced off the cavern. "Carrie-Anne, Carrie-Anne."

A shot rang out, tugging back the head plate of the queen in a spray of lemony blood. The woman spun around to see that, having wrestled the courtesan inside the burrower, D'Angelus had launched a grenade from the nose cone of the machine.

"No!" shrieked the woman.

Her bubble burst.

"Saintless crawlers." D'Angelus spat out the side of the cockpit, as if ridding himself of the taste of murder. All around him, the locusts clung to the walls, newly petrified. "Show 'em fuckers who's boss, hey, Das?" He gave the navigator's elbow a knock.

From behind his bug-eyed goggles, Das looked far from certain. He went back to messing with the controls. "We gotta get out of here, boss. There's too many of them and we lost all those men…" His voice hitched and trailed off.

"And now I've taken out the crawlers' queen." D'Angelus

showed his dead men's teeth. "I got the whore. Only thing I'm down on is the wolf girl."

"You mean the rabid dog coming straight for us?" said Das, voice aquiver. He shrank down into the foot well of the cock pit among the peddles and levers.

D'Angelus, though, was frantic with excitement. His eyes ate up the bounding form of the wild girl, the pendulous teats that swung beneath her lean brown body, the savage show of her. So thoroughly naked. So utterly abased. He longed for her, every thread of him stretched to capacity.

Below, the Sirinese was calling something in between deflecting the blows from the swine man and the lashes of the ladyboy's sharp whips. Something about danger and the need to slide the glass shield of the burrower back into position, lock it and seal out the wolf girl. D'Anglus was impervious to the cry.

He watched the beast of a woman tear up the ground between them. Wasn't she magnificent? How her claws ripped over the dusty rock!

"Come to me, bitch," he cooed.

The shot when it came was at close range and to his chest. D'Angelus looked down, hands puddling in the red gore. He glanced questioningly at the she wolf. She bounded up onto the nose of the burrower and paused alongside the HawkEye, who stood there, a curl of smoke escaping his rock rifle.

"But... but…" D'Angelus's lips produced a childish puff of air then gaped. He fell off to the side. Seconds later, the soldier's boot kicked him hard, exploding nose and cheekbone. And then he was face-to-slavering-face with the wolf girl.

Through the agonies that wracked his body, D'Angelus tried out a bloody smile. She was here at last, dragging him down off the burrower into a crush of limbs. And then her face was so very close to his, the tangled mane ticking and arousing his bleeding skin. Something drove into the depths of him, unravelling his inner workings.

"My love," he said, and meant it as the savage girl showed

him his guts between her teeth. Biting down, she began to feast.

The whips sliced into Jaxx's face, creating two fresh scars – good and evil etched into opposing cheeks. He gritted his black teeth. When the ladyboy next lashed out, he grasped both whips, withstanding their terrible sting against his palms as he did so, and began to reel the ladyboy in. The swine man charged. Jaxx yanked on both whips, ripping them from the ladyboy's hands. He dived forwards onto his stomach – avoiding the swing of the swine man's fist in the process – and spooled in the whips, taking hold of the handles. Flipping back up onto his feet, he revolved the ropes about his waist and kept the ladyboy at bay with a couple of slashes. The kid seemed to know he was beat and charged for the circus tent, avoiding Jaxx's whip cracks with a show of nimble acrobatics.

He was alone with the pig then. The awareness of witchcraft derived from his Sirinese roots told him that some force was keeping the swarm at bay for the time being. Out the corner of his eye, he saw the creatures clumped against the walls. A thin pall of dust cocooned the circus and the area immediately outside of it. He'd a sense of the other players nearby, the HawkEye cradling the whore as he retrieved her from the cockpit of the burrower, Das signalling him in a generous wave of panic, the blood bag that was once D'Angelus, split open on the rocks, a feast for the squatting wolf girl.

Despite the swine man's grotesque appearance, Jaxx judged him an excellent opponent. The swine took the bite of the whip to his arm, his chest, and he cried out like the man he once was and not the pig he had become. There was pleasure in their fight, thought Jaxx, taking the weight of the swine's fist against his jaw and tasting his own blood. He smashed his butting plate into the pig's snout at full force and saw the blood gush, the small piggy eyes water.

But their battle would be concluded some other time, Jaxx decided. With the magnificent calm that was so characteristic of his violent culture, he stepped back and bowed.

"Blood enough for this day," he said, and turned sharply on his heels. At his back, the swine attempted a final weak swing which didn't connect then seemed to come to terns with the pause in their battle.

Hearing the burrower clear its throat of dust and rumble into life, Jaxx ran across the rock plain. He climbed the metal ladder in two steps and swung inside the cockpit. Das slammed the glass hood back in place, shutting out the bugs and freaks.

"Jeepers, Jaxx. Thought I was gonna have to leave you." Das sighed heavily and peered over at Jaxx from behind his insectile goggles. "D'Angelus is gone. So's the rest of the boys. Reckon me and thee should scoot."

Jaxx nodded. Through the wind shield he saw the woman who had disguised herself as a Zen monk, then lain with him beneath the stars. She was standing in the lake, a short way out from the shore, the black water up to her knees. Her hands were raised in supplication, as if commanding some unseen force. Or was it in homage to the slain queen whose carcass sprawled across the opposite shore? He remembered the terrible waking nightmare he had experienced when he'd pressed deep inside her. Men torn limb-from-limb by demons. Had that been a vision of Hell, or a window on the future he'd just caught up with?

He dismissed the fact. It was a diviner's trick. He'd found the warmth of her body a far more fascinating gift. Not that she was his to rescue at that moment. She had another lover, whom she searched for in this shadow-land. Their time together had run out.

"Let's get out of here," he said.

Das snapped up a couple of switches in the control bank, tugged on and lowered a large lever by his hip, and eased the drive column forward. The burrower rattled over the sheet of rock. A few metres short of colliding with the circus tent, the machine lowered its nose and drilled down.

"Come now, Rust! Leave off your meal. Swarm'll dive any second." Pig Heart lolloped towards the wolf girl, sweat pouring off his jowls.

The girl glanced up, mouth blackened with visceral, hands burrowed in the man's stomach. Her eyes were dazzlingly bright.

She ran towards Pig Heart, strong limbs powering off the rock, and together they charged in at the tent flap.

The pitch crew worked to wind in the hose. Inside Cyber Circus, the air felt swollen and humid. The boiler fizzled away below the calliope. Large bubbles tumbled against the glass or popped when they reached the surface near the rim. Everywhere inside the tent was given over to preparations to fly. Pitch crew clambered high up on the gangplanks, double-checking the newly patched hide. Herb was installed on the calliope's balcony like some goblinesque Maharaja watching over his domain.

"Everyone inside?" Pig Heart hollered at the ringmaster.

"Apparently so." Herb nodded at the HawkEye, who stepped in at the tent flap, Nim's prone body slung across his arms. "She dead?" Herb called down, voice tinged with sadness.

"Alive," the soldier shouted back. "Paralysed by a locust's sting. There a cure for that?"

Herb looked lost suddenly. Pig Heart joined Rust in eyeing the ground a moment. The idea of Nim spending the remainder of her days locked inside an inanimate body seemed a brutal way of existing.

But then a woman's voice rang out. "I can heal her. I need bobbisroot, lock lime and a whole lot of rock salt." It was the woman who had posed as a Zen monk. She'd ducked in at the tent flap an instant before it was stitched shut, wearing such a look of sorrow that Pig Heart thought she might just crumble to dust and blow away on the spot.

The woman walked towards backstage, where the pitch crew stood ready to roll shut the great steel shield. She paused and glanced back. "We should get moving. The locusts won't mourn their queen for long."

Pig Heart tried to make sense of the woman's place on their craft – was she a prisoner still, or one of the crew? He dragged a hand across his jaw and slopped away the drool that hung there. While the ringmaster merely nodded, the HawkEye strode backstage and Rust bounding after.

Stopping just inside the gateway between the circus ring and backstage, Pig Heart ordered his men to stay their hands. "Herb!" he hollered across the vast expanse of the tent. "What about the Scuttlers?"

His question was lost to the suck and drawl of the ship's giant bellows in the engine room, the bubble of steaming water in the boiler, the gentle flood of air to the float bladders, and the pipe of the calliope.

"Roll 'em to," Herb told the crewmen and the great steel shield rolled shut.

High up in the eaves of the cavern, Ol, Tib and Rind watched Cyber Circus pitch once then settle and drift away into the caverns beyond.

"Bye, bye," said Ol. She rattled off a little dance with her knock-knees.

"Won't get no key to heaven from the nice lady now." Rind shook her head sadly.

"Won't need one either. We're gonna stay put, bed down with these shitters. Me and Ol will be their shepherds, and you can be their Queen," said Tib. He gave Rind's shell a gentle stroke with a claw. "Queen of the swarm."

Rind smiled, a queer show of teeth in her little old face. *Queen*? She liked the sound of that.

With her brother and sister following in her wake, Rind clattered down the cavern wall and went to meet her people.

NINETEEN

Deralisee was a bustling hive of people, beasts and colour. The Festival of Saints was in full swing. Garlands crisscrossed the streets, strung from gas lamps and the windows of eateries, brothels, salons, general stores, alongside the printing press, farrier, barber, tanner, jail and schoolhouse. Statues of the Saints stood on every street corner – forlorn sculptures made of dirt and dung, then painted pretty. Pilgrims cluttered up the place, come to sample the sacred waters at the natural spring. Saint Azena herself, giver of clarity, was said to have rested at the spot once and partaken of the liquid on offer from a small rift in Deralisee's bedrock. Cashing in on the fact over the centuries, the citizens of Deralisee had established a shrine over the site and developed itself into quite the religious destination. Zen monks milled through the crowds like silent demons. Children gawked. Parents shuffled their families quickly by.

While the Sirinese had their magic men and the Jeridians their sacred spirits, both cultures were happy to congregate at the festival with a common aim. To relieve the pilgrim of his or her dollars. Jeridians paraded, waving great etched banners proclaiming, 'Warrior for hire', 'Have dust? Can handle', 'Gang Stock', and the like. The Sirinese, meanwhile, were more subtle. They kept to the shadows, where they engaged in wagered wrestling bouts or took a rich man's coin and told him his fortune. Come festival time, Deralisee was ablaze with shame, sin, and piety.

"And punters!" Herb had declared when the circus finally took to the western trail again, having waited out the worst of the dust storm at the caverns' entrance. "The dimes flow freely when a man is Saint Blessed," he'd told the company.

And it had sounded good. To haul up for the remainder of the Hamatan season in a spot that was ripe with passing trade. A night's passage it had taken, during which Nim had been ministered by the woman and sweated out the poison, her Jeridian genes helping her to heal. Swinging in over Deralisee's permanent carnival pitch, Cyber Circus had descended out of one of the last blue skies of the year, a colossal beast of brass and biomorphed flesh, to take centre stage amongst Deralisee's bountiful celebrations.

The lights dim. All is hushed inside the green-tinged underworld of the circus tent.

A soft melody begins to pipe from the calliope. Notes that are fine and sweet, like longed-for rain. She appears – a figure in white beneath the blaze of a spotlight. Her dress is enticingly translucent; it skims her ankles and clings to her thighs, waist, ribs and breasts. Her hair is a cascade of orange flame.

When she dances, Desirous Nim seems to ripple like a petticoat pegged out to dry in the wind. So beautifully she arches her bare feet, lifting and lowering her arms like water flowing – and isn't she divine? This exquisite desert flower. This fragile reed.

The drums start to beat. Soft at first, as a steady heartbeat. Building and building over time. The lights dim further so that the crowd are forced to squeeze up their eyes and peer into the gloom. The drums grow ever more agitated, rolling over themselves into sonic waves.

Boom! Boom! Boom! The base drum kicks in. Nim sets herself ablaze and the drums turn tribal. She's shining now from beneath her made-new skin – a light storm of purest white.

Which is when a second figure takes to the stage. An

offbeat beauty. Eyes set wide. Mouth slashed like a scar. Her clothes are pinned tighter at places it won't show, petticoats and a scarlet corset borrowed from Nim. Her stage name is Charm, Conjuress of Seasons. She steps up into the circus ring, and her hands lift and the dust across the ground begins to dance.

The drums beat ever faster. The dust swirls, a magnetised cobra. It breezes out past the edges of the ring, lifts and swooping over the heads of the gasping audience. In time, Charm brings the magic grains back inside the circle and waltzes with them spilt out over her two hands. At the centre of the ring, Nim continues to flood the circus tent with her gleam while Charm directs the dust to ripple in beneath the courtesan's feet.

Liftng her hands towards the spot-lit heavens, Charm agitates the motes to rise. On a wave of pulsing drums and spellbound dust, Nim ascends ten metres above the ground. She pirouettes air-bound. Light spills out from the heart of her over the world of the circus.

The others emerge then from behind the backstage curtain. A ladyboy flashing teeth and feminine wiles as he skips about the ring. The pig man who is yet awkward on the stage but grunts and squeals with bold enthusiasm. A savage black-eyed girl who bounds in on all four limbs, jaw snapping, gore matted in her mane. And the HawkEye, a man of flesh and metal who scans the crowd with his whirring eyepiece and stalks into the centre of the ring. He holds a hand up to Nim and she takes it.

On a balcony above, the ringmaster hops from foot to foot, waving his extravagant feathered hat as the calliope pipes its last song of the night.

"Goodnight ladies. Goodnight gentlemen. Goodnight Saints and goodnight sinners. Goodnight one and all from the sensational, lavational, electrisical, metaphysical Cyber Circus!"

BLACK SUNDAY

Friday April 12, 1935

Wesley Sanders edged the drink onto the table.

"There ya'rl, Miss Nightingale. Iced lemonade, or as Momma's prone to call it, sunlight in a glass."

The eight year old grinned. His teeth were large and very white, as if slicked with whitewash like the exterior of the Grace Presbyterian Church. His cheeks were nut-brown apples.

Carrie-Anne leant forward in her rocker and put her toes to the floor. She smiled back. "Thank you, Wesley. Tell your momma, she sure does know how to soothe the spirit."

Wesley bobbed his cap. He waltzed off down the porch, humming one of those slow sad negro church songs he was prone to. Even after he'd swung through the inner gauze and disappeared inside the house, Carrie-Anne could hear the tune. It seemed to nestle down inside the dry Oklahoma heat and stay there, whispering at her.

She picked up the lemonade, rested the sole of a bare foot against the table and rocked. Julie Sander's eldest, Abraham, had painted the porch a light grey colour before he'd abandoned Bromide for Oklahoma City last fall. That afternoon, the paint shade complimented the troubled sky where blue and lavender clouds roiled.

A storm was coming. What kind, Carrie-Anne wasn't sure. This time of year, it could be hail, could be lightning, could be a twister. But she welcomed it. The weather was unseasonably close. It licked at the nape of her neck where her shoulder-length hair clung, and at each underarm, leaving sweat stains on her new cotton dress. Everything induced slumber. Except the cold lemonade.

Carrie-Anne put the glass to her lips and sipped. She wanted to stay mindful. The back gate needed fixing; she'd set the new yardman on it with instructions to go about replacing the struts. One of her stockings had a run that wouldn't darn itself.

Plus the whole house needed airing.

She'd noticed as much that morning. Rising from her blankets at the tail end of night, she'd descended the stairs and glimpsed the place as with an outsider's eye. Everything was layered with dust. She'd got a rag to it. But as she beat the motes, she'd felt a familiar, inexplicable crackling along her bare arms. Lips parted, she'd held up a hand to the window. In the first rays of dawn, the dust had appeared to dance near but never touch her skin, as if magnetically repelled…Seconds later, she'd heard footsteps on the stairs and Julie Sanders saying in her quiet way, "Sure is dusty, Miss Nightingale. I'll light a flame under the coffee pot then get to helping ya."

Carrie-Anne braced her foot against the table and stayed tipped back on the rockers. Having filled the role of nursery nurse ever since Carrie-Anne first arrived at Boar House, aged eight and orphaned, Julie was like family, as were her boys. Which was how the woman knew to fill the house with the clarifying aroma of coffee and just join in shaking out the dust that morning. Also how she knew to dispatch Wesley with cool lemonade when the gate was still broken, the stocking still torn, the house still dust-riddled.

All the same, Julie's best efforts had failed. With the heat cooking in around her, Carrie-Anne found it impossible to rouse herself to any thought but one.

Where the hell were they?

Even wearing ear mufflers, he couldn't escape the terrible clanking as fragments of rock in the sand ricocheted off the drill. The cockpit shuddered with each impact. His jaw ached from clenching his teeth to stop them jarring. The four-point Sutton harness rubbed the same sore spots it did every run; Virgil imagined Carrie-Anne slavering the blisters with peppered grease. Lust alleviated his discomfort. The excavations were pivotal to his work, but, Christ, he missed that gal. Her baby scent when she soaped the sweat offa her. Those frank blue eyes and wide mouth. He liked her off-beat beauty.

"Stop tugging your little john back there, Virgil, and crank the boiler. That last sheet of bedrock took the best of old Bessie's heat." Straining at the front harness, Josephine Splitz attempted to glare back over her shoulder.

Virgil knew he'd just be a blur at her peripheral vision. He crossed his arms over his crotch all the same.

"Sorry, Jos. Its hot's all. Got me sweating like a hog ripe for slaughter."

Grabbing a battered iron scoop off a hook overhead, he drove it through the coke trough that ran alongside his chair and used the other hand to open the iron flap in the Burrower's wall. A tremendous gush of heat spilt into the cabin. He shook the coke down the shoot and shut the hatch.

"Another couple."

If the old coot'd had eyes in the back of her head, Virgil guessed they'd have been lit up and smiling. Twice more he drove the scoop into the coke and threw the fodder down the boiler's throat.

Reaching overhead, he took hold of a leather loop and tugged several times, feeling the papery air off the bellows feed the cabin and boiler simultaneously. Glancing past Josephine's shoulder, Virgil saw the needles creep up in the rack of brass and glass gauges. The steering wheel juddered under the old girl's hands, and he thought he heard her wince despite the wads of muslin she'd taped around the triangulated steel bar. Any other octogenarian shoehorned into the cramped quarters of the Burrower would've screamed for death's release long ago. But Josephine was a wizen fruit, long past the point of any residual softness. She reminded Virgil of a small hunched Asian man in her navy-blue mandarin jacket, loose pants and soft cloth hat, except her fierce single-mindedness was peculiar to the matriarch.

"Got your mind up top too soon, Virgil Roberts. Long as we're still beneath, we're just one mistake away from being buried alive." Jos's voice got that molasses quality it always did when she wanted to aggravate him for kicks. "Nothing certain in love or geological exploration, I promise you. By the time we break surface, chances are Carrie-Anne will've hooked up with Preacher Richards' son. Great strapping lad, all thighs and neck and buttocks like quartz boulders. Or Jeffrey's boy. Part store keeper, part donkey."

"In place of a lab rat that spends his time parked behind the arse of some old dame," Virgil shot back. His mouth twisted. Jos sure liked to tease, but part of him guessed she might be right. Why was Carrie-Anne laying down with a freak like him? He'd spent so much time underground this past year. His eyes had a skim on them like spoilt milk. Likewise, his skin was colourless through lack of sunlight. Danger was, sooner or later, he'd fade right out.

Even without seeing his face, Jos was astute enough to know what he was thinking. "You're okay, Virgil Roberts. Wouldn't choose you for my bedfellow but Carrie-Anne's got the right to."

"It bother you if I said I wouldn't choose you for a bedfellow either?"

The old gal snorted. Any retort was cut short by a tremendous scraping noise. The steel undercarriage bucked beneath their feet, the motion immediately offset by the concertinaing of the Burrower's riveted steel roof plates. It was a filthy, stinking, terrifying ride, thought Virgil, but Jos's design was immaculate. The torpedo-shaped main carriage had a dual layer of modular pneumatic tiles, or 'scutes' as Jos called them in homage to her greatest muse as a bioengineer, the horn-coated dermal bones of the Armadillo. As a geo-engineer, she'd applied similar tessellation logic to the rotating bit of the twelve foot Tungsten Carbide plated nose cone, likewise the corrugated neck frill that funnelled the spoil out behind as they pressed forward on sharpened steel tracks. The unstable nature of the terrace deposits was counteracted by gills in the outer walls that released a fine mist to solidify the sand. Hot, thin, rust-scented air was siphoned into the cabin from the tunnels. Water bladders were grouped at the backend of the machine like egg sacks.

The turbulence abated.

"Five minutes more. Just time enough to make yourself look pretty for my niece." Jos adjusted in her seat. She handed a metal pot over her shoulder. "And to empty the piss pan."

Carrie-Anne plunged forward in the rocking chair and stood up. She rested her hands against the corner strut of the porch then leant her whole body into it to better feel the vibrations. The keen of ruptured earth was just audible. Dust misted the field beyond the garden.

"Wesley!"

The boy was already at the swing door.

"Momma knows, Miss Valentine. Says she's drawing Miss Splitz's bath and fixing Mister Robert's Gin Sour."

"Good." Carrie-Anne stared at the dry field, littered with entrance and exit wounds inflicted by the Burrower. "That's good," she repeated softly.

The ground shook. There came a sudden explosion of brilliance in the centre of the field as sunlight touched the tip of the emerging nose cone. A geyser of dark sand erupted. The cacophonic whirring of the engine ripped through the air. The Burrower wormed up from below like a giant silver maggot castor.

I shall not run to his side, not this time, thought Carrie-Anne. *I will be the lady of the house, patiently waiting on the porch, lemonade glass in hand.*

Though it was hard to stand still as the terrific machine sledged up into the air, slammed back down and coasted forward, its twin steel tracks sending up two great tides of dust. The engine sound changed to a discordant chug. Steam spurted from the side valves.

"Want me to run down to them, Miss Valentine?" Wesley stared up at her in round-eyed innocence.

"No, Wesley." She stuck out a hand as though to brace his chest. "You know better than to get near Miss Splitz's excavating machine so soon after surfacing. It's a big old unpredictable cottonmouth 'til it cools some. Look!" She felt a rush of longing as jets of steam escaped the rivets of the roof hatch. "Even those inside take their time when exiting," she murmured.

The roof hatch cranked up. Aunt Josephine was first to emerge, un-crumpling herself as she went with all the decorum of a farm hand. She dropped heavily onto the ground, agitating the dust. For a brief moment, she applied her thumbs to her spine and arched backwards. Then she made for the front of the vehicle, kicking out stiff legs as she walked.

Carrie-Anne's gaze returned to the roof hatch. He was visible now as a coil of flesh that stretched out to become a tall, thin figure. Her heart got hot at the sight of him. He raised a hand to wave.

There wasn't chance to respond. Her aunt was shouting and gesticulating towards the huge steaming drill. Virgil answered her and threw an arm towards the house.

He's waving her away, thought Carrie-Anne admiringly.

Sure enough, the old maid turned heel and began to stomp towards the house.

Carrie-Anne watched Virgil slide down off the Burrower's roof. With his shirt sleeves rolled and one suspender dangling loose from his waist, he strode up to the drill and dipped under it, one arm raised as a shield against the heat. Virgil's in-depth mechanical knowledge made Carrie-Anne aware of her own internal workings; he seemed to grasp them too. And while she wanted to keep her eyes on him, her aunt was already at the garden gate.

"…peach of a ride 'til we hit that friggin' boulder. Now the damn drill's breached. Virgil best check the depth of those gorges good and proper else I'll be roastin' his sweet cherry ass on old Bessie." Aunt Josephine plonked down on the porch steps, untied her boots and kicked them off. She didn't falter in her monologue. "…not like we weren't prepared. Hit wet sand and Virgil was gonna switch from steam to soot mix, gloop the walls to stop them caving in. But we didn't find one patch of moisture. 'Course it's bone dry up here on the surface. Just the same, no water bodies, not even fifty foot below? It's strange. Not strange, it's unnatural."

The old woman stopped prattling suddenly. Her hooded gaze fell on Wesley.

"Help your momma black the stove?"

Wesley sucked his lip and nodded.

"Kept the dirt from growin' between them fat little toes?"

The kid caught a foot up in a hand and used his fingers to scoop between the toes.

"Am all clean, Miss Splitz."

The old woman gurned at him and he giggled.

"Here." She held out a fist.

Wesley dropped his foot. He ran over, offering up cupped hands, and Aunt Josephine opened her fist over them.

"Thank you, Miss Splitz." The boy eyed his prize then pocketed it.

Carrie-Anne smiled; she knew the ritual. The treasure was a mundane stone recovered from several miles below ground. Wesley would add it to his collection.

Hand on the stair rail, Aunt Josephine levered herself up. Stalking over to the front door, she paused to cut her eye at Carrie-Anne.

"Told lover boy you'd've shacked up with a new fella by now." She slung her gaze over to the field where Virgil had shifted his attention to the cooling engine.

Carrie-Anne felt panic worm between her eyes.

Her aunt must've noticed.

"He missed you," she relented, and shouldered the flyscreen door and disappeared inside. Wesley followed after like a child bound to a witch by invisible silken thread.

Carrie-Anne rested her forehead against the corner strut.

Eyelids lulling, she watched the ghost of a man at work out in the field. Minutes passed. He became less and less solid. Late afternoon ebbed and swelled around her. A cicada soloed ahead of the insect symphony at sundown. Through the open bathroom window, she could hear Aunt Josephine's prattle and the slow pour from a water jug as Julie endeavoured to clean up her mistress. Wood creaked; to Carrie-Anne, it was the sound of the house groaning under the weight of memories impregnating its walls. She listened past the familiar sounds of her environment, out to the dusting plateau of farmland and the drone of nothingness.

Her flesh crackled. Her eyes shot wide.

Virgil stood on the porch a couple of paces away.

Carrie-Anne's first reaction was indignation at his materialising like that when she expected to watch him approach from the distance of the field, to get used to him closing in. Her anger was blunted by the sight of him, hands and forearms etched in coke dust, shirt savaged at the neck. Lifting her eyes, she saw a death mask of skin so terribly white and dried to the bone. He went against what common decency said a man should look like. Yet his was a salt-preserved masculinity which made her drip away from herself.

Carrie-Anne let go of the strut and wrapped her arms around her waist. Virgil kept on staring. She felt transparent.

"Lose your tongue as well as your mind this trip, Virgil Roberts?"

He smiled and the death aspect was replaced by tangible sensuality. Now she saw a slender man with well-worked shoulders, high cheekbones and generous lips in need of moisture. Only his eyes remained strange with their misted irises and pupils gone over from black to lead grey.

"I was drinking you in, Carrie-Anne Valentine," he said quietly.

The gauze door yawned on its hinges and Wesley emerged from the house.

"Yu Gin Sour, Mister Roberts."

The glass was offered up. Virgil gulped from it, his gaze on Carrie-Anne. She felt his stare graze her flesh like a steam burn.

Bromide had been parched for months now, and in spite of its draw as a spa town not fifteen years past when the railroad carved through the district and millionaire, Robert Galbreath, found a hole into which to sink his oil money. Back then the town supported three general stores, two drugstores, a bank, a meat market, two hardware stores, two restaurants, a blacksmith's and a dry goods. Four grand hotels wined, dined and bed-timed. A public bath house doused and rinsed. Meanwhile, Bromide's unique geology gave rise to a cotton gin and yard, a rock crusher and quarry, a wagon maker, a sawmill, a gristmill, and even a bottler who shipped out the medicinal waters.

But fame is nothing if not fickle. Come 1930, folk moved further afield. As quickly as it was raised, the town was brought to the ground. The excursion trains were cancelled, the bank closed, the hotels emptied. Five years more and Bromide looked set to simply blow away like a handful of dust.

Knees in the dirt, Reg Wilhoit wondered which piece of his town's history he worked up beneath his fingernails. Not much left to see of old Bromide now. Just slim pickings like the Baptist Church, a double-doored cattle barn of a place built of the usual dreary stone whose pews were regularly buffed, as if that would be enough to wipe the grime offa the place. There was the shack of the Post Office, which stank of old maid and kerosene given Mrs Johnson's partiality to warm her knees by a stove. And there were another forty or so dwellings still bothered by human breath. Mostly though, ruins scattered a three mile radius, like markers to a ghost town.

"Ya need a hand there, Mister Wilhoit?"

The old man shone his eyes up. Preacher Richards' boy blocked out the sun.

Reg could guess how he looked to the kid. Seat of his pants

patched. White cotton candy hair around a craggy face. Bent over like that. A marionette cut from its strings.

"Them calipers giving you gyp? Come on." Ben stuck out a hand the size of a rib steak. "Let's be havin' you."

"I'm fine, I tell ya."

Reg tossed out a fistful of dirt; luckily for Ben, no wind meant it sifted back down to the ground rather than flick up into his eyes. Not that the kid noticed.

But he wouldn't, mused Reg. Nice boy like that would've been raised with Preacher Richards' good grace. Yet sometimes manners got in the way. He wished to hell the kid'd kept on walking and not had to go and play Samaritan.

"Move it along, kiddo. Got a cramp in this knee's all." Sidewaysing onto his ass, Reg rapped one of the steel side bars of his left leg brace.

The Preacher's son offered him a big dumb smile. But there was a wary glint to the eye.

"Alright then, Mister Wilhoit. I'll just be at the store getting' Momma her sewing notions. Hollerin' distance if you need me." Ben pointed to the far end of Main. Reg squinted over at the rubble shack of the General Store, one of a handful of buildings to survive fire or abandonment and keep on serving what was left of the community. Same way it always had.

The old man said nothing, just stayed still as a tombstone, ass in the dirt.

"Alright then," repeated the lad. He tipped his cap and set off, letting the sunlight back in like a holy blaze.

Reg watched him go. Then he bent forward and dug his fingers into the dry dirt again.

Virgil drove his knife through the pork. Eying the mashed potatoes, gravy, black-eyed peas, and collard greens, he pressed a little of everything onto his fork.

"Fine pork shoulder, Julie," he announced as the maid re-entered the room carrying a jug of iced water. "You get it from

Bobby Buford's farm?"

Julie flashed her generous smile. "Bobby Buford's, Mister Roberts. Quality hogs he's got penned. Decent price he charges too, 'cept we always exchange goods of course. Mister Bulford, he's all gone on my cornbread and fresh picked tomatoes. It's so warm, see. I got to planting unseasonably early."

"Sure is a helluva dry spell. Not that visitors to Boar House would notice with a garden this lush." Virgil leant in on his elbows, knife and fork laid over one another like a silver cross. "How'd you do it, Julie? How'd you grow vegetables and herbs like you do when the field opposite is shredding its epidermis quicker than a rattlesnake?"

"'Cause I designed the best irrigation system in the state. And 'cause Julie gets a big ole milk churn and hauls ass to the well night and day to keep the system's water butts topped up." Jos jammed her own elbows onto the table. "Sissy boy like you'd struggle to lift that churn five yards."

"Better a sissy boy than a bad-tempered gasbag," shot Virgil from the opposite end of the table.

Jos got a sour twist to her mouth. "Better a bad-tempered gasbag than an incompetent navigator."

"Oh, come on now!" Virgil was peppered on the inside. His skin got some colour to it. "Much as I'd love to look into a crystal ball and know what's gonna hit before we get there, you know as well as me we can hit waterlogged sand or a boulder anytime underground. Because of water pockets, we got the soot mix, and as backup, the tar tap. Because of boulders, we got a Tungsten Carbide drill bit." He raised an eyebrow. "Maybe you need an early night, Jos? All this hard work and staying up late is bound to make an old crone cranky."

Jos stabbed at her greens. She ladled in a mouthful and chewed it up into one cheek. "It's your job to survey the route. Establish the orientation of bedding planes and steer us clear of joints in the rock," she insisted, adding aside, "Julie, you go get your supper now." Her gaze cut back to Virgil. She swallowed the mouthful. "We hit that last stretch of gravel hard and we hit it clumsy. Now we gotta pray there ain't a hairline fracture in the bit."

Virgil dug in fingers at his hairline. "And if there is, it'll blow itself and us to kingdom come." He dragged his hands back over his scalp. "I got my nose into every inch of the Burrower this afternoon. Like the one who built her, she's a tough old bird."

He allowed himself a smile. Sure, he was smarting that Jos felt the need to pin the blame on him – and maybe if he'd surveyed the field's surface for the thousandth time, he'd have guessed at that curl of gravel a few hundred yards below. But, no… Virgil kept his smile in place. Deep down, he knew there was no magic way to see exactly what lay in the Burrower's path, only estimations based on months' worth of surveys of the rock formations up top. He also knew that while Jos'd take a bullet before she'd admit it, they were both dog tired – which was why their usual banter had a caustic edge.

Luckily, there was Carrie-Anne to agitate the atmosphere.

"You know, Aunt Josephine, there hasn't been a scrap of wind these past four days you and Virgil have been down under. Not a scrap. Still the dust creeps in under the doors and windows. I was up before cockcrow this morning. When I saw a fresh layer over this place, my first thought was how come there's any ground left for the Burrower to dig through?" Carrie-Anne threw out her hands to indicate the panelled dining room, and, presumably, the whole house. "Julie and I spend our days sweeping it up."

Glancing at Virgil, she rubbed one side of her nose with her knuckles as if to rub away a soot smear. He recognised the gesture as slight embarrassment and he understood. Carrie-Anne wasn't really one for words. Not that she couldn't hold a conversation if she wanted. Just she was a girl who spoke with her eyes, or a wisp of laughter, or the sorcery of her tongue at his navel.

Jos was talking now. Thanks to Carrie-Anne, the old gal had been lulled into a softer frame of mind. Conducting a symphony of science with her cutlery, she appeared intent on using her niece as a sounding board for the plethora of geological theories Virgil had helped her construct.

"...over-intensive arable farming methods. I told Bobby Buford so two years ago when he still had land worth ploughing and hadn't pigs shitting over every inch of it. Drain the land of mineral, strip it of ground cover, and you're gonna get a wind tunnel. All's needed was a turn up in temperature and lack of rain, and, hell, I told them!" Jos screwed up her face, itself parched of moisture.

"But as I said, Aunt Josephine, there's been no wind. Just this thick baking in."

Carrie-Anne's gaze shifted towards him as she spoke. Virgil felt the same mix of emotion he'd felt when he'd stood on the porch a couple of hours earlier and soaked her in. Everything had misted into the background except Carrie-Anne. The only thing worth seeing. After so many hours spent in twilight underground, he'd fed on the colours offa her. Then Wesley had stepped out onto the porch, and the mist and colours evaporated like a broken spell. Only Carrie-Anne's tangibility had remained. He'd longed to mould her with his hands like wet sand.

"The wind will come," he said softly. He carved at the lump of roast pig on his plate again.

"And when it does, we'll all be blown away like stupid shitting pigs in straw houses," cut in Jos. She scraped back her chair. "Now I've a mind to get Julie to cut me a slice of that pie I smelt baking earlier."

Passing Virgil, she put a hand to his shoulder. "You want?"

It was as close to an apology as he'd get from Josephine Splitz.

Virgil glanced sideways, his mouth softened. "No. No thank you, Jos."

He dared believe she might disappear into the kitchen and

stay there, stuffing her face with pie, while he and Carrie-Anne got to sit together and talk some. But then Jos paused in the doorway.

"Go to the workshop and get all maps sketched in the last two months, Virgil. We musta missed that seam of gravel somewhere. And no…" She raised a hand to block his objection. "Tomorrow won't do. We ain't seeing the warmth of our beds 'til I'm satisfied we're not gonna drill a goddamn minefield in two days time."

"Two days? But that's a Sunday?"

Virgil could see Carrie-Anne turning her mind inside out in search of arguments against.

"I promised we'd all be at chapel Palm Sunday. Our attendance – or lack of it – has been noted, and not just by Preacher Richards. Folk talk, Aunt Josephine, and talk leads to trouble."

"That it does, Carrie-Anne, and it's gonna lead you into a great deal of it right now if you don't stop gassing and get yourself to bed." Jos's eyes shone out like coal chips.

Virgil watched Carrie-Anne intently. His gal would never show that dry old coot what she felt on the inside. Oh no, she'd keep it stitched into the flesh lining over her heart and ribs.

He, on the other hand, knew no such restraint. But just as he would've happily strangled Jos on the spot, the old woman let her shoulders stoop. She looked incredibly tired all of a sudden.

"Please, Carrie-Anne. We're out to save lives here. And that includes protecting our own."

Saturday April 13, 1935

Saturday. Town Day. Once upon a time, Main Street would've thrummed with the footfall of folk who'd journeyed to Bromide to trade, swap and stockpile. The Ice Man would have busied his pick. The Blacksmith would have chipped at his anvil. The pharmacist would have returned a whisper across the counter and deposited some bottle or canister of powder into a bag which he'd carefully fold over. The girl at the Dry Goods store would have dragged the fabric bundle off the shelf and measured, snipped and ripped. In every store and business premises, proprietors and staff would have busied themselves to satisfy Saturday's rush. Meanwhile, townsfolk and families from surroundings farmsteads would have gathered to speculate, commiserate, and nose into one another's business. Once upon a time.

But Bromide had gone from riches to rags. All that remained of Town Day were a series of '*How'd you do*'s, '*See you around*'s, and all the idle talk in-between. Womenfolk ooed and arred in the shade of the porch belonging to the solitary general store. Children chased each other like hot-footed hens or formed puddles of lilting conversation. The menfolk, meanwhile, kicked up dust out on the road, swigged Coca-Cola or root beer, and smoked and talked in the hazy, drawn-out way men are prone to.

"Johnson said his cattle went on and ate the grass despite the dust. Lost half the herd to mud balls in their stomachs," said George West, a pharmacist who'd stayed on after the drug store closed to farm his own patch of land before the drought hit.

Ben nodded. "Franklin Herby had the same, 'cept he bailed a month ago. Packed Rita and the boys up in that old cart that was his daddy's, hitched a nag to it, and moseyed on out. Rumour is he got a great aunt owns a fruit farm in California. So I'm guessin' he's all made up now."

"Don't you be so sure, Ben. I'm inclined to believe the news on the radio and as far as folk makin' their fortunes out west, yeah, they get work on the fruit farms but they don't make enough offa it to keep a bag-a-bones donkey in feed." Quarry worker, Samuel O'Ryan, eyed the preacher's son. *It hadda be nice to still have the shine of youth on you*, he thought to himself. *All that belief life's gonna come good in the end. All that gullibility.*

"Yeah, I guess." Ben bowed his head. But something must

have itched at him and he added, "Ask me, folk should have more faith."

"Easy for you to say when your daddy's the preacher. Come judgement day, you and your daddy'll be sitting pretty on the right hand of the lord. Rest of us, well, we'll starve to death and find ourselves looking up at ya from the pit of Hell," hollered Dixon Goodwin, tinker and sometime yard's man, who had the devil's gift for saying exactly what would stir a man.

"Pit of Hell? Ain't we there already?" Samuel beat his hands. His laughter had a sour note, but was echoed by the harrumphs of the others.

Drawing on his cigarette, eyes pinched against the smoke, Dixon kept on staring at the preacher's son.

"Can't but wonder though, Ben. While the rest of us are working the scrap of land we got left, or raising swine on soap weed, or fixin' to leave the only home we've ever known, how'd you and your daddy manage to keep your shoes so nicely shined and sweet potatoes on the table? No, no, now…" Dixon raised his hands against an undercurrent of complaint. "I ain't criticising Preacher Richards. He's a man of the lord. I'm just interested to know if the preacher's boy thinks he suffers like the rest of us."

Ben eased back ox shoulders. "Me and my daddy seen suffering aplenty, Dixon. We take relief supplies to farmsteads as far out as the abandoned Indian academy. We're the ones that dig a hole for them that have died of the dust pneumonia, who say a prayer o'er them. As for our shoes being shined, I was raised to mind what my neighbour thinks of me. As for sweet potato…"

"Why're you picking on Ben here? Flea biting your ass?" shot Samuel, who apparently saw no good reason why Ben should explain what food ended up on his father's table. The quarry man added, "You know darn well if there's any fresh vegetables to be had around here, they're from Miss Splitz's homestead."

George and a couple of others nodded.

Dixon hacked and spat into the dust. "Just 'cause I got a

spot as the new yard man out at old woman's Splitz's place, you think I'm in the know?"

"Aren't ya?" shot one of six quarry lads sat in the road.

"Aren't I what?"

"Aren't you the one to fill us in on the place?"

"Whadaya wanna know?" Dixon kept a smile behind his teeth. No harm in splashing out a little gold dust about Boar House and its residents. He plumped out his chest. "The old gal's machines? They're helluva big, I tell ya. Steam-breathing hogs the lot. She's got 'em holed up in a workshop out back. As I heard it from their last yardman, place is lined with tools plus a whole host of thingamajigs Miss Splitz engineered alongside the hired help – guy called Virgil Roberts?" Dixon weighted his voice just right. Outsiders were the worst sort of intrusion when folk were down on their luck.

"This… Virgil. He a relation?" piped up another quarry lad.

Dixon ground his smoke under a boot heel. He breathed in slow and took his time. Wasn't often folk listened without him having to shove his opinion up under their noses.

"No relation," he confided.

The men hushed. Dixon could hear the womenfolk over at the store, their soft laughter alongside the chirruping of children.

"Josephine Splitz hired him in from some big college outta state," he said to the men surrounding him. "Place called Stanford."

The quarry boys kept on chewing their tobacco like calves on the cud. Only Ben got a knowing look. Dixon paid him no mind.

"Anyways. Pair of 'em have butchered the field in front of Boar House good and proper with a great big drilling machine. The Burrower they call it. This Virgil and Miss Splitz, they climb inside and drive it underground for days, leaving Miss Nightingale to keep house."

One mention of Miss Nightingale and he'd really got their attention now, these men with unsatisfied needs and empty pockets.

Not everyone was seduced though. Dixon dragged the back of his hand across his nose and got a whiff of disproval off Ben, Samuel and George.

Samuel beat his big hands again. This time the gesture was threatening. "I ain't interested. Folks' business is their own."

"Unless it has a bearin' on others!"

Reg Wilhoit made his way into the group with that stiff-legged, foot-scrapping motion of his. He halted, one hip at an awkward angle. "Jos should be forced to stop with the crazy machines. Liable to get someone killed."

The quarry boys had sense enough to hunch their shoulders and look away. Samuel swallowed the last of his soda, eyes scrunched shut against the sun's glare, then peered on over at the newcomer.

"It ain't up to us to tell grown folk what to do in their own time on their own land, Reg," he said quietly. "Just as no one had the right to warn you off working them machines before they decided to take a piece of you?"

"Thought I was helping Jos mine for new branches off Bromide Spring," Reg embarked, deaf or bloody-minded. "Ten years ago, folk thought we could breathe new life into this town's dry and weary bones and tempt the visitors back. Least that's the way I saw it. 'Course it wasn't me that got to go underground in a giant metal worm."

"That the problem, Reg?" Samuel's tone stayed gentle. His words were more caustic. "You jealous some outta towner gotta ride in the big machines?"

"And lose my life, not just a pair of useful legs? No thanks, Sammy. I got crushed enough under that iron hoisting crane ten years ago. Just as well too. I've learnt to stand back and see Jos Splitz for what she really is."

Dixon wore a sly look. "Miss Splitz, hey? Well, what'd ya know. Seems even old folk gotta get their kicks." He let his mouth hang open.

"Mind outa the gutter, Dixon Goodwin. I'll tell ya what Jos Splitz is. She's a conjuress! A leech!" A fleck of spit escaped Reg's sunken mouth. Shifting his balance awkwardly, he cast wild eyes about the group. "Not one of ya's got the first clue what that dame's doing over at Boar House."

"I know plenty," cut in Dixon with a grimace that suggested it was his time to talk and weren't no cripple gonna shake him off his perch. "I know Miss Splitz is spitting mad at Virgil 'cause he might've broke something on her burrowing machine. Heard her riding him for it when I went to the kitchen last night to get a glass of lemonade offa their house negro. I know Miss Spitz calls us farming folk a bunch of shitting pigs, blames us for killing off the land and leaving ourselves with nothing but dust."

Dixon wove his words well. There wasn't a man present who didn't tuck a frown into their face or sheesh through their teeth or curse a dry old coot who'd got no right to judge.

Reg rounded on the group, dragged feet drawing snake-coils in the dirt. "There was nothing natural about the way that big old crane unpinned from its earth footings to come crashing down on me…"

"We gotta go there again, Reg?" It was the turn of George, ex-pharmacist, failed farmer, to roll his eyes.

Reg rolled his own back. "I know, it's the word of a mad old cripple against those respectable whores at Boar House."

"Shut your mouth, Reg. There's an awful bad smell coming out of it." Samuel threw out his arms. "Wasn't a soul near you when the accident happened. Said so yourself all them years ago." His stance was reinforced by mutterings from the quarry boys. Miss Splitz could go hang, but no one badmouthed a doll like Carrie-Anne. Not when there were so few young and single women left in Bromide for a fella to set his hat at.

"Yup, I sure did say as much." Reg drawled his words. He seemed to burrow into himself. "But there is change afoot and Miss Splitz and her apprentice are at the heart of it. I feel them breaking through the earth beneath our feet more often these days. Vibrations offa those great tunnelling machines work their way up through the flesh and the metal and make my legs cramp."

"What they burrowing for anyways?" said a quarry boy.

"My daddy says they are investigating why the land's gotten so barren in these parts. And, yeah, you're right about hunting out more branches of the Bromide Spring, Reg, but way I heard it, Miss Splitz's thinking is to siphon water from deep below ground and find a way to feed it in beneath the crops since surface spray 'd evaporate too quick." Ben realised the entire group was fixated on what he had to say. He faltered. "Well, it goes something like that."

Reg scrubbed at his cotton hair with two hands. "Except maybe it's Miss Splitz's mining activities which drained the land in the first place. Ever think of that?"

Over by the store, the women were creating their very own storybook, layering it with soft tones and sudden laughter. The children had sticks and were offering up war cries. Reg's inconstant eyes flicked about the now-hushed menfolk.

"Nah, you didn't think of that, hey?" He nodded sagely. "As I said, a conjuress and a leech."

The garden at Boar House was as sweet-smelling and fertile as any botanical institute. Either side the lawn was a great spread of Indian Blanket, hundreds of small pink suns tipped with gold. The leafy vines of Morning Glory tendrilled the wooden fence, flowers peeping out like midnight-coloured eyes. Potato ferns filled eight large beds. Peppers and egg plant gave off their grassy, sap-like scent.

While the rest of the panhandle was barren, Boar House garden flourished for two reasons, the first of which was Josephine Splitz's patented sprinkler tripod and underground irrigation system of interlocking copper tubes fed from giant water butts, and the second being that, when it came to dirt and what grew in it, Julie Sanders had the Midas touch.

"Tastes like the blood of summer." Carrie-Anne manipulated what was left of the tomato with her tongue.

"Here." Julie dug a hand through the vines and snapped off another. She offered it. "A fresh sacrifice?"

Carrie-Anne put the fruit to her nose. It smelt of the rich red dirt of her childhood, when the plains of wheat and prairie grass were flowing.

"They're going under again. Virgil and Aunt Josephine, I mean." She kept the tomato under her nose like smelling salts. "I asked them not to since it's Palm Sunday tomorrow. Their absence from church'll be even more marked than usual. Folk are already noticing."

"Then folk should learn to mind their own!" Julie snapped. She stared over at Carrie-Anne and added blankly, "Yeah, I see the glint of disapproval in your eye. A housemaid shouldn't talk so about good white folk as fix their hair and attend the preacher's sermon every Sunday."

Carrie-Anne frowned. "I didn't mean that, Julie." She cupped the tomato in a palm. "You surprised me was all. Most days, you're a ball of hot roast sunshine. It's odd to see you in shadow."

Julie raised her large bovine eyes to the endless blue overhead. "I apologise, Carrie-Anne. Something's hunkered down in the air these last few days, niggling at me. Might just be a woman's flush? Might be the dry heat?" She lowered her gaze to Carrie-Anne, who felt its touch like a mother's hand. "What I do know, chile, is we can't take much more. A storm's needed. Even hail'd be better than this devil's blanket we're under!"

Carrie-Anne popped the tomato into her mouth and chewed. Following Julie to the nearest vegetable bed, she knelt alongside to help shovel dark composted manure around the bean poles and fledgling sunflowers.

"Remember those great rocks of ice that came slamming down in March? The tale of Nancy West's little girl run ragged trying to keep the chicks from being crushed out in the yard. They lost half the poor mites in one storm." She indicated the plants with her trowel. "Don't reckon this crop'd survive either."

Julie sat back on her heels stiffly and used the corner of her apron to dab at her temples. "This crop, no. But we'd start again. Trade what we did have for what we didn't."

Perhaps noticing Carrie-Anne's muddled look, she chuckled all of a sudden. "Chile, I'm playing with you. I don't take one inch of this land for granted, nor the good Lord blessing me with the knowhow to raise crops on it." Julie got a fresh trowel-full of manure and leant in to the plants.

"You know all about the way dirt beds in around Boar House," Carrie-Anne said softly.

"Well, I ain't alone there." Julie kept on working. Sunlight rained over her skin like a downpour of black diamonds.

Carrie-Anne pinched up her eyes. She didn't want to dig inside herself, was afraid to, and instead rocked back on her heels and moved to the neighbouring bed, umbrellaed with the pinnate leaves of the Mississippi peanut. Bending down, she trailed a finger along a leaf coated with blown-in dust. The particles expelled to either side of the leaf at her touch.

"Watch you don't step in grasshopper poison." Julie stood up, supporting her lower spine with her hands as she unfolded. "Mix of molasses, bran and lemons I scattered at nightfall couple of evenings back."

Gazing at the ground, Carrie-Anne noticed wads of vegetable matter distributed between the rows of peanuts. "Say a spell too?" she teased.

Julie tucked a smile into a corner of her mouth. "Carrie-Anne Nightingale. I worry about your soul."

"Well, there is some sort of magic at work in this garden, Julie. Beyond the boundary of this fence, I've seen field peas and tomatoes blighted by the wind, potatoes like coyote dung half-cooked in dry dirt. But here, all is plump and ripe and perfumed. You're a weaver of dreams, Julie." She gestured to the nearest clump of grasshopper poison. "A potions mistress."

Julie snorted. "Gotta keep Miss Splitz in fried okra and cornbread's all. Then there's the extras we trade for canned goods at the store. You know how partial Miss Splitz is to pineapple chunks. She always saves the juice for Wesley. Soft old thing."

Carrie-Anne didn't contradict. Aunt Josephine was as much of a dragon as any giant machine birthed from her workshop. But she did occasionally expose a chink of humanity, such as the stones she brought back for Wesley from below the surface, or her reserving pineapple juice for the boy, eying him as he supped as if she was a kid herself feeding treats to a puppy.

The wizen old prune also had an acid way with words which Virgil thankfully seemed to relish where his predecessors had been burnt.

"My aunt's certainly got her own brand of kindness. I wonder if she always appreciates Virgil's worth though. He's one of the state's top geological surveyors, you know." Carrie-Anne got a shine to her. "He's got the papers to prove it."

"Don't need to persuade me Virgil's worth something, Carrie-Anne. He wrote the letter of recommendation that got Abraham a teaching post at Douglass High in Bricktown, Oklahoma City." Julie picked up the wicker basket she used for cut flowers and fresh vegetables, and deposited her trowel in it. She started back towards the house; Carrie-Anne watched the peculiar twist to her hips as she walked. Julie was arthritic. She was also a polio survivor.

Carrie-Anne followed after.

"I love him, you know!" She blurted out the words, afraid they'd drive tiny hooks into her tongue and stick there.

Julie swung around. In place of shock or elation, she simply jutted her chin as if to say 'that so.' Then she turned heel and started again with that jarring gait.

"Is that it?" Carrie-Anne flushed. She'd built up to the revelation, weighing her options in terms of who to confide in before settling on her old nursemaid who was sure to have grace enough to understand. Why was Julie acting so?

"I don't get it." She ran alongside. "It's not like we're hurting you, or Wesley, or even Aunt Josephine." Julie didn't stop marching and Carrie-Anne was forced into a sideways polka as she spoke. "He's a good man and he's got my heart taped up. No escape for me from this one, Julie. But what's so terrible about me and Virgil Roberts anyway? You know his worth. Said so just now."

Reaching the foot of the porch steps, Julie stopped suddenly, mouth parted as she tugged air into her lungs. "I gotta spell it out for you, chile? Well okay. You mix your environment according to your mood. Move one speck o' dust from this spot to that. Shake it all up any which way you feel."

"I have absolutely no idea what you're talking about!" spat Carrie-Anne. Her chest ached.

A flame was struck in each of Julie's beautiful bovine eyes. "You could cause real damage, chile. I'm just not sure how the dust'll settle on this one."

"Think I'm playing with Virgil, don't you?" Carrie-Anne felt the insinuation bite at her on the inside as if she'd swallowed live termites. "Good Lord, Julie. You raised me!"

"That's not what I meant…"

"Whatever else could you mean except to suggest I'd go all blue-eyed and brainless on Virgil, get him hooked then look for something, for *someone* better. How dare you, Julie! After the kindness my aunt has shown you and your boys. After her treating you like a family member and not the slave that you really are."

Her words were as violent as if she'd lashed Julie round the jaw. Carrie-Anne knew it, felt the poison seeping in as the housemaid she loved like her own flesh and blood got cold in the eyes.

"Yes, mam," said Julie evenly. She turned away and climbed the steps to the porch, where she pulled open the inner gauze on complaining hinges and disappeared inside the house.

Carrie-Anne stood alone in the garden. A light breeze brought in dust from the field which danced about her ankles.

Cicadas droned in the long grass outside the workshop. A moth performed its tortured tarantella around a kerosene lamp hooked on a nail to one side of double doors. The sun had left its heat on the place like a layer of hot grease.

Inside the workshop, nothing moved except the dust motes. Chisels, mallets, pliers, hammers, and wrenches lined the walls like a field surgeon's medical kit. A large scarred workbench held a mechanical arsenal: grimy gears, cami-leathers like stomach linings, chipped china cups full of nails and nuts and bolts, bushels of wire, wirewool, chainlink, hose, valves and fuses. The floorboards were strewn with the lost limbs of iron smoke stacks, greased levers, punctured flotation balloons, sled tracks, even a pair of outsized bellows like an ogre's shoehorn.

Grease and metal filings perfumed the air. All was still but for dust fall.

Virgil had his hand at her throat. Time drew out like a strand of spun sugar. His eyeballs flickered. Blood drove inside his ears.

Slowly, he eased his hips against hers. A welt of heat spread through his groin as she rose up onto tiptoe. Her flesh glistened. He leant in, bruised his lips against her fragile jaw and found the soft wet sacramental hollow of her mouth. It wasn't enough. He wanted to get past the physical, the hindrance of blood and cartilage, skeleton and skin. Raking his hands through her hair, nails digging in at the baby softness of her skull, he meshed his lips against hers until she gasped.

It was her tongue's touch which quietened him, its curl of motion at the sliver of skin connecting his upper lip and gum. He felt tethered, and a new depth of need as she worked his shirt free of his pants and imprinted his spine with her fingertips. His own hands were awkward extractions of flesh; he fumbled with the buttons of her dress as she moulded his shoulder blades under her palms. Sweat soaked in at his shirt collar. Her dress fell away.

He stepped back to gaze at her every niche and curve. Her breasts were white fruit burred with damson-coloured seedheads. The pour of flesh to her hips was slight. A half-moon of tiny brown freckles arched above her belly button. Soft brown down spread out from the cleft between her legs.

Dragging his shirt up and over his head, Virgil bundled it into the hollow of her lower back as she drew him back against her. The sour tang of sweat worked up between them; she dragged her tongue along the underside of his chin like a saltlick.

He drove his head down and she curved her spine, offering each breast to the ebb and flow of his mouth. At the same time, her hands cupped his ears so that he was back in the dark with the iron drone of the Burrower. With one difference. Here above ground, the heat was breaking out of him as much as it was tunnelling in.

She moved her hands away and his lips found her throat again. It was a small bewitchment, a brush of mouth against skin which always made her fold herself into him. He flung his shirt aside. His fingers skimmed the rough warm wood of the workbench and spooned her buttocks which tensed at his touch. She carved at his hipbones, digging her fingernails in ever so slightly at the underside of his belt before dragging them diagonally down in a tingling swipe. His gasp was a thin dry reed of air.

Dixon Goodwin stared down at the patch of ground and clucked his tongue. The pipework he'd exposed was the colour of rust in the moonlight; he guessed it was copper. Nice choice of metal for water transportation, even if it was an expensive material to sink below ground. Of course, the old gal, Jos Splitz, belonged to one of Oklahoma's oldest, richest bloodlines. A few lengths of copper boring wasn't about to see her bare-handed, even when her fellow Okies were sell-their-mother desperate.

So, the secret to Boar House's fertile ground was an

irrigation system? Dixon kept hold of the trowel he'd found in a basket outside the kitchen, twirling the handle between two palms. There hadda be, what, a couple of acres of garden tucked around the house, every bit of it fed by those underground pipes? It was a helluva thing, and not just to afford the raw materials but to engineer and physically locate them. He shook his head like a fly-bothered mare. Jos Splitz was a withered old gourd, but she'd the wherewithal to keep herself afloat while all around were going under.

But who'd got the muscle to install that rig? There was this Virgil character, this brain from outta town. Vampire morelike by the look of him, Dixon snorted to himself. And Boar House had its slaves, though rumour was Jos Splitz behaved like an old witch in her professional capacity, but she was a pussycat in terms of how she ran her household.

Dixon twisted his mouth aside and spat. What good was kindness to the sow or the rooster? Didn't fatten them beasts any faster. Sameways with the black man; kindness only made a slave waste time on smiling. His daddy had taught him that much. Few folk wielded a lash as neatly and as effectively as Dixon Goodwin Senior.

But whether them soft-handled Negroes installed it or the ghost face Virgil, all that was of interest was that Jos Splitz had gotten herself a means to pump water into dirt. Except, where'd the water come from?

The night had stitched itself in around him but there was a weak glow coming off a kerosene lamp over by the workshop. Dixon narrowed his eyes, noticing a ridge of earth running parallel to the brick path. He dragged a forearm over his forehead. He mightn't be worth much to folk in Bromide, but he'd a tendency to work things out.

Walking slowly along the path, his footfall soft, he traced the ridge to the far side of the workshop, where it broke ground to emerge as a series of the rust-coloured pipes. These plumbed into two vast water butts located side by side and interlinked by a vertical winch system hooked up to five large buckets.

Dixon stroked his throat. One thing was for sure. Jos Splitz wasn't feeling the effect of no drought. In fact, she was sucking up the juices of the land while the rest of the state died of thirst.

The question now was what to do with that knowledge.

He walked back around to the front of the workshop. The kerosene lamp gave out jaundiced twilight, and it occurred to him what a curious thing it was to find outside the workshop at that hour. The old gal was hee-hawing in her bed like a sun-baked mule; he'd heard the housemaid remark on it. So, some fool musta lit the thing for the ghosts, or more likely, as a deterrent against starving hobos, of which there were plenty.

One side of the double door's latch wasn't quite caught in its slot. *Careless keepers make for loser-weepers*, Dixon thought acidly.

He was about to secure the door when it occurred to him that a late night check of the grounds, along with the investigation of any mysterious circumstances, might well fall within the duties of a yardman. He gave the door a gentle push and stepped inside.

Great black rafters overhung a room divided into two separate work areas by a mottled, semi-opaque glass sliding screen. Since this 'wall' was at most eight foot, he was able to see the upper section of the vast machine referred to as The Burrower at the far end of the workshop. Moonlight filtered in at high narrow windows, reflecting off the tip of a colossal metal bore like an exploding star.

Dixon tucked his arms in tight to his body. Either side of him were shelves laden with cartons, jars, bottles filled with some milky substance, balls of string, small plump sacks lined up like Humpty Dumpties, and boxes containing preserved weed, bark strips, tubers, cotton bolts, and all manner of weird in-between.

"I'll be damned," he whispered, leaning in to study a jar. He wasn't much for learning but his daddy had insisted on him getting his alphabet licked. "U... S... E. Use. A.T. At..." He spelt out the words phonetically. "M.I.D.N.I.G.H.T... Use at midnight?" Puzzlement wormed up at his brow. The contents looked like something scraped outta pig sty.

Dixon peered closer at the racks of jars. Seeds, burs, dried flowerheads... it hadda be a gardener's store. Carrie-Anne liked to mix dirt, he thought, remembering how her cotton dress had scooped tight across her buttocks as she'd worked her trowel into a flower bed that afternoon. But no, that didn't sit right somehow. Carrie-Anne was too refined to stock that queer larder. What he did suspect was that this corner of the workshop had been given over to the house negress who used it for potions and witchdoctoring.

Coloureds know no betta than to side with the devil. Their womenfolk'll entice ya and ride ya with all kinda words and intoxications. Sap the spirit from your manhood and leave ya outta dry.

His daddy's words played over and over in his head. Dixon felt parched even as sweat glistened at his brow. Placing one foot carefully behind the other, he started to back off from that devil's altar.

It was the small catch of breath which made him pause mid-step. He listened intently. There. A whisper of sound, girlish and sensual. Momentarily he was afraid that the housemaid's brews had attracted some intoxicating spirit come to steer him to sin and feast on his soul. Then he heard a second murmur, a man's baritone that was distinctly human and coming from the other side of the glass screen.

The baking heat crested and broke over him as, through the thick lichened glass of the sliding screen, he made out the outline of their rutting bodies. His nostrils flared. It hadda be the sorceress, squeezing the life from some poor soul between her flanks.

An old parlour chair rested on two legs against the screen. Dixon eased it back down, placed one boot on the seat and tried out his partial weight on it. Reassured the chair would hold him, he stepped up level with the top of the screen and tentatively peered over.

The air was torn from his lungs. In place of black flesh, he saw the bow of a pale breast, the crush and rise of white thighs, and unsoiled nails that cut in at a man's spine, causing him to buckle and thrust harder. As moonshine spilt out into every corner of the workshop, revealing an ocean of dust motes, he saw Virgil Roberts with his pants down and Carrie-Anne Valentine's angelic face twist in grotesque ecstasy.

Sunday April 14, 1935

There'd been many occasions in the past when Carrie-Anne and Julie had exchanged words. When she'd pulled the rags from her hair and worried out the ringlets an hour before Great Aunt Rita's annual visit. Or when she'd cut down a bed of sweet potato fern to use as a posy for her 'marriage' to a five year old Ben Richards. Or when, more recently, she'd scolded Wesley for beating a carpet near the spot of lawn where she was resting. Listening in from the porch, Julie had puffed up like a prize-fighter and stomped on over. "Carrie-Anne Valentine!" she'd embarked with a shake in her voice. But even though Carrie-Anne demanded then cajoled then begged her to continue, Julie seemed to think better of her anger and just take herself back off inside the house. It was a different story yesterday afternoon. Then Julie had decided to stick around and say her piece... although, as it turned out, it was Carrie-Anne who dug up sentiments that should never have been voiced.

Arranging her gloves on her lap and leaning back against the hard pew, Carrie-Anne was haunted by Julie's blank expression when told to remember her place. And it occurred to her that she had seen that look before, on the faces of the field Negroes who toiled and starved and hated their master.

The thought festered. Boxed in on either side by Mrs Lisa Goodwin's plump respectability and old Mrs Johnson's hoary bones, Carrie-Anne felt jostled into a slot that didn't fit.

Somewhere at the back of that dull stone coffin of a chapel, Julie and Wesley were amongst the other coloureds standing because the lord's house didn't see fit to offer them a chair.

"Your aunt is not with you," shot Lisa Goodwin suddenly. Her tone sat the wrong side of polite.

Carrie-Anne watched Preacher Richards lean in to discuss the sheet music with his wife, the organist, and willed him to start his sermon.

Old Mrs Johnson peered over her. "Josephine Splitz? Ain't she dead?"

Lisa Goodwin bundled her arms beneath wasteful breasts. Her eyes betrayed a mind full of nasty. "Word is she's alive but no one's seen hide nor hair of her at chapel for three months. What do you say, Carrie-Anne? Is your aunt still with us?"

Carrie-Anne sensed the weight of her respectable gloves on her lap. Humming lightly, she rocked forward onto her toes and back.

"Is she dumb?" Mrs Johnson squirted sideways, sucking her bottom lip like a teat. "You dumb, girl?"

"Dumb, no. Ignorant maybe." Lisa Goodwin's hot fat fingers branded Carrie-Anne's arm. "Your coltish act don't work with me, girl. Just like your aunt, think you're better than the rest of us. In her case, because she got brains and money. In yours, because you've got beauty and you know how to *spread* it."

A mind full of nasty, thought Carrie-Anne. She kept humming, imagining the tune dispersing through her like sunlight.

There was an undercurrent in the chapel that morning, half-whispers that left a shadow on the glorious day outside. Young men, who usually snatched off their caps and shuffled whenever she walked by, had watched her with a new, hawkish intensity. One even spat on the floor. Everywhere she'd looked, she'd seen the folk of Bromide grouped about the chapel walls like a swarm; they'd stung her a hundred times with their barely disguised distaste.

Let them judge, she decided, stilling herself as the Preacher took to his pulpit. They'd find fresh meat inside the month. What's more, she couldn't help agreeing with them in part. Aunt Jos should've honoured Palm Sunday, should've cared enough about events on the surface to let alone what lay below. But instead, at 6.00am that morning, the Burrower had lowered its nose and descended with a tremendous roar of grit and steam. And she'd been left to drape herself in fresh cotton, put a tea rose behind her ear, meet Julie's stone-faced silence and come alone into the lion's den.

It's a dark spell, Carrie-Anne thought to herself. Virgil's fresh absence so soon after the last, Julie's cold-shouldering, the hungry, bored minds of the townsfolk. *A dark spell. But soon the clouds will pass.*

She fixated on a shaft of sunlight streaming in at the nearest chapel window. Dust whirled in its soft golden element. She could hear the preacher's voice as from a distance, and for a moment she imagined that she was back on the porch again, head resting against the corner strut, listening to the stillness of the plains. Virgil had come to her then… just as he came to her now as a memory of tenderly bruising lips and franticness. She smiled secretly.

"Smears up her mouth even now," hollered a male voice, piercing the illusion so that she refocused to find a sea of eyes turned towards her.

"What's that?" Her voice sounded set adrift.

"Dixon, please." Preacher Richards gripped the lectern, his face lined with irritation. "This sermon is about aiding your fellow man not abusing him. If there is tension in our community, let us resolve it at an appropriate time and without resorting to verbal attacks." After a brief pause, the preacher held his arms out from his sides. "My words are a lesson in scripture. They illustrate that…"

"'Their god is their stomach... their mind is on earthly things.' Ain't that what you read out just now, Preacher

Richards?" Dixon Goodwin rose up out of his seat on the far side of his mother and stared over at Carrie-Anne, an angry crease between his eyes. "Some folk fatten themselves like hogs while the rest don't have a bean."

"Need I remind you this is a house of God, Dixon, not a two buck brawl pit?" said Preacher Richards in the deep voice he reserved for children who couldn't sit still in the pews. There was a waver in his tone though. Anger at the interruption or something else? Something like fear he could not control his flock?

Carrie-Anne wanted to start humming her song again. She wiped her gloves between her palms. Heat pawed at her.

"You better sit your backside down, son," said Lisa Goodwin quietly. Carrie-Anne detected a trace of indifference, pride even. *Yes, I have raised my son well. He takes a stand when no other will. He is the rock all others hide behind.*

"Sure, Momma. Just as soon as I get the measure of what Preacher's teaching. 'Their god is their stomach?' Well, I'm here to tell ya there's one home near Bromide where that sure does apply. Boar House. Seen it with my own eyes. I work there as a yard man…"

Not anymore. Carrie-Anne dabbed the moist hollow of her throat with the gloves. Not content to pour his eyes over her – oh yes, she'd felt their weight, familiar, uncomfortable, and a sensation she'd laboured under before several years ago – it appeared that Dixon wanted to invent some hocus-pocus about those she held dear.

Go on then, she urged. *Expose the darkness in the hearts of Boar House's occupants. Tell these good folk all the horrors you have witnessed.*

"Take a seat or leave, Dixon." Preacher Richards was flushed. His son, Ben, got to his feet at the fore of the congregation – Carrie-Anne marvelled at the height of him and thought again of the potato fern posy she'd picked as a child. Had time ebbed so quickly that Ben Richards was now built like a quarterback while a squirt of a kid could evolve into a creep like

Dixon Goodwin?

"All I'm saying is there's a reason why they're growing crops while the rest of us are struggling to harvest soap weed. More than that, ain't we preaching abstinence from earthy things?" Dixon jabbed two fingers at his eyes. "Out there, I seen filth. I seen fornication. I seen witchcraft."

A few folk gasped audibly. Carrie-Anne felt a squeezing tight up inside. She resisted twisting about in her seat and staring at the back of the chapel; best thing she could do in that moment was sit soldier-straight and offer no emotion.

"Witchcraft?" Preacher Richards's eyes appeared to supplicate his wife from her seat in the organ pew. Whatever he saw there must have reassured his indignation because he rose up out of the girdle of his hips and asserted, "A vicious accusation, Dixon, and not one that we abide inside the lord's house. I repeat, I must ask you to leave. Mr and Mrs Goodwin…"

The preacher would not win over Lisa and Dixon Senior. They rose to stand alongside their son, oozing superiority and righteousness.

"Preacher, my son's got news about Josephine Splitz and her kin which is of interest to this congregation," said Dixon Goodwin Senior, a barrel-bellied man with a circlet of white hair and the same bristled baby face as his son. He planted his hands on his hips and revolved at the waist. "So I ask ya, folks. If my boy says what he's got to tell ya is in keeping with the preacher's sermon, shouldn't the rest of us rightly hear it?"

"This is not the time or place to discuss disputes between individuals," embarked Preacher Richards. He was immediately shot down.

"…Ain't no matter between individuals. This is town talk." Dixon Senior thrust a finger towards the back of the chapel. "This is about one of 'em negresses and her pantry of potions in Jos Splitz's workshop!"

There was a second expulsion of air from listeners' lips. Ugly words were spoken under breath.

Dixon Senior rubbed a hand around his bald spot. "You seen it, ain't you, son? And that ain't all he seen? Tell 'em about the giant maggot, a burrowing machine that sucks up all the water."

Was she labouring under a brain-fever or were folk speaking in tongues? Carrie-Anne glanced back at Julie; the woman had the look of a startled jack rabbit and was working hard to push Wesley away. Carrie-Anne recognised why; when coloured folk were accused of something, only way to protect those they loved was by disassociation. Wesley didn't get a bit of it though and kept wriggling his head up under his mother's arm, all the while nervously flashing that broad smile of his as if he'd found it got him fuss before and he figured it might work now.

Carrie-Anne stood, her upper body bathed in the rich sunlight so that she was forced to squint against its brilliance. She tried to speak. Her throat clamped around her vocal cords.

"I am in no way a scientist, Mr and Mrs Goodwin, Dixon." She nodded at each. "But it is my understanding that my aunt and her assistant, Mister Virgil Roberts, have been excavating below ground in a bid to find water and to understand what it is about the land beneath our feet which has left us in such dire straits."

"Except, you ain't in dire straights, are you, Miss Valentine? Not only have you water to feed the soil where you wanna, but a sorceress to raise them crops up with spilt rooster blood, devil's weeds and every other kinda wickedness. 'Use at midnight.' That's what I read, Miss Valentine. Written stark clear on a label it was. Use at the devil's hour!"

Dixon's expression was seven ways of wrong. And he wasn't alone. More voices were cutting in.

"What a slave doin' with her own store while we're left to scrape around for seed and other provisions?"

"Always said Jos Splitz was lead-lined."

"Heart of stone, that one."

"Except when it comes to coloureds. Then she's soft as marshmallow."

"Coloureds with the know-how to mix magic? That's a straight up sin. Ain't no defending that."

The eyes moved from Carrie-Anne to Julie. There was fragility in the air. One audible breath and the line between peace and pandemonium would be muddied.

"Exodus 22:18. Thou shall not suffer a witch to live," said Lisa Goodwin, soft as the wind.

Carrie-Anne felt as if she was suffocating. So much white flesh crushed in around her like pulped pages from a bible.

"Enough with your accusations!" she spat. Her heart pulsed violently. Forcing her way past old Mrs Johnson, who shrunk into her desiccated bones, Carrie-Anne strode to the back of the chapel. Twice, a figure stepped into her way. Twice a voice told them to let her be. Through the smear of angry human shapes, she made out Samuel O'Ryan and George West. Good, honest men in a town awash with hokum.

She found Julie, fear and unshakeable knowledge etched into the lines of her face. Wesley was a phantom limb at his mother's hip, arms encircling her.

Carrie-Anne reached out. The air inside the chapel turned shroud grey; she parted it with her hands like scissors slipping through silk. When her fingertips made contact with Julie's wrist, she felt the housemaid shiver in spite of the tumbling waves of heat.

"Let's go home, Julie."

Out the corner of an eye, she saw a figure lurch from the back pew in a jilting motion. Cold dread poured down the inside of her ribs. She would not meet that vile stare. She would gather up Julie and Wesley to her side and she would walk with them out of chapel that day and deliver them safely home.

"Know what else I saw?" continued Dixon, a serpent at her back. "Last night, I was checking the grounds as is my employment when I find the workshop unlocked. Lotta fancy engine gear in that shack. This day and age, lotta folk in need of stealing such. So I slip inside. And I hear this ruckus. Any idea what I'm talking about, Miss Valentine?"

Eyes swirled towards her from every angle. The sun went in.

As Dixon went on with his sordid description, Carrie-Anne sensed the young men of Bromide wipe her from their palms like chaff. In a barren town, she had been the one sweet-smelling flower they could admire and dream of owning. Except now she was gone over. Another clean thing corrupted.

Their agitation was immediate. No insult was spared inside those hallowed walls. She was Jezebel, Salome, the Babylonian whore, and every other breed of temptress. But their anger was good. Anything to deflect attention from Julie.

Carrie-Anne made her way to the chapel door, Julie's blistering handhold in hers, Wesley bundled into Julie's folds... Only to find the exit was guarded by its own gargoyle of hunched flesh and mangled bone.

"About time the witches of Boar House paid their dues," said Reg Wilhoit. His voice was a tar scrape, thickened over time. Hands that used to twist up inside her blouse and maul at her unformed breasts were pressing into and over one another, moulding the situation into his preferred shape.

"Move aside, Reg." She concentrated her revulsion, taking strength from it.

"Time to pay, little lady." A foul whisper. A forward shuffle on crumpled limbs.

"Stand away from the door." Her eyesight blurred as a great hollow wind seemed to drag itself up beneath the underside of the chapel door and shriek past her ears. *The sky is darkening,* she thought, *where I dreamt only of light.* Far below the surface, her aunt and Virgil were crushing through the sand and rock in an effort to find fresh reserves of water, in an effort to save the lives of these nasty, vicious souls who would dig them out like louse and burn them for trying. *Keep them below*, she implored the subterranean world under their feet.

Reg teetered. He kept his sneer stitched in place.

Beneath her fingertips, in the creases of her palms, at the tender flesh of her lips, the baking air reverberated. Dust drifted out the corners and alcoves where it slept, leaving a soft grey charge in the atmosphere. Heat surged in at every chink in the chapel walls, gushing and churning and soaring all around her. Sweat bled from Carrie-Anne's temples, and the dust, so much dust, roared like the battle cry of an archangel.

The latch snapped up on the chapel door suddenly. Someone pushed it open and Reg was elbowed aside in a rush of zigzagging steps.

A young man's face appeared, cherry-toned by the midday heat.

"Preacher Richards!"

Carrie-Anne heard the preacher's sombre acknowledgement, and through her black rage, the man's hesitant explanation.

"Preacher, I hate to interrupt service but my daddy says I gotta tell ya there's a dust cloud growing out to north and it's a fierce un. Bigger than anything my daddy ever seen. Folk might need to get off home now, tie down what they need, forget what they don't. There's a helluva storm coming."

"Drag on that soot mixer, Virgil Roberts!" came the shout from up front of the Burrower. "You feel it, you Mary-Anne? We've gone and hit wet sand."

Scooping his fingers around a small leather loop that hung alongside the larger one linked to the air duct, Virgil hauled down on it. As he did so, he tucked his head into his right shoulder and tried to peer past Jos's front seat. The view was limited, but he got an idea that the soot mix was piping through the gills either side of the main hub thanks to the black spray coating the viewing pane.

"Lights… Hit the lights! Christ, man, if you ain't gonna cease daydreaming over Carrie-Anne, I'm gonna pack her off to Michigan. She's got a bitch of an Aunt Rita out there. Nibbling little ferret who'd have Carrie-Anne married off to some rich bilious bastard quick smart, I can tell ya."

Virgil paid Jos no mind. He felt to the left of his chair for a triangular brass panel containing one squat flip-switch. It was an awkward location for a seemingly essential mechanism, except, as Jos has instilled in him a thousand times over when he had first started working for her, what real need was there for light when the bore that went before them was as blind as a mole. Best to feel their way through the earth's materials, acclimatise themselves to the rat-tat-tat of sand, the plug and crack of rock, the lumber through shale-sounding gravel. But, on occasion, even Jos's curiosity could not be contained, and that's when she called for him to fumble for the switch and flood their murky world with light.

A blaze of illumination accompanied his tug on the switch. Virgil blinked wildly against its burn.

Jos, on the other hand, seemed insusceptible to alterations in light and dark. Yet clearly she benefitted from the refreshed view.

"There. Sand, And wet sand too. How's the tunnel bearing up?"

Virgil revolved a polished wooden handle to crank the drive shaft that ran up the back of Jos's seat. The whir of clockwork was just audible over the grind and sluice of the Burrower in motion. Lanterns affixed to the roof of the cabin as well as a number of spots integrated into the corrugated iron floor flickered then strengthened. Virgil stared at a rack of dials above his head. Indigo and ruby glass shields protected fine spindles which twitched or held firm.

"Whiskers say we're okay for now," he stated in the loud clear voice Jos had beaten out of him. "A little fallout to the right of that rock gorge few moments back."

"Then we're gonna haul anchor and get ourselves a sample of that pretty wet stuff, my boy." Jos half-leant back, her vinegar features squeezed up in an attempt to express happiness.

It was Jos's job to steer the Burrower, as it was to dig the twin steel sleds at the undercarriage into whatever matter lay beneath in an effort to slow then cease their motion. Virgil watched her leathered hands punch, skip and tug their way around switches, wheels, plungers, knobs, gears and levers, and the rest of the coke-dusted motorisation bank.

"Keep an eye on those whiskers."

Jos eased off on the steam release and drew the Burrower to a juddering halt.

The engine wheezed noisily then idled. A faint sensation of crushing in threatened to overwhelm Virgil. He pushed that to the back of his mind. It was just his imagination... or an innate knowledge of how preternatural the circumstances were that had brought him below ground. Somehow it was more eerie to be at a standstill in that freshly-cut tunnel, the illumination from the floodlights spilling either side of the colossal bore. All that lay ahead and behind was tight-aired darkness, hence the detection of any faults in the tunnel walls being left to a backend full of softly sprung copper spines, or 'whiskers' as Jos was prone to call them. If matter sifted down too heavily, the weight of it would trigger a kick-back action in the spine, and, with it, a clockwise shift of the farthermost dial in the rack above his head.

All was still for now.

"Dig your little horn into the belly of this beast, Jos," he said softly, doing a mental check of the fill level of the coke channel to his right.

Jos worked a small fly wheel in the ceiling 45 degrees right. There was the slightest rocking motion as the sample needle took its two foot worth of rock sample then withdrew. Jos rewound the lever in the opposite direction.

"Wet sand… No time to shake hands on it now, Virgil Roberts," she tossed over a shoulder, and in a tone which implied he had attempted to. "We're only a couple of lengths below the surface. Best get you back to that strawberry of a niece of mine. You sure do seem to like the taste of her." The old gal snorted, like a smaller version of her vast grunting machines. "Lets shake free of this sand and haul on up."

It was difficult not to wipe his glad, tired eyes, not to pat the whorled dragon on her shoulder and say, 'Well done, Jos. Well done you wise old dear', not to dream of ice chips pressed to Carrie-Anne's lips, her jugular, her glistening sternum, not to just sit and sigh and sleep.

Instead, Virgil dove the scoop hard through the coke, ripped open the iron flap in the wall and shook off the fuel, feeling his skin flush and hurt with the heat. The engine bubbled under, then roared in its gullet as Jos manoeuvred the twin steel tracks free of their footings and the tremendous hammer of a machine thrust forward and up.

"Tell you one thing, Virgil. That water gotta come from someplace. Don't know if you been over the way of the old Indian Academy recently?" Jos made a sound like spit had caught up in her throat and spun there. "Now there's some suffering. I've been hiking up there with a backseat of beet and sweet potato and the rest whenever I get a minute. 'Cept what do you do? Help the few or try to fix the root problem? That's what we're aiming at, ain't we, Virgil, boy? Let's hope we gotta a break through, hey?"

Jos Splitz. A devil of a woman on her dried up exterior. A polished silver heart on the inside. Virgil broke out a smile.

It was such a small, simple instance of happiness – snatched away the very next second. A noise, like the scream of a great wind buffeting a hide of metal scales. The Burrower shuddered and the whole cabin seemed to tear forwards an inch then sling back several feet. Virgil heard the wind cut from Jos's throat; the old gal caught it badly, sucking and choking to guzzle down air.

"You alright, Jos. You alright, girl?"

What the hell had they hit? A sheet of bedrock? Wasn't possible at that angle. He'd surveyed that stretch of land like a mother knowing every inch of her baby's skin. Wouldn't do to risk that nosecone on a more difficult stretch. Something was hard up against them though.

"Jos? You gonna answer me there?"

Unclipping his harness, Virgil manhandled himself up to lean a short way over the front seat. Jos's head lolled towards him as he dug a hand into the metal boning of her chair, eyes closed so that she looked like a husk of a woman whose clockwork had just run out.

No chance to move her. Never was. The notion of a stalemate underground was something they'd both signed up to. He had no choice then but to attempt to work the motorisation bank by stretching his limbs at grotesque angles. The pain cut at his mind like a lash, but he succeeded in engaging the gears and driving the Burrower hard forward. At impact, his ribs jolted against the driveshaft that fed the lights, plunging the cabin into darkness.

Virgil gulped down the baking air and tried to calm himself. He'd promised Carrie-Anne they'd surface by midday, that she would have her afternoon of shared breath underneath a ripe gold sun. If Jos would just wake up. If the Burrower could just work its way home.

His stomach crunched around a sickening mess of feelings. The pitch black thrummed.

I ain't never seen a glimpse of Hell on Earth like it. Rolling in it was, from the direction of the old Indian academy out north, a great black cloud, thick as flies swarming. How far it stretched I ain't sure, but miles it was. A mouth that yawned back on its jaw and scooped in everything in sight. And the scream, like demons loose upon the land.

"We've got to get back," Miss Carrie-Anne said. "Let's go now, while they've no time to intervene." And she steered me outta the chapel and into Mister Roberts' automobile. Plopping Wesley on my knee, she got that engine whipped up and we were back out on the road in no time, the darkness snapping at our heels.

"It's a good thing Miss Josephine and Mister Roberts planned a short trip. They'll be back up top now. Sat on the porch worrying themselves sick I shouldn't wonder, and who can blame them. Dust cloud like that on the horizon…"

I kept on yapping like a screech owl because Carrie-Anne, she got that soulless look like I'd seen whenever her strangeness came over her, alongside which, the talking helped trample down the fear that burned inside 'a me like a brand. Wasn't the way of things for a coloured woman to be accused of devilling and not end up as some sorta strange fruit hanging offa tree. Not that that stopped a man from attacking a person any way he found how if he got a mind to.

My thoughts were softened by the sense that Wesley'd got a fever to him. I felt his shakes above the jitterbug of the engine and turned my chatter to a lullaby. That soothed them both, Wesley going soft as a raggedy-anne and aslumber while Carrie-Anne took up her own hum of a song.

She stopped though. Her face turned to mine.

"I'm sorry, Julie. Seems I don't get far into a day anymore without stirring up pain in one person or another."

I saw tears fall like longed-for rain, and I noticed the way the silvered dust in the air danced about her head like a halo.

"Hush, chile. Ain't no bother."

"I made the dirt keep the Burrower below," she exclaimed, wild about the eye. "I wanted to keep them safe." She glanced deliberately at the rear-view mirror, and I went the way of her eyes to see for myself the great stain on the summer sky.

"What if I can't get it to let them go?" she sobbed.

There'd always been peculiar ways to the girl. Ever since she was a child, I'd seen how the light would get supped up then spill out from her with one glance. How the lay of dust would alter when she tried to sink her duster in amongst it. How the dirt would mix its own swirls when she skipped by. But what of it? I'd got nothin' to teach the girl about the Lord's good brown earth in that way. Raising crops, I knew a good fix or two, since taking care of Boar House garden was kinda like it was my own bit of freedom. Might never be more than a maid in the kitchen, but when I grew them crops, it seemed as if I was master at last.

But Carrie-Anne, perhaps them folks weren't broad of it. She had a way for rearranging the flow of things. I'd witnessed as much the day I saw Reg Wilhoit lay his hands on her ten year old bones, all up over her he was, and I wanted to make some commotion but didn't know the best way how. It was then that the earth shifted, and that great iron crane swooped down on Reg and crushed the juice from his limbs.

Yes indeed, Carrie-Anne Valentine had a gift. But no matter what folk'd said in chapel, there weren't no spells or hocus-pocus. If there hadda been, I might'a known how to ease her now and bring back the sun.

Somehow the girl managed to steer us home. As the motor cut, I scooped Wesley up into my arms and put a shoulder to the door. The wind was awful strong now and battering at the long-dead prairie. Birds tried to fly ahead of it; the pull of that great black mouth was too strong. I hadn't got the wings to take flight, but Boar House would do for me and mine like a wall of stone.

"Gotta get inside now, Miss Carrie-Anne."

The girl, though, was rooted, hand on the open driver door, her stare taking in the empty porch.

"Why haven't they surfaced by now? The danger's passed. They should be surfaced."

The words seemed to bite into her flesh, and she was gone suddenly, striding out towards the field.

"Miss Carrie-Anne! Miss Carrie-Anne!"

The dust was too thick to see past my own hand. A mighty cold swept in. Wesley was a tugging piglet at my neck and shivering so. With backwards glances, I fought my way up the steps to the porch, burst in past the gauze, got a grip on the front door and shut the howling out.

It was the blinding mercury where the sun's glow hit the nosecone which drew Ben Richards to gather up a few of Bromide's best men and take them out into the field. For the breadth of an afternoon, the men toiled against the welts of the dust dunes. Long into the amber eye of the evening, they worked to expose the Burrower's cockpit. It took the quarry worker, Samuel O'Ryan, twenty minutes more to put a crack in the toughened glass hub.

When they'd laid the bodies of Virgil Roberts and Jos Splitz on the ground, those men found space in their lives to stand and stare a moment, and wonder who else among them would have travelled far below the ground in that steaming dragon. Some wondered if the two dead had indeed tunnelled in search of life-giving water. A few feared a modicum of truth in Dixon's tale of draining the land. One wondered if the field of bore holes had contributed to the death of Oklahoma's farming land, its seas of dust. Ben Richard, whose face was etched with the rawness of the storm like a charcoal map. Across the field and the churned garden, he saw Miss Splitz's housemaid and her boy stood still as waxworks at the carnival and just watching.

He strode on over.

Shreds of Indian Blanket flowers carpeted the porch steps, which creaked a little as he climbed as if weary.

"Julie Sanders?"

Keeping her hand on her boy's shoulder, the negress turned her face towards him. She was a living well of emotion. Fear and loss flowed and ebbed across her face.

She struggled to keep the boy back but he broke away.

"Yu need take these back, Sir?" The kid held out a palm with five small pebbles in it. "Miss Splitz. She found them underground."

Ben squinted down. "Nah, boy. Keep 'em."

He dipped his head and peered over at the housemaid.

"Ain't no sign of Carrie-Anne, but we'll keep on looking."

"I reckon she's gone, Mister Richards. Back to the dirt

from which she came."

"Well, we can hope she didn't suffer." Ben tucked back the bob of pain in his throat. "Meantime, my daddy says how's about you and Wesley settle yourselves with us for a while. You can always come right on back at the first sign of Carrie-Anne."

The housemaid tucked her son back in under her arm. "Yes, Sir. We'll pack a few things and say our farewell to Boar House. But first, if it's okay with you, I'll just watch a while longer."

"'Course, Julie. Take your time."

The Preacher's boy strode off down the porch steps and through the tangled remains of the garden. Dust lay over everything as if the garden and house had been asleep for a thousand years. There was no bird song, no evening insect chorus. Only the distant voices of the men and the emptiness of the clean-swept plains.

Author's Acknowledgements

For every circus there must exist a ringmaster, someone to shape the weird and colourful chaos of acts into a plausible show. For me, that person is my husband, Del Lakin-Smith. Words of thanks can never begin to repay his unconditional love and support. Oh no, for that Jack Daniels is required!

A special mention must also go to our very own wolf girl, Scarlet. Thank you for staying untamed and reminding me that imagination should not be subject to rules or caged – a message my mother, Carolyne Lakin, would surely have approved of.

Another force of nature is my publisher, editor and very dear friend, Ian Whates. With Ian at the helm, Newcon Press has taken genre publishing to new and glittering heights and I am delighted to be on board.

I must also pay tribute to geologist, mechanic, self-survival expert and all round good guy, Marc Williams, whose studio reengineering helped root Cyber Circus in reality.

Talking of the real world, I am indebted to a spectacular troupe of writer colleagues and friends: Sam Moffat, Paul Skevington, Helen Sansum, Cath Hancox, Donna Scott, Neil Bond, Natalie Wooding, Alex and Emma Davis, Brian Marshall, Mark Dakin, and Ian Watson. Likewise, thank you to Tamsin Baxter and the rest of the clan – Nick Lakin, Dave Lakin, Grace Lakin, Jasmine Lakin, Carl Baxter and Nyall Baxter - for your care, concern, bolstering, and always being there.

A final circuit of the ring in honour of my father, Nev Lakin, to whom this book is dedicated. Thank you for nurturing my appreciation of the natural world and for teaching me how barren life would be if it all turned to dust.

About Kim

I still live in the family home I was born in. Ivy House has always been one of those piles of bricks and mortar with its own personality. As a child, I was terrified of its numerous dark corners, creaking floorboards, rattling pipes, spiders the size of dinner plates (only a small exaggeration) and lights that flickered. Without realising it, I was busy building my first stories of monsters out to get me, ghostly apparitions and other bloody ghouls. As a partially deaf child, I found my imagination more of a curse than a blessing and spent many a sleepless night peering out from under the bedcovers.

My fascination with the shadow world extended to my love of theatre and dance. Following in the footsteps of my grandmother, Doreen Roberts, a former ballerina, I filled my spare time with dance lessons. When not en pointe, I was at the Burton School of Speech and Drama taking part in lessons, productions, competitions and exams. Real school was somewhere I couldn't get out of quick enough, but on stage I felt free.

True freedom came when, at age 16, my hearing magically resolved itself. At the same time, I found a new place to dance – the nightclub. It's fair to say I went off the rails for a good while, and I'm not sure I ever got back on.

1990 was marred by the Gulf War and lousy fashion. Having failed my A levels in spectacular fashion, I travelled to Accra, Ghana, and took up a post as a teacher's assistant at the Ghana International School. My visit was not the romantic gap year presented in glossy brochures. Alongside the beauty of the country and its people, I was introduced to the harsher side of life, to poverty, self-survival and racism.

On my return, I decided to make the most of the

opportunities I had been blessed with. I signed up at Stafford Collage for two years and did a 360 on my previous A'level results. Having studied English Literature, Theatre Studies and Stage Design, I found a new passion in the form of playwriting. In 1993 I enrolled at the University of Glamorgan on their Combined Studies course. Why 'Combined Studies' sounded better to me than 'Humanities' is lost to history. I do know that my time at Glamorgan was transformative work-wise and on a personal level. I loved everything about South Wales from its connections to my welsh granddad to its glorious summers to slate grey rooftops slick with rain to the misty fairyland of the valleys. My studies took in America's Wild West, Jazz, Religion, Media Studies, Theatre, Gothic Literature, Women Writers, and a new, major influence – Transgression and Sexuality.

Just as I was discovering the wonders of academia, real life came crashing down about my ears. My mother was diagnosed with advanced bowel cancer. Inside the year, she had passed away, as had my grandmother. It was a bleak period and I threw myself into my degree, rejecting the more emotional creative writing for academic study. For two years I immersed myself in feminist theory and the study of anything I found challenging and wanted to understand – pornography, S&M, transvestism, transgender and sexuality, subjects which developed in me a passion for otherness and a deep-rooted desire to promote understanding.

All the same, a year into my PhD, something didn't feel quite right. I missed using my imagination and applied for and was awarded a scholarship to study for an MA in Writing at Nottingham Trent University. While ecstatic to write fiction again, I felt a sense of loss for my academic studies and the time I had spent as a lecturer at Glamorgan.

Set loose in a fiction writing environment again, I had a bloody good time meeting likeminded folk and trying to write in a structured, plot-driven format. Award-winning author and lecturer, Graham Joyce introduced me to the graft behind the craft of writing. He also enjoyed calling me a procrastinator – a red rag to a bull – and pushing me as damned hard as he could to take writing seriously.

Things clicked when I met my husband, Del. Not only did Del encourage me to take up writing fulltime, but he also introduced me to Nottingham's Rock City, a world where I finally felt at home. Rock music had always been part of my life but I had never shared in the vibrancy and dark brilliance of the alternative scene. Celebrating difference, freakishness and absurdity, the tribes of goths, emos, rockabillies, punks and skaters sparked my imagination like never before. When I became pregnant with our daughter, Scarlet, Del and I moved into Ivy House, located a good distance from Nottingham. But the legacy of the city's alternative underbelly stayed with me. The result was my first novel, *Tourniquet*, an ode to the tribal mentality of the alternative scene and what it means to belong. I had no concept of fitting into 'Fantasy' or 'Horror' or 'Science Fiction' at the time. I just wrote the story I wanted to tell.

May 2006, Del suggested we attend a local writers' event, the very first Alt Fiction. He was keen to hear Richard Morgan's reading and I desperately wanted to meet Storm Constantine. Not only did we share a love for the alternative music scene but I was a great admirer of Storm's short fiction magazine, *Visionary Tongue*. Trembling with nerves, I approached Storm in between readings and was over the moon when she asked Del and me to join her for a drink. Within two weeks, Storm had read the manuscript for *Tourniquet* and wanted to publish it. I couldn't have imagined a more perfect home for *Tourniquet* than Immanion Press. Likewise I had no idea that our daytrip to Alt Fiction would see us join the genre convention circuit and meet so many wonderful, talented and colourful new friends.

One of these precious encounters was with Ian Whates at Fantasycon 2006. I don't know at what stage in the evening Ian and I started chatting, but we've been chatting ever since. Those who've seen Ian's home library could attest to the fact that if anyone could juggle a successful writing career with running a genre publishing house in the form of Newcon Press, it was Ian. I was delighted when Ian accepted my short stories 'Heart Song' for Newcon's anthology of women writers, *Myth-Understandings*, and 'The Killing Fields' for *Celebration*, celebrating 50 years of the British Science Fiction Society. I also enjoyed working with Ian on the BSFA's Matrix magazine before home and work commitments meant I had to step down.

Something that came to the fore around this time was my reoccurring desire to ground stories in science and mechanics. An interest in steampunk led me to explore gaspunk in my 2009 BSFA nominated short story 'Johnny and Emmie-Lou Get Married' (*Interzone #222*). New influences filtered through into my writing – a love of cars, machinery, and action scenes from films like *Mad Max, Pitch Black, Fast and the Furious,* etc – alongside a fascination with the notion of the lone warrior in a post-apocalyptic setting. These themes dominated my YA novel, *Autodrome*, the novella, 'Queen Rat' (from Echelon Press's forthcoming *Her Majesty's Royal Conveyance* anthology) and my short story, 'The Harvest' in *Further Conflicts* (Newcon Press, 2011). This is not to suggest I completely bypassed my gothic inclinations. 'Unearthed' and 'The Shadow Keeper' (*Black Static #12* and *#13*) were both very much in the traditional horror vein, with my latest short story 'Field of the Dead' appearing in *The Mammoth Book of Ghost Stories by Women*, (Robinson Publishing, released October 2012.)

This crossover between SF and dark fantasy was never more evident than in my new book, *Cyber Circus*. Originally conceived of as a twin novella to my short story, 'Black Sunday', *Cyber Circus* grew into a novel in its own right. The world of Sore Earth and the weird circus within it drew on all of my favourite inspirations – dystopian landscapes, lone warriors, theatre, fight scenes, cyborgs, and the many glorious shades of otherness. Looking at the story now, it is not so hard to see how Desirious Nim and her burlesque act developed from my love of dancing as a child. Or how Hellequin's biomorph implant is just a logical extension of the hearing aid I suffered wearing in childhood – and was fortunate enough to discard in adulthood. Lulu's gender lawlessness, cross-species love affairs, violation of sexual boundaries, piercings and tattoos – every piece of the story has evolved from a piece of me. Slice me open and you'll find a seam for every tribe: geek girl, gearhead, hippy chick, SF nerd, environmentalist, other.

In the future, I hope to return to the worlds of Sore Earth and Renegade City. After all, a writer is only ever as good as his or her next book. Sitting at my desk in Ivy House, I'm still conscious of the flickering lights and creaking floorboards. The difference is the same darkness I once feared now fuels the strange little stories I write.

Bonus Story

Hellequin's Arrival

Telling of the HawkEye's first encounter with Cyber Circus

HELLEQUIN'S ARRIVAL

The sun razored down. Hellequin wriggled free of his backpack, easing it to the ground and taking out his water flask. He was sorry to drain the last dregs; life on the road meant never knowing when he'd stumble across the next water source. Within seconds, he was thirsty again.

He stowed the empty flask and slung the pack back up on his shoulders. If the vermin exterminator he'd encountered earlier was to be trusted, he'd another half a day's travel before he reached a township. Hellequin became aware of a dulled sense of dread. Dread of the wretched thirst he'd experienced all too often when he and his squad had drunk their canteens dry. Dread that he'd find water and have to keep living his half-life of vibrant vision and muddied emotions.

He trudged on. The sky was the same soft blue as the tiny prayer beads common to the Sirinese. Brushland stretched either side of the dirt track, undulating like sand dunes. He was surprised by a lack of dustpaddlers – lizards the size of a man's hand with hoary skin and large webbed toes. They were common enough to have provided him with a sparse meal over recent nights; he roasted them whole in the ash of a bind root fire. But he saw no sign of them today, or the wrinklenecks that had accompanied him across the miles in anticipation of fresh carrion. Instead, Hellequin had an impression of being utterly alone and he was grateful for the fact. His emotions were stunted to such a degree that it was possible for him to empty his mind and wait for madness or death, whichever claimed him first.

Time slipped away. The track grew steeper. As the sun dipped low, the first wisps of purplish dusk crept across the sky.

A speck of red appeared at the crest of a hill a mile or so ahead. Hellequin's steel eye whirred in rapid rotation, zooming in on an envelope of bright red paper aloft in a windless sky.

He put his hands on his emaciated hips and watched the lantern pass overhead. Others followed in its wake. Soon the sky was peppered with glowing red lanterns, as if they were some primitive attempt to replace the sun.

Thirst gnawed at his throat like a parasite. Hellequin dismissed the phenomena and was about to press on when he heard the first strains of music. For an instant, he wondered if the madness was beginning to settle in; the notion of music in that wasteland seemed nonsensical. He walked towards it and, yes, there it was again, mechanical notes drifting in across the distance.

His first thought was water. As much as he had enjoyed his lonely hours on the road, he was engineered towards self-preservation – added to which, he caught the seductive whiff of roasting meat and syrup soda in the air.

He quickened his stride. Soon the slope levelled out to become a desolate plain of quartz rock. Esparto grass grew in clumps. Red harvester ants navigated the path at his feet. Hellequin saw these details in rapid bursts of magnification. But it was the giant circus tent which focused his attention.

The canvas had a sun-bleached, dilapidated look. The shabbiness of the exterior was in contrast to the streams of colourful lights suspended between the two posts of the striped roof. A large flap was hooked back in the side of the tent. Music exuded from within. Recognising the mechanical cadence from visits to touring fairs in his childhood, Hellequin had visions of steaming pipes, fluting pipes, bellows and automated clashing cymbals.

He felt in a pocket of his faded blue frockcoat and found a fistful of coins. Enough to buy a hunk of the roasted meat. Maybe in place of the syrup soda, he could persuade one of the circus workers to fill his water flask. It also occurred to him that he'd like to rest up nearby. The atmosphere was oddly comforting, a reminder of more innocent times perhaps, or could it be that he simply liked how the coloured lights played across his Hawkeye lens?

Not that he could just stroll up to the tent with his biomorph implant on display. Hellequin cupped a palm over the unnatural eye and suffered sparks attacking his skin until it got too uncomfortable. He took his hand away and grimaced.

While he'd been willing to startle the lone exterminator on the road earlier, he drew the line at revealing too much to the families making their way inside the tent. The blue frockcoat he wore could be any old soldier's uniform; this far east, the Hawkeye were less mortal man than myth. But his steel eye was not so easily ignored.

Removing the scarf which served as a neckerchief to guard against the savage sun, he held it across his left eye and tied it around the back of his head. Time to play the wounded soldier again.

He approached the tent and the music lit him up on the inside like some secret incantation. He could not have tasted the notes more clearly in the air if he'd inhaled a pinch of Dazzle Dust. The metallic flow seeped inside and seemed to bolster him. He felt inexplicably linked to its source. Something excited the amalgam of flesh, bone and clockwork tucked into his brain folds, something that whispered, "We are alike. We are biomorphia."

Shaking himself awake, he put the sensation down to being blind in that now essential eye. It confused his balance to have the Hawkeye implant out of action, more so since the mechanism refused to settle and kept attempting to readjust. The music combined with the noise of the crowd drowned out its tinny whirring.

Hellequin joined the throng of dust handlers, exterminators and mine workers. Children ran about the place like roo rats. In his wounded soldier guise, he attracted reverential nods from the hoards. He knew those same munificent looks would turn to dumbstruck wonder if he removed the scarf from around his head. Reputed to have been instrumental in bringing about the end of the civil war, the Hawkeye regiment were seen as selfless men who gave up their natural sight and sanity to save Sour Earth. As the one individual who'd endured the implant procedure as punishment, Hellequin was less comfortable with hero-worship.

He hunched in an effort to disguise his unusual height and approached the food stall. An iron spit threaded with skinned roo rats was suspended over a low burning fire pit. The carcasses were a glorious nut brown.

"Whole rat, please."

A carnie worker tore one of the crisped bodies off the spit, struck it through with a skewer and held it out.

"Five cents old soldier."

Offering a dollar, Hellequin pointed to the water barrel behind the stall. "Syrup soda won't slate my thirst. Fill this up for me instead, fella?"

The man eyed the passersby. "We usually only sell water by the cup. Our king pin, Herb, catches me filling canteens, I'll be keelhauled. But seeing as you look in need…" He filled the flask, keeping his gaze on the mouth of the tent.

"There you go."

"Much obliged." Hellequin moved aside, allowing the next customer to step up. A flat shelf of rock jutted out from the uneven surface a short distance away; Hellequin took a seat and drank deeply from the flask. He let the fluid settle in his stomach a few moments then began on the rat carcass, savouring the meaty mouthfuls as if partaking in a feast for the Saints themselves. Oil trickled between his fingers. He lapped at it, not wanting to miss out.

When his hunger and thirst began to abate, he slowed the motion of his jaw, watching the last few stragglers disappear inside the tent. His eye was drawn to the roof of the tent and movement at one of the masts. He couldn't quite make out the detail of the figure, but he wanted to. In spite of the lengths he had gone to protect his identity, he couldn't resist inching the bandana up slightly. The Hawkeye twirled audibly, telescoping in just at the moment the woman held up a glowing red lantern and released it. As the airborne light drifted off into the shadowed sky, the woman appeared to radiate her very own extraordinary rainbowed lustre. Poised aloft the circus tent, she shone out like a star. Or a warning beacon. Hellequin magnified in on her translucent skin, her meshwork of blue veins, her scintillating eyes.

Seconds later, she dipped down and disappeared.

He slid the bandana back down over his eye just as a voice said, "Its two dollar entry but I'm sure them marks'll squeeze up on the benches to fit an old soldier in."

It was the carnie worker from the meat stall. One of the pitchcrew, Hellequin reckoned, judging by the man's work-a-day shirt and pants and his muscular arms.

Hellequin finished picking clean the last bone and threw it onto the small pile by his feet. "I'm liking the atmosphere here," he said softly. For the first time since had he left the barracks, he was at peace. The mechanical music soothed the ragged edges of his neural network. He liked the smells and colours too. In a world of crumbling, dusting things, it promised frivolity and amusement and the wondrous.

"Ah, don't let that bad eye stop you from seeing our great and marvellous show. Herb's got himself a right queer collection of acts – aerial artists, clowns, dangerous beasts, and one helluva showgirl." The pitchman winked. "Desirous Nim in the flesh is worth the price of admission alone. She's electrifying!"

Hellequin felt a spark-surge. Inside his mind, he replayed the image of the glowing woman. Beautiful. Ghostly. Desirable.

He stared at the tent. 'Cyber Circus' proclaimed the painted banner suspended under the eaves of the roof. Would it be too great a risk to venture in? Could he enjoy the show like any other patron, or would someone detect the whir of his hooded steel eye and expose him as a Hawkeye – yet another freak on display?

Taking one more swig of water, he corked the flask and used it to indicate the open tent flap. "Go on then, fella. Lead the way inside."

FURTHER CONFLICTS

A beleaguered army unit fights a very alien war and is forced to mourn one of their own; the crew of a Russian ice submarine faces an uncertain future in a dystopian world; a war artist lifts the lid on what's really going on in a disturbingly plausible future; a warrior returns home from galactic conflict only to face his greatest ever challenge; a missionary doctor harbours an alien fugitive against all advice and reason…

Thirteen tales of extremes of human striving, of ingenuity, brilliance, desperate action, violence, and resolution. Thirteen tales of Conflict, of Science Fiction at its absolute best, from some of the genre's most accomplished writers: Dan Abnett, Eric Brown, Tony Ballantyne, Colin Harvey, Philip Palmer, Stephen Palmer, Gareth L Powell, Andy Remic, Adam Roberts, etc.

Features "The Harvest" by **Kim Lakin-Smith**, in which a school is threatened by the dreaded Harvesters and a resourceful teacher must somehow ensure the survival of both her wards and herself, and "Unaccounted", a rare short story from South African author **Lauren Beukes**, winner of the 2011 Arthur C. Clarke Award.

"There are no weak links in *Further Conflicts*. Although the anthology varies widely from exuberant battles to disorienting freakishness to deeply pensive tales, the stories are all fiercely brilliant." – *Warpcore*

Available now from NewCon Press, as a dust-jacketed limited edition hardback, signed by all contributors, and as an A5 paperback.

www.newconpress.co.uk

Fables from the Fountain

Edited by Ian Whates

A volume of all original stories written as homage to Arthur C. Clarke's classic *Tales from the White Hart*, featuring many of today's top genre writers, including **Neil Gaiman, Charles Stross, Stephen Baxter, James Lovegrove, Liz Williams, Adam Roberts, Eric Brown, Ian Watson, Peter Crowther**, and **David Langford.**

The Fountain, a traditional London pub situated in Holborn, just off Chancery Lane, where Michael, the landlord, serves excellent real ales and dodgy ploughman's, ably assisted by barmaids Sally and Bogna.

The Fountain, in whose Paradise bar a group of friends – scientists, writers and genre fans – meet regularly on a Tuesday night to swap anecdotes, reveal wondrous events from their past, tell tall tales, talk of classified invention and, maybe, just *maybe*, save the world…

"*Fables* is probably the closest I've ever seen to a multi-author anthology reading like a single-author work. There's not a poor tale in here." – *The Future Fire*

"Highly recommended for anyone interested in a good tall tale told well." – *The Green Man Review*

Available now from the NewCon Press website as both an A5 paperback and a special dust-jacketed hardback edition signed by all the authors on two bespoke signing pages. Limited to just 200 individually numbered copies.

www.newconpress.co.uk

TOURNIQUET:
TALES FROM THE RENEGADE CITY
KIM LAKIN-SMITH

Renegade City. Futurist Gothika. Mecca of the damned. Where über rock-band, Origin, is deified and the world's dark subcultures coexist under the umbrella faith of 'Belief'. But Roses, the great Gothic messiah, is dead, the tribes are in turmoil, and Renegade's own home-bred rebels, the Drifters, are quickly becoming a law unto themselves…

"Its combination of Goth and gadgetry, music and mysticism will have a new generation of mosh pit prophets drinking up every word." – *SF Crowsnest*

"… a cloacal, treacly mix of gothic thriller, urban paranoid examination and scarred, black magic treatise." – *Conrad Williams*

"Lakin-Smith… overlays it all with the realities of various subcultures. Each provides a different mix of the same locale, coming together like the beats on an industrial track." – *Yatterings*

Renegade City: a different Nottingham in a different world.

Tourniquet is Kim Lakin-Smith's stunning debut novel, available now from Immanion Press.